his black tongue

mitchell luthi

Sentinel Creatives
www.sentinelcreatives.net
The physical edition 2022

Copyright © Sentinel Creatives 2022
The author asserts their moral right to
be identified as the author of this work
This work is entirely a work of fiction.
The names, characters and incidents portrayed in it
are
the work of the author's imagination. Any
resemblance to
actual persons, living or dead, events or localities is
entirely coincidental.
All rights reserved. No part of this publication may
be
reproduced, stored in a retrieval system, or
transmitted,
in any form or by any means, electronic, mechanical,
photocopying, recording or otherwise, without the
prior
permission of the publishers.

Also from Sentinel Creatives

The Ritual (by Mitchell Lüthi)
The Zealot (by Mitchell Lüthi)
The Jethro Parables (by Justin Fillmore)
Write Like Hell: Dark Fantasy & Horror Anthology Volume 1
Write Like Hell: Dark Fantasy & Sci-fi Anthology Volume 2
Write Like Hell: Kaiju Anthology Volume 3
Lovecraft in a Time of Madness

CONTENTS

His Black Tongue	1
The Bone Fields	100
The Knights of the Non-Euclidian Table	170
The Breeding Mound	220
Necropolis	284
The Blessed Tomb	313

His Black Tongue

1349

A young man had become possessed by a devil. The thing within him burst into loud lamentation and departed from the man. At once the youth's eye fell out on his cheek, and the whole of the pupil which had been black became white.

Saint Augustine

Rain fell that day from clouds that scarred the sky like bruises on a newborn's skin. It washed away the dust, and the rot, and the smell that lingered over Val de Havre, a thin strip of land somewhere north of Reims. It had been a plague year. As had the year before it and the year before that, too. What the rain couldn't sweep away, the mud claimed. And its tithe was a handsome one, this year, the year of plagues.

In the centre of the valley, jutting out of the soil like freshly unearthed bones, lay the town of Enfaire. It was a small town, built the previous century, with high walls to repel Englishmen, and deep wells to survive siege. Spindly towers peeked out from behind its ramparts, facing the wooded hillsides that surrounded the valley like the gnarled tips of a ribcage around the sluggish heart within.

On the edge of the valley, beyond the empty fields that surrounded Enfaire, a shadow peeled off from the forest. It moved quickly, keeping ahead of the gathering storm clouds, and slipped onto the muddied road just as a bell began to toll out from within the town.

As it grew closer, the shadow became recognisable as a pair of silhouettes and then as the figures of a tall, gangly man and a younger woman. The woman wore a simple blue coat over a padded tunic and carried a walking staff in her one hand, while her other was wrapped around a small shoulder bag. The man moved with a slight limp and muttered beneath his breath as he tried to keep up.

Pierre Dubois was not a young man. And hadn't been one for a very long time. His face was creased with lines, from years of happiness, and sadness, from days of too much sun and too little. He wore his grey hair clipped short, and a well-kept beard framed his jaw.

"This is it then, eh?" Pierre let out a steaming breath and leaned against his own walking stick to stare at the town. "Those gates have a decided look about them, Remi. What shall we find behind them, I wonder? Another tomb sealed in the names of Pestilence and Death?"

Remi shrugged, walking ahead of him. "There is no sickness here."

"So they say, so they say." Pierre wiped his nose and looked up as the first drops of rain began to fall. "Would that the absence of Pestilence were so inextricably bound to the absence of Death. But I fear that is not the case. One may still reside in a place where the other does not!"

"It's either that or the storm," said Remi. She turned back on the road, tugging her hood over her hair as rain pelted the mud around them. "These fields will be flooded by morn, and us drowned in them if we stay outside. So, a hearth and roof... or this stinking mire?"

"Ah! But for a roof over my head and a fire to warm my feet, I might be convinced to share a room with the Reaper," said Pierre. "If only for a night."

"And for a belly full of food?"

The old man laughed and trudged toward his companion. "For that, I would be tempted to dine with the Devil himself!"

Remi snorted and shook her head. "Sometimes I think you'd damn your own soul for a half-loaf of bread and a spoonful of honey, Pierre. I hope your faith will never be tested such... But I do not think the Devil waits for us in Enfaire."

"No indeed," said Pierre with a smile as they approached the town gate.

A shallow river framed the town's eastern wall, running alongside the road like a serpent's coils. The current was split by an island of stone and masonry, the one half disappearing through a sluice gate in the walls, while the other followed the road north, toward the edge of the valley. Its banks were already starting to overflow, and water flooded out onto the road, quickly turning it into a quaking mire.

Pierre and Remi hurried through the mud, slipping and sliding in the ooze as the first rolling booms of thunder split the sky. Pierre groaned miserably to himself as he braced against the rain, pulling his hood tighter around his neck until they finally took shelter beneath the gate's stone overhang.

"Let's see if anyone's home," said Pierre, with a glance to his companion. He rapped the head of his staff against the wooden gate and then huddled back against the wall.

After a brief pause, a small shutter slid open, and a yellow eye peered down at them from behind a meshed viewing port.

"What you want?" came a penetrating voice through the gate. The eye swivelled from Pierre to Remi and then back to Pierre and blinked. "Can't you see the gates closed? The rot's not welcome. No visitors!"

Pierre smiled up at the eye, drawing back his hood. "Our humble pardons, monsieur. We are simple travellers on our way to the

Pilgrim's Road. We seek no alms. Let not my designation of 'Begging Friar' dissuade you from that fact. We ask only for the safety and shelter of your walls and for a single night."

The eye narrowed and blinked again. "Begging Friar? Franciscan?"

"Indeed. I am Pierre Dubois of Auvergne. And this is my charge, Remi of—"

"Just Remi," said his companion, tilting her head.

"Auvergne? You're a long way from home, Friar. And these roads aren't safe anymore." A furrowed brow appeared through the viewing port as the gatekeep swapped eyes. "Brigands, rapers, godless men, even those bastards from across the channel hound us here. And at night… Well, you're lucky you got here before sunset."

"So you will grant us entry?" asked Pierre hopefully.

"Aye, Friar," said the eye. "I don't know the punishment for denying entry to a man of God. But I'd prefer not finding out."

"Most wise," said Pierre, letting a smile crease his features. "Most wise indeed."

The eye blinked again and then disappeared. A moment later, the viewing port slid shut, and the gates groaned before creaking open inwardly.

"I hope you two haven't brought the sickness with you," said the gatekeep, emerging from out of the shadows. His eyes, which had appeared yellow from behind the shutter, were instead a mustard green. They rested above a nose that curved like a beak, giving him an appearance that would have been regal if not for the weakness of his chin. The gatekeep heaved a shoulder against the wooden frame, scraping it through the mud, and waved them in.

"But friar or no," he said as they entered Enfaire, "I'll fling you both back out the moment I hear so much as a sniffle from either of you and face God's judgment for the crime."

"That won't be necessary," said Pierre with a thin smile. "We have been fortunate in our travels, and you will find no pustule or boil upon our skin. Only the ravages of age and the bruises of youth."

The gatekeep chuckled at that, closing the wooden doors and barring them, before guiding Pierre and Remi into the yard. The rain was starting to let up, but the air was cold, and steam curled around their faces when they breathed.

"I'll take you to the Prioress," said the gatekeep. "My shift's about done, and she'll want to know what news you have from outside. If she had it her way, the gates would stay open to the world, plague year be damned."

"A generous woman," said Pierre, matching the gatekeep's pace as they crossed onto a cobbled road. From within Enfaire's walls, the town was revealed to be octagonal in form, built in rows of concentric circles around the imposing structure of the aedificium, which pierced the skyline like a half-buried nail. Rows of windows covered its upper floors, growing more numerous in the upper echelons. Craven forms squatted beside one another beneath the sills, stone gargoyles leering lecherously from up high.

The priory's bell tower was hewn from the same yellow rock as the building itself but had been appended to its western flank and jutted out awkwardly. It seemed to Pierre that the tower had been added as an afterthought rather than built as the priory's focal point.

Their guide—who had told them his name was Clemens—led them from the cobbled road across a narrow bridge. Dark water coursed beneath the stone arch, carrying debris from upriver, where the storm had already hit. Roots and saplings were swept beneath the course way... And other things, too.

Pierre paused on the bridge, blinking away the rain as a familiar shape was dragged down the river by the current. A body? A swollen corpse to be interred within a watery tomb? No... Just a muddied clump of roots. He shook the vision from his mind, taking a cold breath before he followed Remi and Clemens into the town proper.

The dwellings to either side of the road were small but comfortable looking, and Pierre waved at a grubby child who appeared from out of the nearest doorway. The boy made a face at the friar before his mother swept him up with an arm and disappeared back into the house.

"That child was as fat as a pig," said Remi softly so that only Pierre could hear.

"And the mother, too," Pierre replied before turning to the gatekeep. "Your town has been blessed with both health and abundance. But your fields outside are as sallow and bare as the rest of the province?"

"I suppose we been lucky, too," said the man, nodding his beaked head. "The Prioress heard news of the plague before it reached Val de Havre, and so we filled our granaries. Now we can fill our bellies, too—until it runs out, anyway.

"She sounds like a remarkable woman," said Pierre, exchanging a look with Remi.

"That she is," said the gatekeep. And then, noticing their expressions, "She got a letter from one of the cities. Maybe Paris, maybe Lyon. Must've been right at the start. But she's not one for sitting on her hands, our Prioress... Where'd you say you were heading to again?"

"We're taking the Pilgrim's Road," said Pierre. He adjusted the collar of his hood against the cold and met the gatekeep's eyes. "We have business South. In Lourdes."

"A strange time to be undertaking such a journey." The gatekeep frowned. "Is it as bad as they say? In the South? There's strange talk about—of sick men falling into their graves, only to be seen amongst the living again a few days later. But I've heard other things, too. Darker things..."

"I've heard the stories," said Pierre. "Probably the same ones as you. There is witchcraft and devilry at work in the south, of that I have no doubt. But to speculate idly without seeing it for my own eyes invites rumour and falsehood, and we must be above that, Clemens!"

The gatekeep nodded at that and led them past the last few dwellings, to where the road grew wider, into the trading district. Most of the town's workshops were still open, even in the face of the coming storm. And Enfaire's residents moved between them, collecting what goods they could before night fell upon the valley.

There was a feeling of nervous anticipation, Pierre thought. The people here moved quickly, keeping their heads down against the rain, eager to get back indoors. He couldn't blame them. The cold was starting to get into his bones. But there was something else, too. A slight tension that only made itself felt when Pierre let his gaze rest on the folk for more than a brief spell. Their eyes were all hooded, turned to their feet as they braced against the cold. Like the boy and his mother, they looked well-fed, but there was a tinge to their skin, a yellow sheen that hinted at malnutrition or some other ailment.

Further down the road, he spotted a black-handed smith working the furnace, and in the store beside his, a portly baker replenishing his shelves with bread loaves. The baker's eyes were set deep against his pudgy flesh, and even from a distance, Pierre could tell they were red-rimmed and weepy. Apprentices moved in the shadows behind their master, keeping out of his way lest they earn a clip behind the ear or a harsh word.

"I thought the sickness hadn't reached you here," said Remi. Pierre followed her gaze down one of the alleys and pursed his lips. Nearly a dozen caskets lay resting against the adjacent walls, and the sound of a hammer on wood rang out from a small shop at the end of the passage.

"Your carpenter has been busy," said Pierre, directing a questioning look to the gatekeep.

The man looked uncomfortable for a moment and then shrugged. "It's not plague, if that's what you think. Nah, those are suicides."

"God be merciful," Pierre intoned beneath his breath. He made the sign of the cross with his free hand and leaned into his cane with the other. "To be spared the rot of plague, only to find your mind ensnared by another sickness. It is a great tragedy."

"So many," said Remi softly, and then louder: "Why are there so many?"

"The Franciscan isn't far wrong," said the gatekeep, picking his words slowly. "We have been spared some things… but, sometimes I think it woulda been kinder if we'd suffered through the plague like everyone else. Better that than… this… this… Perhaps you oughta hear it from some learned figure in the priory, lest you think I fib! But come, before night falls and you find out for yourselves! Then you'll see that no lies have passed these lips!"

Pierre and Remi exchanged another bemused look but held their tongues and followed after the gatekeep. As the last shadows of dusk began to merge with the gloom of night, they crossed into the priory grounds.

The Prioress was not who Pierre had expected. For starters, she was far younger than anyone of her station had any right to be. If he had to guess, he'd have put her within a few years of Remi. And Remi was little more than a child herself! But the Prioress carried herself with the dignity of her post, even if she lacked the grey that usually accompanied it.

"You must tell me news," she said. Her eyes smiled when she spoke, dancing from Pierre to Remi. "It has been so long since I heard word of the outside world. Please, you must tell me all!"

"I'm afraid there's little good to share," said Pierre. He'd noticed the young Prioress's skin was flush with colour, with health. "Paris has seen the worst of it. But the sickness covers all four corners of France, perhaps the world."

"This saddens me greatly," said the Prioress. She shook her head and waved them in through the great wooden doors of the aedificium. "But come, you must be tired from your travels. Eat, rest! There is plenty here for all."

"It seems your small town has been spared the brunt of it," said Pierre as they followed the Prioress across a courtyard and back beneath the vaulted ceiling of the priory.

"By the grace of God," she replied, but her smiling eyes darkened, and she hesitated.

"Sister?"

The Prioress seemed to find her resolve and met Pierre's gaze with her own. "Tell me, friar, where does your path take you?"

"We are headed south, to Lourdes. As I told your gatekeep, we go to do the Lord's work."

"Lourdes?" The Prioress frowned and raised a thin brow. "I have heard the stories coming out of Lourdes, from even before we closed our gates to the world. They say a devil has made the town its own and that there are no good men left to bury the dead."

Pierre shrugged at that. "There is no soul so lost that can no longer be found."

The Prioress nodded her approval, but another shadow crossed her face. "We have stories of our own here. Perhaps you have heard those, too?"

"Only rumours of rumours, and some suggestion that not all is well from your gatekeep."

"If only they were just that: rumours, but I am afraid not." The Prioress tugged at the hems of her habit, bunching the fabric between her knuckles as they approached a steep flight of steps. "All is not well in Enfaire. As you shall find once the darkness of night covers our fair valley, and devils walk the earth."

Pierre glanced at Remi as they followed the Prioress up the stairs. The look on his companion's face was one of puzzled curiosity, and Pierre was sure that his own face reflected the same bemusement.

Their route took them past the Epistolary, where a handful of nuns sat transcribing from the dusty pages of great leather-bound tomes. One of the scribes looked up, a pale-faced youth with a curl of blonde hair sticking out from under her cowl. The nun held Pierre's gaze as they passed beneath the windows of the

Scriptorium but quickly blinked away when she spotted the Prioress.

"These devils," Pierre began, following the Prioress through another vaulted passage, "they come from across the Channel? Or are they pagans?"

The Prioress paused, shaking her head. "You mistake me, friar. The things that torment this land are no allegory—no words of mere fantasy. When night comes, our valley sees itself transformed, leaving only a hellscape in its wake. The stench of sulphur and rot grows thick, and flames dance within our forests. Only then, when the mad flutes and drums rise with the moon… only then do they emerge. I speak of no men-of-sin. These are crooked beings and broken things which hunt and prey upon anything that falls outside our walls. Even the dead… it is said… rise in unholy rapture to join them. These are the devils who have forsaken our land, and we along with it."

Neither of them slept that night. They sat up in their cots in a small cell beneath the bell tower and listened to the world outside through a small window in the wall. At first, there was nothing, and Pierre felt his nerves slowly starting to ease as the night grew old. He was considering sleep when Remi's hand shot up, and she shuffled over to the window.

"Do you hear that?" she asked, peering into the darkness.

Pierre tilted his head, his brow furrowing as he listened to the world beyond their cell.

"I don't hear any—"

"Shh!" Remi waved her hand at him again, this time beckoning him toward her spot beneath the window.

"Alright, alright," said the friar, grumbling as he clambered across her cot. But he stopped complaining mid-way and snapped his eyes to stare past his companion. He thought it was the wind at first, a low howl sweeping the valley from across the mountains. But as the sound grew louder, he started hearing other notes... ones that no natural phenomena could ever account for.

"Voices," said Pierre softly.

Remi nodded, her gaze still fixed on the dark landscape beyond Enfaire.

"But from where?" asked Pierre. "There are no—"

A roaring drone cut through the air, splitting the night like a scythe cuts through barley. It was followed by a sudden quaking, as if the world itself was being torn apart. A red glow, as bright as the Summer sun, blotted out the valley, forcing Pierre to blink back from the window. The light shone into their room, and the friar felt his hand start to shake as he slouched back down next to Remi.

The voices, no more than a sibilant whisper at first, had broken out into a brazen cacophony. Mad laughter joined the chorus—and then screams, too. When Pierre focused, he could just make out the rhythmic pulse of a drum resounding across the field and the mangled harmonies of strange instruments.

"This is the place then, isn't it?" he said.

"It is," nodded Remi.

"And that is…."

Remi leaned forward and slammed the window shut, blocking out the worst of the dread opera. She turned to Pierre, a determined look on her face. "The Gates of Hell."

THE DEVIL'S BARGAIN

The Devil never runs upon a man to seize him with his claws until he sees him on the ground, already having fallen by his own will.

Saint Thomas More

Pierre sat opposite Remi on a smooth wooden bench inside the priory's main hall and stared down into his bowl. Neither of them had slept much the night before, and he could feel the fatigue settling on his bones like a wet blanket. Remi looked how he felt, and her red eyes blinked back at him when he looked up at her.

"This could be worse than Lourdes," said Pierre softly. Others had entered the halls—nuns and scribes, as well as young novitiates from an abbey nearby. They were breaking their fasts and talking animatedly amongst themselves, the horrors of the night before not reflected in their tone or mannerisms.

"And I said the Devil does not wait for us in Enfaire." Remi snorted and shook her head. "But no... Lourdes is cursed with an affliction beyond even this."

"Worse than Hell's dominion?" Pierre looked unconvinced. "This may be something we cannot solve, Remi... Something that even you cannot fix."

His ward shrugged at his words but, seeing his expression, let out a sigh and leaned forward in her seat. "It is my duty, even in the face of such odds. It is as your Avignon Pope declared: we must surround ourselves with light to block out this plague and the devils who conjure it. And so we must."

"And you are this light?"

"You know that I am, Pierre." Remi turned to stare at the hall and its other occupants. "But I am just one, and the darkness we face is thick and will not be easily shifted. I will need your faith in me."

The Franciscan sighed, stirring at his porridge with his spoon. "And you shall have it, little saint. But this place... I confess: there are few things that I have seen to match the depravity that lurks beyond its walls. None, in fact."

"Faith, Pierre! That is all I need. I have not led you astray so far, have I?" Remi let a smile cross her face and glanced down at Pierre's bowl. "But I would be careful of eating anything rendered from this soil if I were you. Don't you think?"

The old man scowled to himself and pushed away the bowl just as the Prioress and another figure approached their bench. Margaux looked flush and healthy, her skin almost radiant against her white cowl. The young woman beside her, by contrast, was pale with thick rings under her eyes and black curls that stuck out from beneath her hood like balls of twine.

"I am glad to see you are both still with us," said the Prioress. Her eyes danced from Pierre to Remi and then to Pierre's bowl before tilting her head to look at the friar. "You must stay the morning. I have arranged for Sister Lucille to show you the grounds after breakfast."

Sister Lucille tilted her head. "Father."

"Thank you," said Pierre, smiling at the sister, before turning back to the Prioress. "If it is possible, we may ask to extend your hospitality a few days more. I have… questions."

A darkness settled upon the Prioress's face, but it quickly disappeared behind her polished smile. "And I will be happy to answer them, father. But I fear you will not be satisfied with what I have to tell you."

"I am sure any light you have to shine on my thoughts after last night will be most illuminating," said Pierre, folding his hands in his lap. "To see such things in the flesh, why, it quite beggars belief… Yes, I have many questions and would be most gladdened by your assistance."

The Prioress smiled again thinly. "Of course, father. But please, that must wait until after breakfast," she said, turning on her heel to leave with Sister Lucille, "once you have seen the grounds."

"Aye," said Pierre, glancing back down at his bowl. The porridge was still steaming hot, and flecks of honey had been drizzled over it in place of sweet sugar. His stomach rumbled, and he made to reach for his spoon before catching Remi's eye. His ward raised a brow at him and then shook her head.

"Fine," said Pierre gruffly. "So, I guess I will starve here, too, while we investigate what has surely become the Devil's land. And for what? An empty stomach!"

Remi snorted again, rising from her seat. "Come then, starving friar. Let us see what Enfaire by day has to offer. Perhaps we can find you some crumbs to fill your belly with!"

† † †

"So, you have decided to stay, then?" asked Lucille as she led them from the priory's steps.

"Aye, for a little while," said Pierre. He squinted past the sister into the morning light and town beyond. The clouds were slowly clearing, and sheets of light crisscrossed the valley, creating a golden haze that hung over it. Pierre paused as he looked beyond Enfaire's walls, at the fields and forests that surrounded them. The earth was a churned mess of mud and upturned soil, and the banks of the river had flooded entirely. Roots, and even small trees, had been dragged down into its filthy waters, damming the river in places and causing large pools to form along its banks.

But Pierre could see no sign of the hellfires that had dotted the forest the night before, nor the tell-tale scarring of the earth where great beasts had walked. Val de Havre was clean. Or as clean as it had always been, anyway.

"It has been a time since we last kept guests," continued the sister as they walked. She was taking them down a winding footpath toward a postern gate nestled into the priory's outer wall. "You must forgive us if we seem hesitant toward you. Many have begun to associate the outside world with…."

"Devilry?" suggested Pierre.

"Quite so," said Lucille. "But they will behave when they see that you are with me."

"What of the novitiates?" asked Remi, slipping out of the gate behind Lucille. "I have seen no Abbey or Monastery in these parts… Are they not guests?"

"They are from Elem," said Lucille. She squeezed shut the gate behind them and started walking toward the village, waving at them to follow. "But they live with us here now, preferring the protection of our walls."

"Yes," said Pierre, hurrying to keep up. "Your walls… Why is it that the horrors that occupy your valley spare you and those in the town?"

The sister shrugged her bony shoulders and turned to look at the friar. She walked with a slight limp, he noticed and seemed to favour her one leg. "Prioress Margaux says that it is because our faith keeps them at bay."

"And do you believe that?"

Lucille shrugged again but turned away from the friar. "Who's to say why these things happen the way that they do. All we can do is be thankful that we have been spared. And that the plague has not visited us in our homes and beds. It is the price we pay, I think."

Pierre merely nodded at that, but Remi gave the sister a sidelong glance, though if she had any further questions, she did not ask them.

For the remainder of the morning, Sister Lucille showed them through a series of neatly kept gardens before leading them toward an old chapel house on the edge of the town. It had been built at the top of a low hill overlooking the churning waters of the river that encircled Enfaire. The church's walls were chalky white and made from a thin wood that had seen better days. But it was clear that its windows had been engraved and installed by a master craftsman, and the glass still shone as though new. Scenes from the creation stared down at them as they walked toward its doors, and Pierre felt goosebumps rise upon his flesh when he saw a panel depicting the Morningstar's fall from heaven.

The Adversary's once glorious wings were crooked and bent, and his hands and feet blackened as though by tar. The expression on his beautiful face was one of rage, even as he was dragged from the heavens by his father's avenging angels. Pierre thought, for a fraction of an instant, that he could hear their triumphant horns ringing in his ears and their spiteful laughs. He shuddered and looked away.

The sister explained to them that the old church had been the original place of worship in Enfaire before the priory had been built almost a century before. In its long history, it had survived fires, and floods, and even a lightning strike. Its stone steps were still scarred by the damage it had caused. But once the priory had been established, the church was abandoned. And now it simply sat at the edge of the town, watching over Enfaire like a lone sentry in the distance.

Pierre knelt down to examine a stone carving at the church's entrance while they waited for Sister Lucille to adjust her boots. The statue was of the Mother Mary, though, in the place of a lamb, she carried a goat. The creature's square eyes stared back at him dully, but there was something about the bust that made Pierre feel uneasy, and he moved his gaze from it.

"Your boots are bound," commented Remi. She sat on the top of the steps to the church and watched the sister tighten the wraps around her feet with curiosity.

"There is no good leather here," Lucille replied. "And no travellers to trade with since the plague. But plague or no, the mud gets into everything. We do what we can to preserve what little we have."

Pierre frowned at her words but didn't linger on them long. And a brief spell later, he was hurrying after the sister and Remi as they moved back onto the path.

"Do you know why this has happened, sister?" Pierre asked as they finally entered the town itself. "Surely such a thing cannot simply happen. There must have been an event to trigger it... Perhaps a ritual or a summoning of some kind?"

"The Prioress did not tell you?" Lucille raised a brow, moving out of the way as a wagon and mule trundled along the road toward them.

"She did not," Pierre called over the rumble of the cart, "though she promised to answer what questions we have after you have shown us the grounds. But forgive me, I am old and have little patience for...."

"Patience?" Lucille smiled, and it was not an ugly thing.

She was silent a moment as they passed grocers and other folk who were going about their daily chores. The cobbled road sparkled beneath them as they moved deeper into the town, the rain having washed it clean. But still, a faint smell lingered in the air, and Pierre could not identify its origin.

"It was a witch," said Lucille finally, once the road began to clear. "She burdened us with this curse. She damned our town."

"Must have been a powerful witch," said Remi, wrinkling her brow. She walked just a step ahead of Pierre and Lucille and turned to look back at the sister. "It is no small thing to open a door to the other side. And a greater thing to keep it open."

"She was very powerful indeed." Lucille sighed and stopped to lean against a low wall surrounding a strip of open land at the end of the road. "She had us all under her spell for a time until Margaux identified her for what she was. But by then, it was already too late. She had sunk her hooves into our soil and become too powerful for us to stop."

Pierre rested his arms against the wall beside Lucille and stared into the yard. His eyes set upon a row of stones sticking out from plots of unkempt grass, like broken teeth in uneven gums. He could see more of them centred around a pair of saplings in the middle of the plot. This was no empty patch of land, he realised, but a graveyard.

He chewed on his lips and glanced at the Sister. "And yet, the witch is gone, yes?"

"She is," Lucille said. "After her trial, she unleashed havoc upon us. We were only spared her wrath through the sacrifice of a few brave souls who managed to trap her and cast her into the flames of a pyre. It was then that she cursed us. And on that first night after her demise, demons stalked our valley. It has been the same ever since."

Pierre made the sign of the cross and whispered a prayer to himself as a small procession entered the yard from a gate on the other side. They carried between them a small wooden casket, too small to carry anyone larger than a child.

A man—perhaps the father—led an elderly woman and two girls toward the corner of the yard, coming to a stop at the foot of a hole he'd not noticed before. Pierre thought he could hear their tears from across the yard and let out a sad sigh.

"Have you contacted the Inquisition?" Remi asked, her eyes fixed on the funeral. The hole the family stood in front of was isolated from the other graves, and there was no priest or nun to stand beside them. A suicide, then, Pierre concluded.

"Their ears have been deaf to our calls," said Lucille. There was frustration in her voice, and she growled out the last words with vehemence. "No one has come."

"We have come," whispered Remi softly from beside Pierre. The Franciscan found himself nodding. If no one else would help the people here, then it was up to them.

Across the yard, the family had begun to lower the casket into the ground but paused at a word from the father when he noticed they were being observed. Pierre tilted his head and looked away, feeling embarrassed, but the man was already striding across the yard toward them.

"Father," he said when he reached the wall. His face was ashen, and his lips dry and chapped. But it was his eyes that would haunt Pierre's dreams in the years to come. They were bright green and rimmed by so much red it seemed all the man's blood vessels had ruptured and now threatened to overwhelms his pupils entirely.

"I am most sorry for your loss," said Pierre, meeting the man's eyes. "Your child will be in my prayers."

"And mine, too," said Remi.

Lucille muttered something beneath her breath but nodded sadly when the man's eyes swept over her.

"Thank you, father. But it is not your prayers I ask for, though I will gladly accept them." The man wrung his hands together and looked at Pierre anxiously.

"Speak, my son, or I can offer you nothing," said Pierre, but it was with a sinking feeling that the friar realised he already knew what was to be asked of him.

The man wiped his nose with the back of his hand and said his piece. "It's only, father, if I could trouble you to say a few words over my son's grave… If'n you'd preside over it, my wife and I would be eternally grateful. I would consider myself in your debt, even."

Pierre glanced over the man's shoulder, taking in the little family standing over the casket, before blinking back to the father.

"Surely the Prioress or one of her Sisters—"

"They will not," snapped the man. His eyes suddenly narrowed, and he flicked an angry glare toward Sister Lucille. "They refuse."

"Ah," said Pierre. He would need to be firm here but careful if he was to avoid provoking the man's wrath. He looked close enough to the edge of his tether already.

"My son," he said solemnly, "I cannot preside over the burial of a suicide. I can only keep the boy in my prayers and hope he finds salvation by other means."

The father blinked at him and then shook his head. "My boy is no suicide, friar. He took a fall, that is all. Broke his neck tumbling down the priory roof."

Pierre's brow furrowed, and he glanced at Lucille. "Sister, is this the truth of it?"

"You have my word," said the man before she could reply. "I would not lie, not standing over my boy's grave. Not today."

Sister Lucille pursed her lips, hesitating before she inclined her head. "He speaks the truth. It was a great tragedy, and your son has been in my prayers ever since."

The man's jaw flexed visibly at her words, and for a second, Pierre thought he was about to leap at the nun, but the second passed without the promised violence. "Keep your prayers, sister. There is nothing the priory and your ilk can offer me and what's mine anymore. I ask only for the friar's words."

"And you shall have them," said Pierre, stepping out from behind the wall. He raised a placatory hand, placing himself between the man and Lucille. "I shall fulfil your request."

"Truly?" The man sucked in a deep breath and wiped his nose again.

"It is my duty." Pierre nudged open the cemetery's gate and waited for Remi and Lucille to enter ahead of him. "Come, take us to your family and let us lay your son to rest."

The man nodded again, his watery eyes looking like shallow pools against his pale skin. There was a hint of green to his flesh, Pierre noticed as the man turned to walk back to his family. A sickly sheen that seemed to afflict everyone in Enfaire... Everyone, that is, aside from Margaux.

"Sister," Pierre said softly as Lucille passed through the gate. "I would be curious to know why it was that you, the priory, refused this man's son his last rights?"

Lucille paused, knitting her brow as a sad look covered her face. And then, "It was the Prioress. She forbade it."

"The Prioress?" Pierre frowned. "Why would she do that?"

"I couldn't tell you. Only that she did."

Pierre let the picket gate swing shut as he turned to walk beside the sister. The cemetery's groundsman had let the grass between the tombstones run amok, and it sat in tall clumps, nearly up to the friar's knees in places. The cemetery had an abandoned feel about it, and the Franciscan was not surprised to see the lettering on all the nearest gravestones was dark and faded.

"It is not within her power to deny last rites." Pierre slowed in his steps as they neared the father and his family. "And even if it were, I can see no reason to deny them to a child. I will need to hear her reasoning for this and report the matter to his Holiness."

Lucille was silent as they came to a stop beside the open grave. The little family had huddled together beside the casket, looking to the red-eyed man for reassurance.

"He says he'll do it," said the man, nodding at the Franciscan. "He'll say the words."

His wife looked like she might burst into tears at the news and looked to Pierre with gratitude in her eyes. And still, that subtle green sheen to her skin….

"Friar," said the man, gesturing to the grave. He held a shovel in one hand and knelt down to grip the handle of the casket with the other.

Pierre cleared his throat and took his place at the foot of the hole. He cast his eyes over the gathered witnesses, finally resting them on Remi, who gave him a reassuring nod. After a short breath, Pierre crossed himself and began the last rites.

"Requiem æternam dona eis Domine," he intoned, trying not to wince as the man dropped into the hole, dragging the casket with him. "Domine Iesu Christe, Rex gloriæ, libera animas." Pierre paused at a splintering sound that emanated from within the grave—from the casket. The father spat out a slew of curses and leaned down in the mud to examine the box. It had split down the middle, caving in where the wood was weakest.

"I'm sorry, friar," he said, looking up from the mud. "There's nothing for it. I'll need to go and fetch another lid from Marcus."

"Wait," said Remi, staring down into the hole. She had a look on her face Pierre had seen before. Nothing good ever came from that look.

31

"Open the casket," she said, moving toward the hole.

The man sat frozen for a second, watching as Remi clambered down into the grave beside him, but he finally found his wits and shook his head. "What purpose would that serve?"

"I must see." Remi gave him an apologetic look and then kicked open the broken lid before the man could move to stop her.

A gasp escaped Pierre's lips, and he heard the boy's mother let out a horrified cry as the contents of the casket were laid bare for all to see.

"God help us all," whispered Pierre, crossing himself again.

Wrapped beneath a thin layer of white sheeting lay a malformed figure that only barely resembled a young boy. Its arms and legs were emaciated and curved in on themselves, while a row of ribs protruded from his chest like the ridges of a mountain peak. The boy's flesh had turned to rotten grey, and maggots had already started to eat through it in places. But it was the wings! The accursed wings that had emerged from the child's back that made Pierre want to turn away from the sight.

And eventually, he did, only to find the boy's father's red-rimmed eyes staring back at him. There was horror upon the man's face—and despair.

"My boy," he said, barely more than a grunt. "What has become of my boy?

AND ALL HIS ANGELS

Alas! Of what kind is that place of wailing and gnashing teeth... at which even Satan shudders? O Woe! What kind of place is it, where the unsleeping worm dies not? What dread misery to be sent into outer darkness?

Saint Ephrem of Syria

Dusk fell upon Val de Havre like a final breath, rolling over its hills and forests before the day even knew it was over. Shadows stretched across the churned-up fields, slowly merging as they crept up on the town. The muddy pools of water along the river banks had started to dry, and workers from the town had broken up the dams that formed around them, letting the waters run freely toward Enfaire's sluice gate once more.

Pierre sat with Remi atop the priory's eastern ramparts and watched as the last rays of sun faded from the valley. The old man rummaged through the folds of his robes, retrieving a small pouch from within. He produced a pipe from another pocket and began the task of stuffing it while Remi paced in front of him.

"You suspect her, then?" he asked, tugging experimentally at his pipe. Satisfied that it wasn't packed too tightly, he cupped its bowl and lit a match against the wind. A tendril of blue smoke coiled out from his mouth before it was dispersed by a stiff breeze coming from the mountains.

"Who else?" Remi waved a hand at the town below, not missing a step as she considered Pierre's question. "These people are sick, and they don't even know it yet! They all bear the same signs. The red eyes and pale skin, maddening dreams and suicidal thoughts. But that is merely a symptom of the real ailment that afflicts them: a sickening of the soul. I have seen it before… though never like this."

"But the Prioress," Pierre sighed into his pipe, nearly spluttering on the harsh tobacco.

"She knew about the boy. Why else would she have forbidden her sisters from performing last rites? She didn't want them to see what had become of the child. And then there is her skin… How is it that she remains so flush with life while others become feverish and sick? She is feeding off of it… off of this place."

"Aye," said Pierre, scratching at his chin. "What you say makes sense, though it saddens me to say. But who is she? Some apprentice to the hag who cursed this place? Or another member of her coven? We must consider that she may not be acting alone."

"I do not know," Remi admitted. She came to a stop in front of Pierre and turned to stare down at the priory grounds. "But whoever she is, she wields incredible power, and her roots are deep in this place. To turn the land into a hellscape each night... that requires more than just magic. If she is a witch, then she is one who has the Devil's allegiance. And that is not to be trifled with."

Pierre followed her gaze down into the yard below. Figures moved across the grass, making for the Great Hall or completing their final chores before night truly fell upon them. Others worked along the part of the river that coursed beneath the priory's walls, clearing up the last of the debris left by the storm. It would not be long before the dinner bell rang, summoning them for supper. The friar's belly groaned at the thought. He still hadn't eaten.

"What is to be done?" he said, lifting his gaze back up to stare at his ward. "Should we not consider, perhaps, calling upon the Inquisition for this matter? I know you do not believe in their—"

"They will burn half the town and imprison the rest in their efforts to sanctify this place! They will persecute the innocent and turn Enfaire into the very hellscape that resides beyond its walls!" Remi spun on her heels, her hands clenched at her sides. Her eyes seemed to glow for a second, even as the light around them finally faded. "No, Pierre. It is not the Inquisition who shall be called upon to free these people from the demons who haunt them. It is we."

"Aye," said Pierre, taking a deep drag of his pipe and letting the smoke spill out along the walls. "I thought you might say that."

✝ ✝ ✝

That night, they watched from the priory walls as the curse of Val de Havre manifested itself once more. Only this time, they did not hide away from the sight. Remi was adamant that they would watch the display in full in the hopes that it might reveal some detail about how and why such a thing had come to be. Pierre had reluctantly agreed to join her, and so it was that he found himself on the parapets, watching as the valley was transformed into a scene from out of Virgil's Aeneid.

Shapes that affronted the eyes emerged from the forest, walking in time to the mournful choir that heralded their arrival. Cries of pain, and of pleasure, followed the shadows out from the gloom and were soon accompanied by the slow reverberating toll of a drum. If Pierre focused, he thought he could just make out what sounded like chains being dragged across stone. But the sound made his skin crawl, and he tried his best to ignore it.

Just as his eyes were starting to adjust to the gloom, a blinding red light tore across the valley, forcing him to blink away. It was like staring into a furnace, and even with his eyes shut, the horrible glow remained. There was a cracking sound—a splitting of the world—and then a distant horn blew into the night. Or was it another cry? He couldn't tell. The floor beneath his feet started to rumble, and he was forced to lean against the parapet, shielding his eyes while he waited for it to pass—hoping that it would pass.

Just when he thought the masonry would surely crack, and the stones tumble out from beneath him, the quake ended.

Pierre opened his eyes hesitantly, slowly blinking as he tested the brightness. The world had taken on a velvety tinge, and shades of red of varying intensity and vicissitudes now covered the valley. In places, it seemed like pools of blood had replaced the air, hovering in clotted balls that made Pierre's stomach churn. A torrent of fire now existed where the river had once flowed and coursed at no lesser speed before fading away at the foot of Enfaire's wall. The forest seemed a blur in the distance— shadows upon shadows, ill-defined shapes on the horizon. But it was the field that drew Pierre's attention, and then his breath, away.

Black pits covered the earth like wounds, stinking holes that vomited noxious fumes. They shuddered as they belched out the foetid air, quivering and reforming as they imposed themselves upon the world.

Around them, gibbet posts had been erected or else grown from the ground itself. Scores of them had emerged and littered the fields like bales of hay after a successful harvest. But of course, there hadn't been any harvests and wouldn't be any until the valley was purged of the evil that had stirred beneath it.

Pierre squinted at the nearest cage. It was a fair distance, but he thought he could see the outlines of a shape—of a figure contained within. Whoever had raised the fires of hell had brought the damned along with it.

The posts grew denser as they neared the centre of the field, laid out in concentric circles in some blasphemous mimicry of the town itself. But in place of the priory and its tower, another pit had formed. This one was larger than the others and spat out a green mist of unknowable origin. As Pierre watched, something began to emerge from within the toxic vapours. Some abominable form, which became many, and then myriad as they were spewed out from the gaping womb of the earth.

Black wings beat against thick, leathery skins. Hooked talons pushed off against the edge of the pit, propelling wicked bodies into the air until the sky was momentarily hidden from sight. The things swarmed like bats, clustering together until they formed a great spiralling pillar—or perhaps a tower, to mirror that of the priory's in the centre of Enfaire. A horrible screeching followed their flight, and glowing yellow eyes cut through the haze that surrounded the pit.

"Demons," Pierre murmured, reaching for the crucifix that rested beneath the folds of his robes. "By what right do they have to walk the earth when the Lord himself has condemned them to the fires beneath?"

Remi shook her head, her eyes still fixed on the formation of flesh and talons. "It is as I feared. A bargain has been struck between the devil and the witch. This is no mere summoning but a rift between our world and the one beneath."

Pierre flinched as his ward's eyes snapped to meet his. They flickered with energy, with a light that not even the abyssal red tinge could subdue. But there was something else in her eyes now, too: rage.

"It is like a wound," she said. "If it goes untreated, it will only grow more rotten until the only cure is amputation."

"How do you amputate a whole valley?" Pierre asked, bemused.

"With fire."

✝ ✝ ✝

The next morning, Pierre and Remi left the priory before the breakfast bell and headed back into town. Their destination was Enfaire's solitary archive. Their purpose: to examine the records of the first witch trial and anything they could find relating to the hellscape that dominated Val de Havre by night.

Sister Lucille had given them directions but was unable to lead them herself due to other duties. She had told them to be careful, scribbled down an address, and left the friar and his ward to navigate their way through the narrow roads in the morning mist.

The first pale-faced townsfolk had just started to emerge from their homes when Pierre and Remi arrived at the archives. Those who had poked their heads out stared at the friar and his ward with unveiled disdain, and it was with a sense of relief that Pierre pushed open the door to the archives and clicked it shut behind them.

"Well," he said, looking about the gloomy lobby, "it appears Sister Lucille was correct about the people of Enfaire being less than welcoming."

"They do not trust us," said Remi, walking ahead of him. "And after what they have seen, I cannot blame them. Can you?"

Pierre shook his head, memories of the nightmarish vision he had witnessed the night before still fresh in his mind.

The lobby widened into another pair of rooms, with a cylindrical iron staircase in the middle of its floor that led, presumably, to further rooms above and below. Pierre let out a soft sigh as he took in the archives. Row upon row of shelves lined the walls, with boxes of unorganised books and ledgers crowding the space between them. A thin layer of dust covered the nearest shelf, and the Franciscan frowned as he ran a hand across its surface before staring down at his fingers and groaning.

"We may not find what we're looking for here," he said. "Not in this disorganised… Well, not in this mess."

The sound of a throat being cleared made Pierre glance up guiltily. A frail-looking man had appeared from behind one of the shelves and was staring at the friar with an expression that indicated his last words had not gone unheard. Pierre gave him an embarrassed smile as he dusted off his palms, wiping them clean against his robes. The archivist was old and thin, with wiry grey hair that reached to his shoulders. He wore a simple tunic that had started to fray at the sleeves, and his hands were covered in the same dust that Pierre had just wiped from his own.

"The archives would be less of a 'mess'," said the man, "if I had more hands to help me with them. You wouldn't happen to be those hands, would you? No... I thought not. What is it that I can help you with, then?"

"Ignore my friend," said Remi with an apologetic smile. "Sometimes, he does not know how to keep his tongue from talking about things he does not understand."

"Indeed," said the archivist, his expression softening. "Not an uncommon habit, I'm afraid. Now, what is it that you are looking for? Perhaps I might be of some help. This mess, after all, is my own."

Pierre shrunk into his robes but met the archivist's gaze when it fell upon him. His eyes were strangely young, with flecks of grey and blue and not a little humour in them.

"We're looking for the records of a trial and perhaps any writings you may have on the events that preceded it."

The archivist rubbed the cleft in his chin with a forefinger, wrinkling a brow. "That shouldn't be too hard to find. We haven't had many of those here. Magistrates are a rarity this far north, and we like to settle things amongst ourselves most times anyway. What was the name of the accused?"

Remi hesitated, but the pause was so brief that only Pierre noticed. "We would like to see the transcripts from the witch trial if you have them? And anything relating to that time in the valley."

"Which one?" asked the archivist, seemingly untroubled by the request.

"There was more than one?" Pierre racked his brain, trying to remember any mention of a second trial, but neither Sister Lucille nor Margaux had mentioned it.

"Oh yes," said the archivist. "We have been unfortunate enough to witness two witch trials in our humble history. They happened in quick succession, with only the second trial reaching a verdict. And then there was the burning. A nasty business."

"Who was the first accused?" Remi asked.

"I couldn't tell you," said the archivist with a shrug. "The first trial was conducted in the Magistrate's chambers, and the identity of the accused never revealed. It's a strange thing, I'll grant you. But not so strange if you consider some of the older families that live in these parts. They would have paid a pretty penny to keep their own from the public's scrutiny, even if they couldn't thwart the law itself. If the name were mentioned, it would have been redacted from the court records."

"We would like to see them both," said Remi, Pierre nodding beside her. "And any records you might have about the execution too."

"As you wish." The archivist turned on his heels, waving a hand at them to follow him between the crowded shelves.

"There isn't much, I'm afraid," he said, looking back over his shoulder. "From what I can recall, many of the records were returned to Reims with the Magistrate. He left in a hurry after the burning... Perhaps the final words of the witch spurred his haste, or else he had a sense of the horrors that were to come. But he left some notes from the proceedings behind in his rush to leave our poor town."

The archivist turned right at the end of the row of books before coming to a stop in front of a large cabinet in the corner of the room. He tugged open one of its drawers and began sifting through a stack of papers. His fingers moved agilely through the reports, and Pierre was reminded of the legs of a spider scuttling over the pages.

The archivist hummed beneath his breath while he searched, a tuneless song that only stopped when he retrieved a pair of thin leather-bound ledgers from the drawer.

"That's it?" Remi glanced back into the cabinet drawer, but the archivist pushed it closed before she could examine its contents.

"As I said, there isn't much. If you want to read the full records, you will have to visit the archives in Reims."

"I see," said Remi, accepting the proffered ledgers. They fit comfortably in her one hand, and Pierre saw the look of disappointment cross her face.

"It's a start," he said, trying his best not to sound disappointed himself. "And it might be all we need."

"It might," Remi agreed, moving to one of the reading desks. She nodded her thanks to the archivist and dropped the ledgers onto the table. "There's only one way to find out."

The Magistrate's notes, it turned out, were extensive and highly detailed. He had recorded everything, from the number of audience in attendance to the trials, to the nature of his breakfast and the impact it had on his disposition that day. There were other notes, too. Bulletins and notices from the week of the trial had been folded into the ledgers, as well as letters from the town heads requesting the Magistrate's assistance. Their pleas had been desperate, referring to the 'great evil that has befallen us', 'the servant of the dark that feeds upon our will', 'A sallow sickness that has taken them, of no earthly origin'. Other such letters made mention of finding 'the Devil's print upon the land' and seeing 'the cloven sign'.

Most learned men would have scoffed at such things, but Pierre had heard much—had seen much in his years with Remi and before. Now he knew better than to dismiss such claims offhand.

The friar scanned the page before him, scrolling quickly past the Magistrate's musings to his recording of the morning's court proceedings. The man had been thorough but had the habit of interposing his own reflections on facts he otherwise might not have. And much to Pierre's annoyance, the Magistrate had been scrupulous in excising the accused's name from the records. Nevertheless, he had resigned himself to reading through the document from cover to cover in the hopes he might be able to piece together some picture of the accused.

He was going through a particularly vivid testimony when his brow began to furrow, turning into a sharp V that made him look fiercer than he was. After a moment, he thumbed the page to keep his place and looked across the table to Remi.

"Listen to this," he said, not waiting to see if he had her attention.

"'I saw her that night, you see. She was up to her knees in filth, digging through the graves like a resurrectionist. I had my club out as soon as I caught sight of her, but even then, I knew there was something wrong. Her eyes glowed inside her skull, like the very pits of hell. Then there was the smell—I do now know if it came from the witch or from the open casket she stood over, but the grave rot was enough to make me retch. That was when the thing inside the casket rose up beside her like it were the

Rapture or something. When I saw its black wings and fiery maw, I must confess that I did run.'"

Remi's eyes narrowed as she listened to the account, and she crossed her arms as the friar finished reading.

"That was from the night watchman who first caught sight of the witch," said Pierre, looking up from the page. "The next morning, when he returned to the cemetery with the rest of the guard, they could find no sign that the graves had been tampered with and nothing of the witch. What do you make of that?"

"I'm not sure," Remi confessed. "Somehow, she is able to raise a hellscape beyond Enfaire's walls... But she cannot repeat the process within and so must rely on whatever blasphemous rituals to try and bring about this summoning."

"It sounds like she succeeded."

"And she's trying it again." Remi ground her teeth, her jaw clenching tight as she stared back down at her own ledger. "The boy we found was only halfway formed, but she intended turning him into a devil full. What havoc it would sow, released upon these hapless folk, while the witch works her spells against their vigour, draining the last of their health for whatever fell pursuits she has in store."

"If it is the Prioress…." The friar shook his head, still unable to believe that such a charming soul could harbour such wicked intent. But he knew witches. Half of their power lay in deceiving. And he would not allow himself to be blinkered to her cruelty.

"If it is her, then we will do what needs to be done," said Remi, turning the page. "We will save this place from the Devil's designs and send her back to his domain."

Pierre massaged his temples and stared back down at his journal. The Magistrate's scrawling text washed across the pages, becoming more detailed as the trial proceeded. Pierre blinked. His eyes had begun to ache from the poor light they were reading by, and still, they were no closer to discovering the identity of the first accused. At least it was warm, he thought, leaning back into the chair. And comfortable… Yes.

His eyes had just started to droop when Remi let out a triumphant whoop and shot up from her chair. The shock at the sudden movement nearly sent Pierre sprawling out of his own seat, and he stared up at her in startled bemusement.

"I think I've found it," said Remi, waving the pages of the open journal at her surprised friend. "I knew there'd be something here. The Magistrate could not have been so meticulous to have erased all mention of the accused."

"What is it?" Pierre sat up straight, suddenly alert. "A name? Is it the Prioress Margaux?"

"No… not a name," said Remi. "A breadcrumb… or the final piece in our puzzle. It is enough, though. Look."

She dropped the journal down in front of Pierre and pressed a finger on a passage halfway down the page. The friar leaned forward over the book and quickly scanned its contents, his eyes narrowing as he read the text. He was familiar with the Magistrate's cogitations, and the excerpt was less formal in tone than his judicial commentary. It was a footnote, really. A passing note on an event that the Magistrate had already decided was unworthy of more than the briefest contemplation, perhaps given that at the time of writing, the man already knew the woman was to be excused from trial.

"'Upon my arrival,' Pierre read, 'I was informed by the Headsman that the guilty party had already been apprehended and that my presence was but a mere formality, as was the trial itself. A mere formality! Hah! Tired from my trip and annoyed with the flippancy of my hosts, my temper only grew from poor to worse when I discovered that the accused had already been beaten near to death by her captors. If she had passed away before I had given my verdict, there would have been hell to pay—perhaps a poor choice of words, given the events that followed. Nevertheless!

As it so happened, the girl survived her captors' 'administrations', and I deemed her fit to stand before me. Tradition and the mandates of the law dictate that such a thing be a public affair. But before the trial was set to commence, I was petitioned by a body I could not refuse! The Holy Church itself, come to seek satisfaction from me, a humble servant of the state!

No doubt interested in keeping their name from such a business, I could not deny their request, even though a certain amount of trepidation filled me at the prospect—I had already read some of the testimony to be levelled against her: accusations of grave robbery, of pagan rituals, and worship most foul, and even, though I do not believe it myself, those who claimed to have seen her consort with a familiar—a serpentine shape that disappeared the moment it was seen!

But the Church cannot be denied, not even in matters such as this! And so it was that the young Sister from the priory was to be trialled within my quarters, with only myself and the witnesses present.'"

Remi's eyes were fixed on him when he looked up from the journal, an expectant look on her face. "Do you see?"

"Yes," said Pierre, seeing no point in denying the truth any longer. "A young Sister, from the priory no doubt. It can only be her. It can only be the Prioress Margaux."

WHERE THE DEVIL DOES WALK

And the great dragon was cast out, that old serpent, called the Devil, and Satan, which deceiveth the whole world: he was cast out into the earth, and his angels were cast out with him.

Revelation 12:9

"I haven't seen her all morn'." The gatekeep scratched at his chin and frowned. "Not since last night, if I think on it. Strange, that. She usually does a walk about the walls before noon."

"She's not in the priory either," said Remi. "And no one in the town seems to have seen her... Or if they have, they're not telling."

Clemens shrugged, closing the door to the gatehouse behind him and stepped out onto the cobbled road. The midday sun had just started to reach its peak, and a warm wind was sweeping in from across the valley. It gave Pierre a headache.

"Well, she didn't come this way, if that's what you're asking." Clemens raised a brow, swivelling his mustard green eyes between the pair of them. "Looking to say your goodbyes before you leave, eh? It's a fine day for travel, even if you are heading into God-knows-what down south."

"Not yet," said Pierre. "We have… a certain matter to conclude with your Prioress. It is most urgent, but she seems to have disappeared."

"I see." Clemens tugged at his undercoat, loosening his top button against the heat. "And you've tried the old chapel house then, have you? She's taken it upon herself to clean the place up. Might be she's snuck off there for a bit."

"The chapel house?" Pierre stared past the gatekeep's shoulder at the hill overlooking the town. The small structure seemed out of place upon the hillside, protruding from the landscape like a thorn in its side. Even from a distance, Pierre could make out its colour-stained windows and broken steps. He remembered the perverted idol of the blessed Mary sat outside its doors and the story captured in the panes above. A chill ran down his spine.

"Oh yes," Clemens was saying. "Seen her wandering the grounds myself. Mostly alone—she's solitary, like—but sometimes with another sister, too. Not sure why, when they've got the whole priory all to themselves. But I find it's best not to question my betters!"

"Then that's where we'll go," said Remi firmly.

"You have our thanks," said Pierre, watching his companion as she strode toward the hill. He turned back to the gatekeep and smiled warmly, clasping his hands firmly. "For this, and for opening your gates to us. A lesser man might not have, given the sickness and worse that lurks beyond these walls. You do yourself an honour."

Remi was already some way ahead, and the friar would have to hurry to catch up. With a final nod to the gatekeep, he bunched up the hems of his robes and followed her.

"You can thank the Prioress for that," Clemens called after him. "She's the one with the heart of gold. A blessing on us all, she is!"

✝ ✜ ✝

"Are you sure about this?" Pierre had hardly caught his breath when they began their ascent, and a bead of sweat dripped from his forehead. The day was getting warmer, and his back cooked against the sun. He wiped away the sweat with the sleeve of his robe and leaned heavily against his staff. "We don't know what we're walking into. You said it yourself: the witch's roots grow deep in this place. It could be a trap."

Remi scowled over her shoulder at him. "What's with you, Pierre? You've been a pain in my side since we arrived." She pointed up at the chapel, still staring at the friar. "A witch has presented herself upon the land, and we have chanced upon her. My purpose, you may recall, is singular. I will remove her from this town like poison from a wound, before it has a chance to fester. I will either do it with you at my side, or I will do it alone. Your choice."

Pierre sighed, but he knew there was no changing her mind. "I didn't survive the shadow and hellfires of Toulouse to leave you now, little saint. No, where you go, I will follow. I urge caution, that is all."

"Your concerns have been noted." Remi paused on the narrow pathway and then smiled back at the friar. "It is no small task that I have been set, but I am grateful for your company and your guidance. We shall be careful."

Pierre nodded, feeling slightly more reassured than before, but the cloud that lingered in his mind would not disperse. There was something different about Enfaire and the valley de Havre. A feeling… a presence the old friar had not felt in a long, long time, though he could not quite place it.

After a moment watching Remi move up the path, he forced the doubt from his mind and followed after.

They approached the chapel house from the east, skirting around its windows before emerging from the path opposite its entrance. A silence hung over the place, and it seemed to Pierre that even the sound of the windows rattling in the wind was muted, deadened by some inexorable force that centred around the church. The friar crouched down in the grass beside Remi and stared at its closed doors.

"It doesn't look like anyone's in," he whispered, more hopeful than anything else. But even then, he knew it wasn't true. Someone—something—had occupied the chapel house on the hill. And Remi wasn't going to leave until that thing had been smote from the land.

A warm gust swept across the hill, tugging at Pierre's hood and forcing him to close his eyes. When he opened them again, the air around him seemed to flicker, and he felt a subtle pressure weigh down on him. The colour in the trees and bushes surrounding the church— even the grass beneath his feet— appeared to him diminished, ashen and faded until the world seemed a shade of grey.

"Come on," said Remi, getting to her feet. She hadn't noticed the change, her eyes so firmly fixed on the chapel house. "It's time we unmasked the hag of de Havre and cast her back into the flames."

Pierre grunted as he rose from his knees, leaning against his staff as he hobbled after her toward the chapel doors. He felt eyes upon him as he moved onto the cracked steps. The friar hesitated and then turned to look around the yard, already knowing what it was he would find.

The grey stone statue beneath the windows seemed to have grown larger and stood near as tall as the chapel itself. The base carving had become more intricate, too, and symbols covered every square inch of the Blessed Mary's robes. But where the Mother had cradled a goat in her arms before, now there was nothing. Her arms were bare, the goat gone.

Despite himself, Pierre leaned forward to examine the statue, staring at the letters pressed into the stone. The words he read were meant for no mortal tongue, and the growing sense of unease that had disturbed him that morning returned. A great evil had forced itself upon the world and made the town of Enfaire its home.

"Remi..." He tilted his head, still staring at the symbols. Another gust of wind blew through the yard, and he flinched at the soft, monosyllabic stirrings that accompanied it. A voice, or many, on the edge of the wind... on the very edge of existence. They called to him through the breeze, pledging themselves to him, promising themselves, chaining themselves to his will, if only he would join them. An image flashed through his mind, of fiery pits and naked, writhing bodies—of fire and void, and an eternity of mangled ruin.

The priest snapped his eyes away from the statue, and the voices dropped. But not completely. He could still hear their murmurs, though they were subdued, and it was easier for him to shut them out.

"Remi," he repeated, louder this time. "I don't think—"

The doors to the chapel house slowly swung open, and Pierre saw the slight figure of his companion disappear inside.

"—this is a good idea," he finished lamely. The old friar spared the blasphemous statue one last glance, heaved out a sigh, and limped into the chapel house.

† ✤ ✤

Remi had been little more than a babe when she'd come under Pierre's care. He'd found her in the ruins of a town, the last survivor of a brutal attack upon its people. She had been unmarked by the fires that still raged and untouched by either the sword or spear that had killed her parents. It had been a miracle.

Knowing that the roads were no place for a child, Pierre had left her in the care of a small abbey on the outskirts of Paris. He visited often and saw to her instruction, ensuring that she was learned in the faith, as well as in worldly matters. He felt a duty to her, but more than that, he saw potential.

It wasn't long before the stories started. At first, it was small irregularities in the way of things—a mended wing, a salvaged crop, aches and pains that faded upon her touch. But as the stories grew, so too did her fame, until Pierre became concerned that she would begin attracting the wrong sort of attention.

The Inquisition was on the move, and the smoke from their pyres stained the sky as far north as Lorraine and Calais. Pierre had done the only thing he could do and sought protection from the Church itself. Far better to pre-empt discovery, he had decided, despite the risks.

He had taken her to Avignon, to the seat of Christendom in France. And there, beneath the vaulted dome of its grand church, her fate had been decided.

First, she had undergone a number of theological examinations in order to verify her morality. Then she had been tested, both in body and in mind. Her knowledge of Christ had been scrutinised, and her dedication to His will examined. She had been deprived of food and water for weeks on end, given nothing more than her Bible and a few words of encouragement from Pierre. Members of the Inquisition itself had questioned her, searched her body for any signs of mutation or witch-marks. Her purity had been checked and confirmed.

Finally, she had been asked to perform a miracle.

Her last test was to be undertaken within the great vaulted chambers beneath the church, in front of the Avignon Pope and his papal enclave. A row of benches and musty old men had frowned down at her from their seats. Doubting her, willing her to fail. They were the representatives of God's will and no one else.

But the Avignon Pope had smiled at Remi, and his eyes had been warm and curious. He was an honest man, at the very start of a reign that was to be burdened by plague and conflict, politics and war. He would smile less and less as his eyes grew colder. That was still to come, however. In that chamber, he had smiled at her and bade her begin, and so Remi had performed her miracle.

After that, there had been no doubt.

✟ ✟ ✟

Colour returned to the world as the old friar entered the chapel, his sandalled feet clicking against the hardwood floor beneath him. The air inside was cool, and the distant hum of voices faded as he passed beneath the doorway. The headache behind his eyes began to recede, too.

Pierre leaned against his staff, squeezing the door shut and turning to look into the chapel. Rows of pews lined both sides of the walls, crammed in wherever there was space. A coat of dust covered most of them, and Pierre could smell the stink of musk, and moisture from a leak, and something else, too. White sheets had been draped over some of the benches, but their wood had still rotten through, crumbling away to form small heaps on the floor.

Silhouettes hovered in the shadows beyond the pews, clay statues half-hidden beneath dirty rags. Pierre gazed at the closest one, trying to make sense of the shape beneath the wraps. It was sharp and angular, with protrusions pressing against the fabric that concealed it from his vision. A chipped hand hung out from beneath the material, but its proportions were wrong, the curling fingers far longer than any humans.

The sound of voices ahead drew Pierre's eyes from the statue and toward the front of the chapel house. An elevated dais stood beneath a pair of magnificent stained glass windows, basking in the yellow glow reflected through their coloured panes. By the podium itself, he recognised the figures of Remi and the Prioress Margaux. They were engaged in heated conversation, and by the harsh, clipped tone of Remi's voice, he knew that things were swiftly coming to a head.

"We both know such a spell could not long survive its caster's death," he heard Remi say as he picked his way through the ruined church. "No, to raise such a hellscape would require life... and deep roots. There can be no other way."

"I will have to take your word for it." Margaux's face was as flush with colour as it had ever been, but her mouth was drawn tight at the corners, and her eyes were dark when she noticed Pierre's arrival.

"Franciscan," she said, tilting her head almost imperceptibly. "Your ward was just telling me about a theory of hers. She does not think the witch is dead."

"She walks among us, yes." Pierre stepped up onto the dais to stand beside Remi. "Without her to channel such fell magicks, the curse of Val de Havre would have been long since lifted. No, there can be little doubt."

Margaux shook her head. "But I saw her burn."

"You saw someone burn," he replied. "It may even be that it was the witch, but she left an acolyte behind... or perhaps it was one of her minions cast onto the flames, to begin with... Only she would know."

"So tell us," said Remi, taking a step toward the Prioress. "Which was it?"

Margaux frowned, shaking her head as she looked from Remi to Pierre. "You can't possibly believe... I would never do such a thing. I could never."

Remi's mouth was set in a hard line as she appraised the prioress, her furrowed brow as deep as trenches. Light flickered behind her eyes, growing brighter as she spoke. "But you did. Do not think we can be so easily fooled as those in the town or that you can hide your blasphemies from us. We will not be blinkered from the truth, witch."

Margaux gasped, her stern facade slipping. "Me? How could... What proof do you have for such an accusation?"

"My dear Prioress," said Pierre, raising a hand. "You wear it upon your very skin. You did not think it went without notice—that you are flush with health while the rest of the town rots? Your evil spreads like contagion and devours life like a parasite."

Margaux hesitated. "I... I thought it was—"

"What happened to the craftsman's son?" asked Remi, taking another step closer. "The boy who fell from the priory roof. What did you do to him? We saw what he was to become."

"Nothing! I did not touch him!" Margaux tried to push past Remi, but Pierre blocked her with the tip of his staff.

"Let me pass," Margaux demanded, blonde curls coming loose beneath her veil. She was flustered, and her voice shook when she spoke. "You cannot keep me here. You have no authority over me. This is my priory."

"But you are wrong," said Remi, rolling up her sleeves. "We claim authority from a higher source, one that even you must submit to."

Margaux hesitated, momentarily taken aback. "Avignone? Rome?"

Pierre snorted. "Higher, even."

The Prioress stiffened, clasping onto the staff to prevent Pierre from prodding her further. There was fear in her eyes. "You are with the Inquisition, then?"

"I wonder," said Remi, ignoring the question. "What chaos had you planned once you were done raising the boy? He was very nearly there, you know... before we had him consigned to the flames."

"May his soul find peace," murmured Pierre.

"You must believe me," said the Prioress, pushing away the walking stick. Her face shone red, even beneath the glow of the windows. "I found him after he fell, that is all. I even offered to perform his last rites. But the family refused."

Pierre frowned at that. "Refused?"

"They wouldn't let me near him... I think... I think they blamed me for what happened. But I'd told him not to climb up there. It wasn't my fault."

"Crooked words from a crooked tongue," said Remi. "We will not be so easily deceived."

"It is true." Margaux looked to Pierre, pleading with her eyes. "I don't know what you found, but it has nothing to do with me. Please, let me go."

"I'm sorry," said Pierre. "Though I know now why the Magistrate was willing to acquit you—a rare thing in a witch trial—you are most compelling."

"The Magistrate?" The Prioress stumbled back, confusion writ upon her face. "What Magistrate? I was never tried. I have never even been accused of a crime—until now."

Remi laughed. "The game is up, witch. There is no point pretending any longer. The Magistrate was not so meticulous as you might have hoped. He left hints and more. We know the first accused was only spared because she cast accusation upon another—your acolyte, perhaps? And we know that she was a Sister, too."

Margaux blanched, her sharp angular features turned down in thought. "A Sister... from the Priory? But that's—"

Pierre and Remi both turned to look as the chapel house door slowly creaked open, and a shadow stepped into the hall. The Franciscan frowned as the air started to buzz, the voices he'd shut out returning louder than before. He grunted as he tried to suppress their calls, leaning deeper into his staff as the effort shook his body. The shadow moved into the light, revealing a slight figure in a white habit.

"Sister!" Margaux called, trying again to push past Remi. "Please! You must fetch

Clemens and the town guard. I think they mean to harm me!"

Sister Lucille cocked her head, her black curls bobbing over the rings around her eyes. She swept the hair back with a pale hand and then smiled, closing the door behind her.

"Ah," said Pierre, watching the sister stride toward them, the voices growing louder with every step. "It appears we were mistaken."

"Lucille?" The Prioress had stopped trying to get past Remi and was watching the nun's approach with a mixture of hope and confusion. "You must get help," she repeated. "They think I am the witch!"

The ache returned behind Pierre's eyes, and he ground his teeth before turning to Margaux. "Who was the sister brought before the Magistrate, if not you? Quickly! You must tell us."

A look of horror crossed the Prioress's face as realisation finally dawned. "It can't be," she muttered, shaking her head. Remi nudged her by the shoulder, and the Prioress looked up, staring down the pews. Finally, she raised a hand, a finger levelled at Lucille. "It was… her."

Lucille feigned a look of shocked hurt as she came to a stop at the end of the pews, and then a grin broke out on her face. "Why, Prioress, have you forgotten your verses? 'Let he who is free of sin cast the first stone.' Isn't that how the line goes? Perhaps you should be careful lest you... slip?"

A sharp intake of breath from beside Pierre indicated that the words had hit home. "He fell," murmured the Prioress, "It wasn't my fault. I... I tried—"

Remi bristled. "You dare tarnish scripture with your tongue? And in one of His Houses, witch."

Lucille laughed. The sound was cold and cruel, and Pierre flinched as it tugged at something deep within his mind. Images from memory flashed before him—of coiling serpentine scales and ichor black talons, a gaping maw lined with bleeding teeth. Deep within his consciousness, he heard something rattle. He shook free the vision, grunting as the ache in his head sharpened.

Lucille flexed her fingers, the smile never leaving her face. "This stopped being a House of God a long time ago, little girl...." She waved a hand, flicking her wrist at the drape covered silhouettes that lined the walls. "See?"

Pierre felt the air stir as some unseen force dragged the sheets to the floor, revealing the figures beneath. They were abominations, foul mimicries of their original forms. Horns sprouted from the head of the nearest statue, and where there had once been a staff, a pair of snakes now dangled. It was Raphael, Pierre was sure. Or it had been. But now, the angel's wings were crooked and malformed, curving in on themselves like that thing they had found within the grave. The other statues had been similarly transformed, and a host of stone gargoyles and demons leered across the pews at them.

"I hope you like what I've done with the place," said Lucille, examining her nails before looking up at Remi. "An improvement, don't you think?"

"Sacrilege," Remi growled, her eyes not leaving Lucille's. "One that shall not go unpunished, witch."

Lucille laughed again. "What do you know of punishment, girl? Do you think you could do to me what hasn't already been done a thousand times and more? Do you think you or your fat priest can break me? With what? Prayer?" The blasphemous nun shook her head and snorted. "No, no, I'm afraid you've got it all wrong. There shall be no punishment for me. Not today."

Remi skipped down from the dais and strode confidently toward the witch. She stopped a step away from Lucille, who was eyeing her curiously from beneath her mop of brown hair.

"Your soul has become corrupted," said Remi. "And I am here to deliver you from it."

"My... soul?" Lucille's eyes lit up with glee, and another cruel laugh escaped her lips. "My soul, she says! I have another secret, little one. Oh, but it is a precious secret. Would you like to know what it is?"

Lucille's arm shot out so fast that Pierre barely saw it move—a flash of pink flesh and something... something that looked like the hooked end of a claw. The blow connected with Remi's neck before she could react, slicing into the skin just above her collar and sending her spinning into the pews. She slammed into the wooden benches with a sickening thud and slumped to the ground, not moving.

"Remi..." Pierre's eyes widened as he spotted the pool of blood gathering beneath his friend's body. Her head hung at an awkward angle, resting loosely against her chest. He turned to the witch, anger boiling in his breast. "What have you done?"

"He works in mysterious ways, doesn't he?" Lucille dropped her arm, staring down at the fingers that had seemed as sharp as razors a second before. She shuddered, flexing her jaw as a grimace replaced her smile, and a shadow shifted over her face, writhing like tendrils about her eyes. Lucille groaned as her flesh rippled like a tepid pool of water that had just been disturbed. She hunched forward, taking a slow step toward the friar.

The pressure Pierre had felt outside the chapel house returned, a pulsing current of power that weighed down on his chest and shoulders. The gibbering voices came with it, scraping against his consciousness as they whispered to him.

"What a privilege," Lucille grunted, pain scarring her features as they bubbled, "to witness my descendancy… few… ever… do."

Pierre blinked, feeling his breath catch in his throat as he watched a shape twitch beneath the witch's skin. Sharp ridges began to form along her face and arms, tearing through the soft tissue as they imposed themselves upon her body. Lucille's jaws opened, extending impossibly wide until they cracked with a gut-churning snap. Sharp, pincer-like mandibles emerged from where her mouth had been, and a row of fangs pierced through her gums.

Her skin started to change, too, darkening with each step she took. She paused, tilting her head as another bout of shakes spasmed throughout her body. The tremors came to an abrupt halt when spiralling horns of obsidian black shot out from her forehead, cutting through the meat and bone that was now falling from Lucille's body like a discarded carapace.

"The Devil's print." Pierre gasped as he watched a pair of cloven hooves burst through the wraps that had bound Lucille's feet, cutting into the floorboards as she stomped toward the dais. Thick clumps of greasy hair covered her legs while jagged scales had emerged all across her midriff and upper body. A tail swished in the air behind her, balancing her growing form as she cast the last of her mortal skin aside.

Finally, with a sound like a stillborn corpse being birthed, leathery black wings sprouted from Lucille's back. A noxious stench accompanied their arrival, and Pierre had to cover his face to stop from gagging.

Lucille's voice was changed when next she spoke. It had deepened, carrying with it the sound of cacophony, of wind, and of the chaos at the edge of order.

"I AM THE HERALD OF THE RED SEA
THE BANE OF THE ISRAELITES
I AM THE MASTER OF TARTARUS
THE WALKER OF THE SANDS
I AM THE SEVEN HELLS
FEAR ME"

Lucille's membranous appendages vibrated softly, shaking off the last of the blood and gore that coated them.

"YOU SEE?" The demon flapped its wings experimentally, turning its caprine head and yellow eyes to look at Margaux. "MY SECRET WAS BETTER THAN YOURS."

LEVIATHAN

And no wonder, for Satan himself masquerades as an angel of light. It is not surprising, then, if his servants also masquerade as servants of righteousness.

Corinthians 11:14

The Prioress fell to her knees, her hand clasped around the crucifix at her neck. Her lips moved in the Lord's prayer, but Pierre could hardly hear the words—the discordant cries in his head were too loud. He could feel the faith emanating from Margaux's body, though. And fear. The concentrated mix was like a hot wave against his skin, and he stepped away from her.

The demon flexed its long talons, scraping them against the floor before folding them back and shifting its gaze to the friar. "IT HAS BEEN TOO LONG SINCE LAST I WALKED THE MORTAL REALM AS MYSELF. FOR THAT, YOU HAVE MY THANKS."

Pierre flinched beneath the demon's piercing yellow orbs. He could feel it gazing into his mind and into his soul—weighing him, determining his worth. There was a soft intake of breath, followed by a bovine snort. The thing that had been Lucille tilted its head as what passed for a strange look occupied its features.

"I KNOW YOU…"

The friar glanced down at Margaux, braving the heat that surrounded her to shake her by the shoulder. "Prioress, please! You must leave this place!"

"I COULD NOT SEE IT BEFORE. BUT NOW I DO."

"The boy..." she murmured, "I couldn't... He fell..." The Prioress remained still, not moving from her knees as the demon stalked closer. Her knuckles were white from gripping the crucifix so tightly, and Pierre could see drops of blood where the silver had cut into her hand.

"LET ME LOOK AT YOU PROPERLY." Wood splintered beneath the demon's bulk as it reached the dais, its long tail knocking benches over in its wake. The monstrosity had grown taller than the pulpit, and muscles as thick as Pierre's body writhed beneath its flesh. The stench of rot followed it, and Pierre recognised it as the lingering scent he'd been unable to identify. It made his eyes water.

The friar stood transfixed as the demon loomed over him, its jagged claws reaching down toward the dais. He cried out as a hooked talon dug into his shoulder, piercing the sleeve of his robes and then his skin like a hot knife. Blood poured from the wound, soaking his arm as it spilt out onto the chapel floor. The pain forced the breath from his lungs, and his head lolled to the side as the demon's claws wrapped around his chest.

The creature lifted him with ease, cradling him in the air before it so that it might better examine him.

Pierre cried out again as the demon's voice entered his head, speaking into his mind as it scrutinized him.

"SUCH A TORTURED SOUL," it said, the orbs in its skull flickering like hellfires. "I WOULD KNOW WHY THAT IS. SHOW ME."

Images appeared before him, memories from his past, but other things, too. They flashed before his eyes, fast enough to make his head spin and his stomach lurch. He saw a city of flames, white walls being consumed as they turned to ash. Bodies lay in piles in front of the city gates, and then a great tide washed them all away. A pyre appeared, its wood already smouldering as the fire licked the feet of the condemned upon it.

"YES, YES, THE FIRES OF GUIENNE. DEATH OF THE WITCHKIN FOLLOWS YOU WHEREVER YOU GO."

The pyre vanished and was replaced by the ruins of another city. Smoke billowed across its streets, concealing the empty houses and crumbling walls. Shadows stirred within the gloom, a procession of holy men moving from house to house. In their hands, they carried crosses, but in their hearts, they bore swords. Screams followed them wherever they went.

"TOULOUSE, TOO, I SEE. I WAS THERE, BUT I DO NOT REMEMBER YOUR FACE. THE REST…"

Pierre's vision swam as he tried to avert the demon's stare. The pain inside his skull had grown insufferable, and the howling voices threatened to drown out his very thoughts. With a grunt, he managed to snap his gaze away from the fiery orbs, his eyes coming to a rest on the stained glass windows that surrounded the chapel house. His brow furrowed as he recognised one of the panels: it was Lucifer's Fall from Heaven.

The scene blurred with his memories until he felt like he was falling from the sky toward a city of fire and ash. Something stirred within him as the demon's hateful gaze scratched at his mind. He could feel his essence being pulled at, diminishing as the hell-thing stretched his soul out, reading it like a scroll. More memories spilt out across his mind, veiled beneath the smoke and clouds as he spun toward the earth. A part of him that had remained hidden, caged away, rattled against its prison, tearing at its bars to get out. He continued his plummet... Only, the earth had disappeared, and a fiery pit now awaited him. Tartarus. Hell.

"A SHROUD COVERS YOUR PAST, PRIEST… BUT I WOULD KNOW IT ALL.

PERHAPS I SHALL FIND SATISFACTION WHEN I CONSUME YOUR SOUL?"

Pierre struggled against the demon's grip as it slowly unhinged its jaws, revealing row upon row of bloody teeth. Its rotten gums were grey and putrid, and streams of maggots fell out from the ulcers that riddled them. A gust of charnel breath buffeted the friar, and he retched bile out all over the front of his robes.

"NOW WE SHALL SEE," the demon's voice rang in his head as it brought him closer to its gaping maw. It withdrew its talon from Pierre's shoulder, eliciting another cry of pain, and slowly loosened its grip on him, letting the friar slide toward its waiting mouth.

"NO!"

A brilliant golden light blasted through the chapel house, pulsing as it swept across the hall. Shadows and filth burned beneath it, and the twisted statues shrivelled and then crumbled away as soon as the light touched them. The demon staggered back against the blinding radiance, sheltering its eyes beneath the crook of a wing. It barked out a shocked curse, further loosening its grip on the friar. Pierre took the opportunity to roll out from between its claws, slipping toward the ground, where he landed with a hard thud.

"WHAT'S THIS?" said the demon, lowering its wing as the light began to fade.

Pierre kept his head down as he shuffled across the floorboards, back toward the dais and the still-kneeling figure of the Prioress. When he reached the pulpit, he risked a glance back over his shoulder and watched with awe as the glow contracted until all that was left of it was a golden aura around a familiar figure.

Remi.

His ward slowly rose to her feet—lifted, it seemed, by unseen hands. She wiped away the blood that covered her neck, but the wound that had caused it was gone, the skin smooth beneath. The girl stared down into her hands, at the life-blood that had sprayed across the pews only a few minutes before, and then cleaned them against her dress. When she looked up, it was like staring into molten pools of gold. Light poured from her eyes, shining with such intensity that Pierre had to look away.

"ANOTHER SECRET," said the demon, unfurling its wings as it considered Remi. "BUT AREN'T YOU A DELICIOUS SURPRISE."

Remi stepped over the scattered pieces of the bench she'd been flung against, walking calmly toward the Fallen. The aura that surrounded her pulsed again, another shock of light that swept through the chapel.

"THE GOD-TOUCHED ALWAYS FILL MY BELLY," said the demon, unsheathing its talons. "AND I SHALL SAVOUR YOU... OH

YES. AND THEN YOUR FAT PRIEST. BUT I THINK I SHALL SAVE THE PRIORESS FOR LAST SO THAT SHE MAY THINK ON HER SINS."

Pierre clambered up the dais step, crouching down beside the Prioress as he watched Remi come to a halt in front of the demon. The beast dwarfed her, standing nearly twice her size and as wide as she was tall. Still, she did not cower beneath its gaze, meeting its fiery stare with her own.

The friar reached out to Margaux but snapped his hand away when he felt the heat emanating from her body. She was near boiling, and yet her skin remained as flush and pure as ever. Her hand was still clutched around the crucifix. The silver had started to warp from the heat of her body and drooped over her nails and fingers.

"Prioress, please," he said, trying to keep his voice even. "This is no place for you... for us. We must go now, before it's too late."

Margaux seemed not to hear him, whispering soft words over and over beneath her breath.

Pierre leaned closer, tilting his head to hear.

"His soul. Spare him his soul. His soul. Spare him."

"Who's soul, Prioress?" Pierre asked, exasperated. He didn't know what was happening to her, but he knew that nothing good would come from staying in the chapel... in Enfaire. "The demon forsook any claim to one a long time ago... Save your prayers. They are wasted on it."

But the sister ignored him, her eyes fixed on some distant point ahead as she repeated the mantra.

"I can't leave without you," said Pierre with a sigh. He shifted on his knees and turned to watch Remi and the demon square off against one another. Their fates were now tied to the fight to come.

The air around Remi hummed, crackling with tension as she stared up at the demon. The hellspawn thing towered over her—all muscle and teeth and razor-sharp claws—but she was not scared. Her aura pulsed again, bathing the chapel house with a golden light. This seemed to amuse the demon, and it let out a haggard laugh.

"I AM BEYOND SUCH TRICKS, FOOLISH GIRL. I HAVE SEEN THE LIGHT OF HEAVEN AND TURNED MY BACK ON IT. YOUR TINY CANDLE MEANS NOTHING TO ME."

"Perhaps this will," said Remi, a faint smile on her lips. She reached into nothingness, her hand fully disappearing as it crossed into the incorporeal realm. Her smile faded, replaced by an expression of steely determination. A bead of sweat rolled down her forehead, the first sign of exertion Pierre had seen since she had been asked to perform her miracle all those years before.

"Your soul," she said between gritted teeth, "is corrupted." She grunted as she began to withdraw the limb, tugging at something from the other side. "And I… am here…" With a flourish of steel and fire, she yanked her hand back from the ethereal plane, her fingers now firmly clasped around the hilt of a flaming sword. "…to deliver you from it."

The demon growled, its black tongue tasting the air as it glared down at its adversary. It flinched away from the current of flame, from the empyrean steel. If Pierre had to guess, he would have said there was a hint of uncertainty in that thing's great, pus-filled eyes. Fear, even.

"You know this sword, don't you, demon?" Remi wrapped her other hand around its hilt, unaffected by the gout of flames that rippled from the blade. The sword was near as long as she was tall, and yet she held it effortlessly. The flames coursed, swelling like lungs after a deep breath. Remi smiled again. "It remembers you, I think."

The demon snorted. "IT WAS ONCE WIELDED BY ANOTHER. BY YOUR BETTER, LITTLE THORN. HOW DID YOU COME BY IT?"

"It was given to me freely," said Remi. "A gift for my crusade against Hell and its accursed minions. Against you."

"THEN I SHALL CLAIM IT AS MY OWN!" The demon lunged at her, propelled forward with a single flap of its powerful wings. Malefic talons extended to deliver a killing blow, slicing through the air faster than Pierre could see. The ground screamed as the demon landed, wood and stone crunching beneath its giant hooves. But not Remi.

The golden saint ducked beneath the demon's sweeping blows, rolling away before it could tear into her skin with its claws. She leapt back to her feet in a single movement and swung her sword with a speed that matched the demon's own.

The creature let out a howl of pain as the burning blade cut into its scales, lurching back to try and avoid the searing flames that licked at it. Black ichor spouted from the wound as it stumbled into the benches, gushing across the floor like a fountain of filth.

"YOU WILL PAY FOR THAT," spat the demon, cradling its side. The hell-fiend did not wait for her reply, bounding forward to re-engage. Remi raced to meet it, adjusting her guard as she sprinted through the pews. She used the burning blade like a lance, swatting aside the demon's claws as they went for her throat and then driving it toward its chest.

The demon was ready for her this time and rolled back on its hircine haunches, letting the tip of the sword pass it by. Remi stumbled as her attack faltered and then tried to skip away. But it was too late. With a bestial roar, the demon kicked out with its one hoof, slamming it into the side of her head with a hideous crunch. The girl went sprawling, her body as limp as a doll as it careened through the air. Her flight was brought to an abrupt halt when she met the wall on the other end of the chapel house, which cracked and then buckled, collapsing over her in a stream of dust and splinters.

The demon snorted, slamming its hoof back down against the ground. "THE FLESH IS WEAK AND CAN BE BROKEN, BUT IT IS YOUR SOUL I WANT. COME, LITTLE ONE, MEET YOUR FATE."

For the second time that day, Remi rose to her feet, pushing aside the rubble as she clambered through the ruins of the chapel house. Pale light shone through the gaping hole in the wall, adding to the glow of her aura. She drew her sword out from the debris, its flame turning a shade of crimson as she took up her guard.

The friar watched on as the two fighters circled each other. They were more cautious now, both having had a taste of what the other had to offer. A bruise was forming where Remi had been kicked, some preternatural strength being the only thing that stopped her from turning into a bloody mist when the hoof had found her. The wound in the demon's side had stopped bleeding, but he could see the white of bone beneath the black ichor that coated it. Remi had cut the hellspawn deep, and it had begun to favour that side.

Pierre spared a glance at the Prioress. Her hands were still clasped around what remained of her cross, but she had ceased her mantra, her eyes closed. There was a subtle sheen that covered her skin now... Not a fever, no. Something... else. Pierre tilted his head and then turned back to stare at Remi, at the golden aura that surrounded her.

Could it be?

The little saint ducked beneath a swipe of the demon's tail, following after it with a vicious swing of her sword. The burning blade gleamed as it carved through its silvery scales, extracting another angry roar from the hellfiend, who lunged forward. Remi pirouetted away, spinning on her heels as she narrowly avoided another kick to the head.

The demon's tail snapped out again, slicing through the air before Remi could regain her balance. This time, its wicked barbs broke through Remi's guard, sinking deep into her waist. The slithery appendage twisted, writhing as it wrapped itself around her body, dragging her toward the hellspawn. Before she could bring her sword down to cut it away, the demon was on her.

"WHAT NOW, LITTLE ONE?"

Remi gasped as it wrapped its claws around her, pulling her into its embrace. She tried to bring her sword up to meet it, but the demon yanked at her arm, breaking it like a twig. She let out a cry of pain as the blade fell from her grasp, its fire extinguished the moment it left her fingers. It dropped to the floor and lay there, out of reach.

"THERE, THERE," said the demon, slowly tightening its grip. "THIS SHALL ALL BE OVER SOON. AND THEN YOU WILL BECOME A PART OF ME. ISN'T THAT SPECIAL? AND I SHALL HAVE WON MY BROTHER'S SWORD."

Remi struggled in the thing's grip, thrashing madly in an effort to get away. But the demon was too strong. It pulled her closer, until she was pressed up tight against its chest, and began to squeeze.

Remi's skin chafed against the scales, and she tried to keep her head away from the sharp ridges and spikes that covered the demon like a suit of armour. The slabs of muscle on its arms and chest rippled as it exerted pressure, tightening its deadly hug.

Her ribs cracked first, collapsing against the tremendous force brought to bear against them.

Then, her unbroken arm started to bend against the pressure, curving in on itself beneath the hell-fiend's vice-like grip. The demon grunted, sensing victory was close. It shifted on its haunches, leaning forward to bring yet more force to bear.

Remi stopped struggling, her arms going limp at her sides. The creature blew hot, foetid breath into her face, and more iniquitous vermin scurried out from the recesses in its mouth.

"SO SOON," said the demon, pulling its head back to stare at her. It sounded almost... disappointed. "I WOULD HAVE THOUGHT TO FIND MORE FIGHT IN YOU, GOD-TOUCHED."

Remi did not reply but lifted her head to meet the demon's pestilential gaze. There was defiance in her eyes—and rage. Her lips started to move, even as red stains gathered in the corners of her mouth. She shuddered, spitting out a gobbet of blood and smiling as the demon flinched away from it.

The hell-thing scowled, shaking away the blood that steamed upon its reptilian skin. "SAVE YOUR PRAYERS, LITTLE ONE. THEY WILL NOT HELP YOU NOW."

The girl closed her eyes, humming softly as her aura flickered. Words filled her lips, a litany that rose above the growling demon, above even the voices in Pierre's head. Her aura flickered again and then disappeared entirely.

The demon started to laugh, its haggard voice filling the chapel house with glee as it unhinged its jaw. Teeth the size of Remi's head slid out from behind the demon's gums, and its repellant tongue slithered out to taste the air.

Remi's voice grew louder as she recited the litany, uttering words of devotion even as the demon drew her up to its mouth. Another sound joined her prayer, another voice that seemed to superimpose itself over hers. It sang with Remi, adding its own notes to her song of defiance. The demon flinched when it noticed it, its eyes growing wide as it searched the chapel house for the source. The beast recognised the voice—feared it. But there was nothing to be found. The voice that had joined Remi's was not of this world.

With a surge of brilliant light, Remi opened her eyes, unleashing her golden wrath upon the demon. The fiend tried to hold onto her, but its claws burned, and noxious steam rose from its flesh. It met her gaze for a moment, and the flames in her eyes grew brighter still. It was like staring into the centre of an exploding sun, and the demon roared in pain as it was flung back by it.

Remi seemed to float back down to the floor, her fall arrested by some unseen force. She pulled her broken arm into place as she landed and knelt down into the rubble to reclaim her sword. Flame erupted from the blade as soon as she touched it, crimson fire mixing with the golden glow of her aura. She hefted the sword in front of her, returning to her guard.

"VERY WELL THEN," said the demon, pushing aside rubble and ruin as it rose back up to its hooves. Its great wings flapped behind it, aiding its rise from the ground, while its tail balanced out its immense weight. "IF YOU WILL NOT BE REASONABLE, THEN NEITHER WILL I."

The demon sunk its hooves into the floorboards, sucking in great breaths of air as its wings stretched out behind it. Already its body was starting to grow, its skin rippling as its bones extended, scales stretching as the thing expanded. Its monstrous horns grew upwards, curling toward the roof like the roots of a tree. Then its belly expanded, slumping over its waist like the gut of a drunkard. The silver plates that covered its midriff stretched, pulling wider and wider, turning a darker shade with the hell-fiend's growth.

The demon chuckled, its voice becoming deeper as it transformed, until the sound was all Pierre could hear. It was tall enough now that its horns nearly scraped the roof of the chapel house, and it was growing taller still. Its bloated figure took up all the space between the aisles, malformed layers of fat and muscle hanging from its frame like candle wax. The hell-thing rapped its bulbous knuckles against the nearest pew and then hefted the bench up by a single claw.

Remi charged forward, not waiting for the demon to finish its transformation. The bloated beast leered down at her, its flabby skin shaking as it swung the bench. It smashed through the pews, sending broken bits of wood the size of daggers through the air. Remi just managed to duck beneath the blow, using her sword as a shield against the splinters that rained down on her, before scrambling to her feet.

"COME TO ME." The hell-fiend raised a swollen black claw, beckoning her toward him. It stood above even the glass panes that covered the chapel house walls, its shadow extending well past Remi to the dais itself.

The demon lumbered forward, each of its giant steps breaking through the floorboards and into the foundations below. Its flabby wings flapped clumsily behind it, too small now to do anything but add impetus to the demon's steps.

Remi swept forward with her blade, slashing at the demon's knees, dancing away before it could parry her blows. Ooze gushed from where the burning blade cut, and the stink of burning hair filled the hall. Remi darted in again, this time using the sword like an axe, chopping at the stout midriff of the demon. There was desperation in her attacks now, and the grooves she left in the monstrosity's leathery skin were becoming shallower with each strike.

The thing laughed, swatting her aside with a clenched fist, sending her flying into the pews. It patted down its waist, looking at the cuts in its stomach before staring at the broken benches to where Remi was getting back up.

"TOO SMALL NOW, LITTLE ONE," it said. "PERHAPS BEFORE I UNVEILED MYSELF UPON THIS WORLD. BUT NOT NOW."

Remi leapt forward again, skipping over the ruined floorboards and flinging herself at the demon. Her sword sang in the air, its fire trailing like the tail of a comet as it came down to meet the hell-fiend. The demon's tail whipped out with blinding speed, unslowed by the added weight and girth. It connected with Remi just beneath her neck, sending her flailing back into the broken benches.

"NO, NO! TOO SMALL!" The demon chortled, flexing its black talons as it lumbered after her.

Pierre felt the heat before he heard the Prioress rise. It was blistering hot, and he recoiled, moving a step closer to the podium as he turned to look at her. The Prioress's face shone with life, resplendent in the gloom of the chapel house. A subtle sheen covered her skin, and he saw a sliver of light ripple across her body.

Sweat dripped from his face as he watched Margaux step down from the dais. The podium behind him began to warp, and the wood beneath her feet scorched beneath the heat. The energy around her seemed to hum, and more golden slivers streamed upon her skin as she moved toward the aisle and its broken benches.

"Prioress!" Pierre called, realising her intent. "Come back here. It's not safe! That thing will destroy you!"

But it was too late. The prioress was already striding between the aisles, making for the bloated form occupying the centre of the chapel. The being hadn't noticed her yet, its eyes still set on Remi as she regained her footing.

"Margaux!" Pierre cried once more, hoping she'd see sense. The Prioress slowed in her steps, coming to a halt mere feet away from the hell-fiend, and glanced back at the Franciscan.

"It was my fault," she said softly. And then louder, "The boy... He fell. And I let him. I could have saved him, but... I let him. Something stopped me." She smiled a sad smile and turned toward the demon. "But I won't let this spawn of hell win. Not here."

The demon finally noticed her and cocked its head, its thick neck wobbling as a grin appeared on its face. "I HAD PLANNED ON SAVING YOU FOR LAST, PRIESTESS. BUT IF YOU WISH TO MEET YOUR FATE BEFORE THE LITTLE ANGEL, THEN I AM HAPPY TO OBLIGE."

It leaned down on its haunches and extended a giant claw, scooping her up from the ground like one would a child's toy. Margaux remained calm as she was lifted, her hands still clasped over the molten ruin of her cross.

The air around her blurred, shimmering as waves of heat flowed from her. The demon did not notice the blistering heat or the golden sheen that rippled upon her skin. Nor did it notice the smile upon the Prioress's face as he lowered her toward its mouth.

Pierre watched as the demon's talons began to warp, curling away from the prioress, just like the wood of the podium had. Scales peeled under the heat, revealing the soft pink flesh and the bones beneath. A spark ignited on the thing's skin, quickly catching on the black tufts of fur that covered its lower body. But the demon did not notice that either.

With a haggard laugh, the hell-fiend unhinged its jaws and dropped her into its mouth, swallowing her whole. Its saggy neck jiggled as she passed down its throat to his belly and a look of fervent concentration set upon the demon's face as it digested her. Then, after a tense moment, the demon opened its mouth and burped.

Pierre's shoulders dropped as he watched the hell-fiend devour the Prioress. There was nothing he could do—there was nothing anyone could do. Remi had managed to get back to her feet again, and her blade was held firmly out before her. But he could see the dismay on her features too. Her aura had diminished, and the torrent of flame that covered her sword seemed less intense than before.

"DO NOT WORRY LITTLE ONES," said the demon. It stroked its belly with a warped talon, chortling as it looked from Remi to Pierre. "THERE IS PLENTY OF ROOM FOR—"

The demon hesitated, a strange look crossing its grisly features. It tilted its head, staring down at the prodigious gut that hung from its midriff. The look of uncertainty turned to one of mild discomfort, and the hell-fiend shifted its head restlessly.

"I—" The demon snorted, blinking its pustule eyes at the tendril of smoke that emerged from its bovine snout. More smoke poured from the corners of its mouth, until the hell-fiend's face was almost entirely obscured by it.

"WHAT IS THIS?" It roared, stomping its hooves in frustration. The thick leathery hide around its midriff bubbled like a pot of water coming to a boil. Large flakes of ashen skin fell to the floor. The demon lurched forward, holding onto its gut as its discomfort turned into agony. A soft glow appeared just beneath the hellspawn's rib cage. The light was enough to illuminate the thousand veins that lined the creature's stomach, knotting together like a city map. But the light showed something else too. A shadow, passing through the demon's insides.

"PRIESTESS," it groaned, scraping at its gut. It sunk a hooked talon into the fatty layers, dragging it like a knife across its belly. The hell-thing took another staggering step forward, its face contorting as it battled with the pain that wracked its body.

Pierre blinked as he watched the demon carve through its own flesh, spilling its guts out onto the chapel floor. More smoke billowed from the open wound, and the smell of burnt meat filled the hall.

The demon let out another horrific groan as a shard of light shot out from its belly, followed by another and another. Blood was running down its legs in great streams, coating the floor thick with slippery black ichor. The demon's entrails hung from it like a foetus before its umbilical cord could be cut. It howled as more light poured from the wound, slicing through its flesh as it spilt into the world. The light was so bright now that the demon's skin appeared translucent, revealing its inner workings even as they dissolved beneath the heat.

"Now, girl!" Pierre called, managing to drag his gaze from the immolating demon to Remi. "Kill it!"

Remi hesitated, glancing back at the Franciscan as he hobbled down from the dais. He waved her forward, urging her to take advantage of the demon's faltering strength. More light blasted through the hellspawn's flesh, but its talons were submerged deep within its belly now, trying to fish out the cause of its agony. It would drag the Prioress out any moment now.

Remi growled, moving into a loping run. The burning sword—Gabriel's sword—hummed approvingly in her hands, its torrent of flame coursing as she closed in on her adversary. She skipped over the ruined benches along the aisles, moving past the bubbling mess at the demon's feet.

The hell-fiend paid her no heed, its own attention focused on drawing out the scorching thorn in its belly. The cavity beneath its chest looked like that of a corpse that had been left out for scavengers to feed on, its rib cage now fully exposed, its guts falling out with every breath it took.

"I ALMOST HAVE YOU, LITTLE PRIESTESS." It grunted out the words between mouthfuls of smoke, spitting blood out onto the floor with every syllable.

The demon barely noticed when Remi scrambled up its side, using handfuls of black fur to ease her passage. Nor did it notice when the girl hooked herself onto the base of its wings, slowly dragging herself closer to its head.

Remi clasped onto a curved horn, feeling the tough keratin beneath her fingers while she tried to find her balance. Her sword smouldered in her other hand, its crimson flame growing brighter as it sensed her intent. She dug a foot into the folds of fat behind the demon's head, grounding herself as she took one final breath. And then she plunged the blade deep into the demon's skull.

Fire erupted from the wound, spilling out from the sword, and from Margaux, and from the demon's own infernal soul. The hell-fiend screeched out in anguish as its bone gave way to the steel, digging into the membranous, soft tissue beneath. It lashed out with a claw, trying to dislodge her, but Remi ducked beneath the swipe, putting more weight behind her sword as it broke through skin and bone.

Remi pulled at the blade, dragging it with her as she started to slide toward the ground. Fire erupted from where the empyrean steel passed, splitting the skin and rot and festering flesh as she pulled it further downward.

The flailing demon swatted at her again, its crooked talons tearing through its own skin as it tried to displace her. With another colossal effort, Remi heaved the sword toward the demon's wings and then leapt from its back, dragging her weapon with her.

The burning blade carved through the demon as they dropped, cracking bones apart with ease and turning flesh to ash. The creature's wings fluttered as they were torn from the spawn's back and then fell to the floor to add to the growing pool of meat and guts. Finally, Remi guided the empyrean blade into the demon's spine, cutting right through it before she kicked off, away from the broken creature.

The hell-fiend coughed out a garbled mess of blood and lungs as it stumbled forward, its body collapsing in on itself even while its brain began to shut down. Its hooves slammed into its own entrails, turning them into paste beneath its gargantuan weight. It seemed to find its balance for a moment, its claws splayed out beside it, holding it steady.

Then, with a mournful groan, the demon toppled over and lay there, still.

Remi rushed toward the corpse, slipping in the pools of black ichor that coated the floor, narrowly avoiding a fall. Her aura was fading, and the empyrean blade no longer billowed with fire in her hands. She came to a stop at the foot of the beast and stared into its gaping belly.

Resting in its centre, her hands still wrapped around the molten silver cross she bore, was the Prioress. Remi let out a sigh of relief when she saw the faint flutter of Margaux's chest. She was still alive.

POSTSCRIPT

Pierre leaned against his staff, watching the gates of Enfaire close behind them. The town's folk had been most generous, and his pack was stuffed with bread and cheese and even a little ham. He remained sceptical of their food, but Remi said it couldn't do any harm—not now that the hag of Val de Havre was well and truly dead.

His ward skipped ahead of him, taking the lead as they followed the path alongside the river. They were headed south, toward the smoke-filled skies on the horizon, and whatever horrors awaited them in Lourdes. The Prioress had asked them to stay, of course, to shelter behind the walls of Enfaire while the world around them fell to plague and ruin.

It had been a tempting offer, and Pierre had been reluctant to decline. Even Remi, with her oaths and duty, had hesitated. The Prioress's face had still been flush with the faith that had spared her from the ailments that beset the town, with the faith that had eventually broken the demon. It had been hard to say no.

But they had business in Lourdes, and if even half the stories were true, the challenges ahead would dwarf the ones they had faced in Enfaire.

"Come on, friar," Remi called, "before we all die of old age."

"Yes, yes," said Pierre, muttering under his breath. "Lourdes will still be there tomorrow."

Actually, there was a chance it wouldn't be, he thought as he knelt down to adjust his robes. The wraps that bound his feet would need changing soon, and he could just see the impression of a hoof sticking out from beneath one of the bindings. He tugged the fabric back into place, tightening it fast before hurrying after Remi.

He hadn't expected to see Abezethibou in Enfaire but had taken some satisfaction in seeing the demon's plans foiled—that scheming bastard had always delighted in his own failings. He'd had it coming.

The God-touched had been another surprise. To come across two in one lifetime—well, it was almost enough to convert him! Even so, it had been a close one. He would have to be more careful in future. Explaining himself to the Courts of Hell after being shat out by one of its Lords would have made for an uncomfortable experience. As if the fall from heaven hadn't been embarrassing enough.

No doubt word would already be spreading through the Seven Circles—Abezethibou was anything but stupid.

Pierre sighed. He'd have a rebellion on his hands if he didn't return soon… Still, he looked over the fields, toward the rolling hills and forests that covered the valley, at the coursing stream and the snow-capped mountain range in the distance. You didn't get views like this back home.

"Pierre!" Remi waved at him impatiently. "Come on, or I'll leave you behind."

"I'm coming!" he shouted back, a thin smile on his lips.

Besides, he thought as he hobbled after the little saint, he was just starting to enjoy himself.

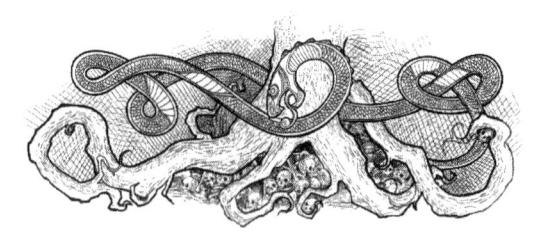

The Bone Fields

LONGSHIPS

Thoril braced against the cold wind and gripped her oar tight as the storm buffeted the longship *Varúlfr*. Beneath them, all around them, the ocean was a broiling black cauldron, heaving its might against their own. It had not yet found them wanting.

Inge hunched up beside her and grinned madly as the sea crashed over the side of the longboat. Her shaven head was lathered with sweat and rain, and the tattoos that covered her skin shone as though freshly inked.

"Njǫrd is in one of his moods again," she called over the wind.

Thoril spat out salt water and wiped her lips. "He is always angry this time of year. Halvor was foolish to make us stay for so long."

She stared along the aisles, past the ragged band of figures that made up the rest of the company. Halvor stood at *Varúlfr*'s helm, unbowed by the frantic gale that hammered the ship. His long hair was soaked through, matted against his head and neck. His eyes remained fixed on the horizon, in search of their sister ship, *Kveldúlfr,* who had disappeared into the storm.

"Halvor's raids are always the most rewarding," said Inge. "That is why he chose to stay, and that is why we chose to come. This old god's anger is a small price for what we have taken."

Thoril nodded. It had been a bountiful raid, and Halvor's company had made enough for them all to secure land and power upon their return home. They had stuck to the coast at first, like any other raiding party, and taken what they could from the farms they found there. But Halvor was ambitious, and they'd soon found themselves sneaking into larger settlements and then sacking them. It had been slaughter, but one well worth the wait. She glanced over her shoulder, towards the covered stern of the boat. She'd even managed to secure a slave on this expedition—her first. He sat huddled up beside two others, shivering into his soaking rags.

"Fritjof better not have gotten himself lost." Inge squinted her eyes against the rain. "Or sailed *Kveldúlfr* to the ocean floor, then we'll never see half our spoils. Afterlife or no, I'll hunt him down and wring his thin neck until his eyes pop out."

Inge had another reason for wanting to see *Kveldúlfr* again. Her lover, Akes, sailed with

Fritjof. The warrior had spurned her advances at first, but Inge was not easily dissuaded. The first night on Bretland soil had seen them share a bedroll, and they'd spent every night together since.

"Not even Fritjof would dare sink his ship when he carries Halvor's cargo. You will see, once the storm relents, then you will see that stupid boy's face again."

Inge slapped her on the back and grinned. "I'm more interested in what's between his legs."

Thoril rolled her eyes and sank her oar into the water. The pull of the waves was getting stronger and she struggled to find a rhythm. Others in the company, Herleid and Ovil—but others, too—had already given up. They sat wrapped in great furs beside sheltered braziers, taking what little warmth they could.

"Halvor will tell us to stow away the oars soon," said Inge, her smile fading. "Then we will need to hold fast until the storm passes, or join Fritjof at the bottom of the sea."

Thoril shrugged. Halvor was too shrewd a sailor to let a mere storm defeat him, but when one's time came, even the trickster himself would be hard put to evade his fate. She turned to the sea and watched as it rampaged and turned beneath grey clouds. For too long she had been away from the open waters, and her mood had dampened with each day they had moved inland. Now that she was back—cold as she was, wet as she was—she felt her spirits soar.

Her eyes narrowed as a wave rose up beside *Varúlfr*. It drew the ship towards it, until they were tilted horizontally against it and a gauzy mist of water splashed over them. Halvor rode the wave expertly, bringing the longship over it before it could crest and plummet them all to their doom. As the wave diminished beneath them, Thoril thought she saw a flash of silver below the surface, the scales of an enormous shape riding alongside them. But when she blinked again, it was gone.

"Land!"

She shook free the vision and looked up as the call rang out again.

"What land is here?" Inge rose from her seat beside her, stepping up onto it in an effort to see over the heads of the rest of the company.

"There is nothing," Ulfgar said from the seat opposite them. He ran a hand over his stubbly head and shrugged. "Not for many days, still. There must be a mistake."

"There is… something." Inge leaned on Thoril's shoulder for support and rose on her toes for a better look. "I see a thin line, barely a smudge, but it has the look of land about it."

"To your oars!" Halvor's voice boomed above the storm. He strode between the aisle, pulling the crew back down to their seats. "We make for the shore, and a break from the storm!"

Inge plopped back down beside her and laid her hands on the oar. Together, they pulled deep against the chopping waters for the smudge on the horizon.

The howling wind relented as they navigated their way into a sheltered cove, where the ocean was strangely dead and still. The land around them was unfamiliar and Thoril felt herself tense as she stared up at the grey crags above. *Where had they come from?* She had never seen this place before, and the maps did not speak of it. Unless the storm had blown them further off course than she realised.

Halvor had them moor *Varúlfr* along the coast, and then set a team to repair what little damage the storm had done. Thoril took up her sword and shield, and walked along the beach with Inge while the rest set up camp. She could see Halvor's pathfinders moving up ahead of them, slipping in and out of the trees that hemmed in the shoreline.

"Maybe they will find us another farmstead?" Inge thumped her sword against her shield and smiled. "Or perhaps a little lord and his castle, too far from anyone to call for help. That would be enough to settle my debt with Dag, no?"

Thoril stayed quiet. Her own debts had been covered weeks ago, and she did not have it in mind to raid again.

Inge stared at her from out of the corner of her eye and then bumped into her with her shield. "You are never smiling, even when things are good. 'Troubled Thoril', that is what they should call you in the songs."

"Only because that hole in your face never closes," she replied, returning the shove.

Inge laughed loud and skipped about her, kicking up clumps of sand.

Troubled Thoril!
Aesirs' daughter did not smile
Troubled Thoril!
Cold as Jötunn, with rage like Freyja

Thoril dropped her sword and shield, and covered her ears. "You sing like a dog, Inge. If the gods could hear you now, they'd cut out your tongue."

"Good enough for the beer halls, but not for Troubled Thoril, eh?" Inge made to push her again, but Thoril raised a hand.

"It's Bjarki," said Inge, following her gaze.

Halvor's chief pathfinder was bounding over the beach towards them, his sword and shield strapped to his back.

"What have you found?" Thoril called as he loped past.

Bjarki slowed, breathing heavily. "*Kveldúlfr*. We've found her, she's up ahead."

"See, I told you," said Thoril, turning to the other shield-maiden. "Fritjof is too much of a coward to lose his ship. He will be sitting fat on Halvor's loot, like Hreidmar and his dwarves."

Inge knitted her brow, her eyes still tracking the pathfinder as he jogged over the sand. "And of the crew, are they all there?"

Bjarki shrugged as he picked up his pace, heading towards the camp. "There is no one."

~~~

Halvor's company—over twenty warriors, all told—stood at the top of a dune, and stared down at *Varúlfr*'s sister ship. Fritjof had moored her on the beach, away from the draw of the tide. Her oars had been stowed away and sails furled, but there was no sign of life anywhere aboard.

Bjarki and his trackers stood by Halvor, engaged in whispered conversation, while the rest of the party edged down towards the ship.

"Do you think an ambush?" Inge's question lacked any conviction, but Thoril shook her head anyway. She couldn't see any of the signs of a fight from the dune; no bodies littered the sand, and there wasn't a drop of blood to be found around *Kveldúlfr*.

"They must have moved inland." She waved her shield towards the dense forest beside them, and then squinted into the gloom herself. A coarse thicket covered the land between the beach and the rock face that loomed above. The trees were tightly packed, leaving hardly enough space for a man and his shield to pass through, and malformed roots snaked their way across the forest floor. Fool that he was, it was unlike Fritjof to leave his ship unguarded, and for what? A walk through parts unknown?

A shout from aboard the boat saw Thoril's eyes snap back to *Kveldúlfr*. Ubba and Katja, two of Halvor's senior blooded-warriors, had clambered up the rungs of the ship and were waving everyone closer. The pair of them were covering their faces, and Ubba retched up something watery before climbing back down.

"I do not like this," said Inge as she grabbed Thoril by the shoulder. The two navigated the steep incline together, slipping and sliding as they made their way onto even ground.

They were among the first to reach the bottom of the rise, and they pushed their way towards Halvor and his trackers, who had moved down ahead.

Ulfgar gave them a curt nod and shifted up to let them through. He was normally the first to crack a smile, but his face was grim. "Might have been better we remained away from this bay." He gritted his teeth and turned to look at the sea. Beyond the shelter of the cove, the storm still raged, and the wind still howled. But beneath the crags of this new island, everything was peaceful. "I am reminded of the tales of *Náströnd* in this place, of the cursed and the damned."

That hall is woven
of serpents' spines
There Níðhǫggr sucked
corpses of the dead
and the wolf tore men
on Dead Body Shore

Thoril shivered. "You are always one to set a mood."

"It is not me." The old warrior thumbed his hand, and then rolled his neck, before meeting her eyes. "Old Ove has felt it, too. We were not meant to come here."

Inge guffawed. "Ove always *feels* something, but sometimes it's just the madness inside his own head."

"Mock him if you like, but he has seen more than you can know, more than you can understand."

Inge shrugged at that, and they walked in silence for a moment, behind Halvor and the pathfinders. Ulfgar took such things seriously, more so than most. To argue with him was like pushing a bull through mud with its horns pointed at you. He bore his faith on his skin, and his shaven scalp was adorned with symbols of protection—Othala runes, the Fe, and tributes to Heimdall himself.

Inge was about to snap back with a delayed retort when she gagged. "That smell."

Thoril made a face and covered her nose with her forearm. "Like rotten fish." Her eyes started to water at the stench that assaulted her senses, but she walked forward gamely, even as others choked and swore behind her.

The rest of the party gathered at the base of the longship, and waited as Bjarki and Ulfgar clambered up the rungs and stared over the side.

"They've left their shields." Thoril glanced up at the rack, which remained untouched.

"That's Akes'," said Inge, pointing her sword towards a red and white shield above them. "They must have needed to move quickly."

Thoril nodded, but she felt the first hint of uneasiness grip her as she watched Bjarki and Ulfgar turn to face the gathered party.

"It is a serpent's brood," Bjarki stated solemnly. He made the sign of the Fe and spat at the boat. "This is Jörmungandr's lot, and we are not welcome in this place."

Ulfgar dropped down onto the sand, and then helped the older warrior down.

"It is an ill omen," he said, once Bjarki was on the beach beside him. A crowd of confused faces stared back at him, until Halvor strode forward and nimbly clambered up the side of the boat.

"Eels," he said simply as he stared down at the hold. "The storm must have seen them dumped in Fritjof's boat, nothing more."

Ulfagr mumbled something from below, but Halvor silenced him with a wave of his hand. "There is nothing of the Midgard serpent here. Do you think we would have found this ship if the World-Snake had come upon it?"

Ulfgar shrugged, and thumbed his palm nervously. "I simply say what I see."

The jarl shook his head, and then stared at the party for a moment, sweeping his gaze across the dunes. "Fritjof is a fool," he said. "We all know this."

Some of the men chuckled at his words, but most were quiet. Ulfgar had put them on edge.

"He has left his ship unguarded and charged off to see what treasures he can find for himself. He means to leave us with his ship, like a nursemaid." Halvor jumped down from the boat and dusted his hands off. "But we are not his nursemaids, are we?"

Thoril found herself muttering her dissatisfaction with the idea along with the rest of the party.

"We will move inland and find the fool, then he can make a bed from the eels he left in his boat!" A grin split Halvor's face as the mood lifted, and raucous laughter was joined by his warriors.

"Come, now," said Halvor once the laughter had receded. "Fritjof can't have made it far."

He nodded to his pathfinders, who moved off quickly into the forest. "There is still a little light before nightfall."

As the company moved towards the tree line, Inge pushed past Thoril and headed towards the boat.

"What are you doing?" Thoril sighed and followed after her friend. "You heard Halvor, we don't have much light left."

"I want to see." Inge dropped her gear into the sand and turned to Thoril. "Are you not curious to see what Jörmungandr has left us?" She didn't wait for an answer before pulling herself up the side of the boat.

Thoril sighed again and dropped her own gear to climb onto *Kveldúlfr*.

The wood had started to rot, and the smell of decaying flesh intensified as she pulled herself up.

Inge exhaled as she reached the top and stared down into the hold. "Gods, Bjarki was right."

"What is it, Inge?" Thoril asked, hearing her tone. She didn't wait for a reply before peering down herself.

The entire floor of *Kveldúlfr* was covered in a writhing, seething mass of serpentine bodies. Their silver forms shifted in the half-light, wrapping themselves around one another in a slippery embrace. Thoril nearly gagged at the sight of them, and turned away as the smell threatened to overpower her.

"There are so many." Inge curled her lips in disgust and watched as the creatures rolled across the floor of the boat. "Fritjof and his company will have much to clean once this lot rots in the sun."

"They will have no help from me," said Thoril. She took one last look at the flowing mass of bodies, and then clambered back down the rungs. "Come! Inge! Or we will be left behind."

THE LIVING AND THE DEAD

Of Halvor's company, four were left to guard over *Varúlfr*, and another two to wait by Frtijof's ship in case of his return. The rest set out into the dark forest, with torches lit against the coming of night.

"I have not seen nor heard any sign of beast or bird in this place." Ulfgar swatted away a gnat with his torch. "Only these bastards."

"Your blood is too pure," said Inge. "But I have the cure." She swigged from her flask and handed it to Thoril. "They will not eat you if your blood is poison."

Thoril shrugged and took a sip, almost spluttering as the bitter liquid went down her throat. "What is this?" she asked, wiping her mouth with a hand, then looking at the flask sceptically.

"Baht gave it to me as a gift before we left. It was all he had left from his journey East."

"No wonder his mind is so addled." Thoril sniffed at the container and made a face. "I would rather be eaten, I think."

"Suit yourself," said Inge, taking back the spirits. "But don't cry to me when your skin is raw from scratching."

Ulfgar snorted. "Inge the generous."

"It is *Inge the Bloodied*, now that I have fought the Christians and stolen their silver." She adjusted the shield on her arm and stared up into the canopy.

They had walked for many miles beneath the outstretched limbs of ancient trees, and there had been no sign of Fritjof or his company. Not long after leaving the shore, Bjarki had found a single path that cut its way through the forest. It was the only way past the near impenetrable undergrowth, and Halvor led them on it towards the great crags they'd seen from the boats.

"There are no stars." Inge frowned up at the branches, and then shook her head. "They hide from this place."

"They're hidden behind clouds," said Thoril. She'd felt uneasy since finding *Kveldúlfr* and its slippery cargo, and didn't need Inge's superstitions compounding that. "There was a storm, remember?"

"Or it is that this place is outside of our own." Ulfgar glanced around him, holding his torch close to the trees. Their boughs and roots were scarred with age, and the leaves seemed to shrink away so close to the open flame. "Beneath the roots of the World Tree, there exists a place of terrible suffering, it is Hel's kingdom."

Thoril rolled her eyes. "But we have not died, Ulfgar. Ove is getting into your head with his stories. Unless you think we sunk to the bottom of the sea in that storm?"

The warrior shrugged. "Who's to say that we didn't?"

"Our flesh!" Thoril pulled down her sleeve and pointed to her bare skin. "Our sweat and thirst! Do you think the dead suffer these things?"

Ulfgar flinched at the tone of her voice and raised a hand in supplication. "It is only a thought, I do not mean to anger you, *storm-maiden*."

"It is not you, Ulfgar." Thoril took a deep breath and rolled her knuckles against her shield. "I am sorry. It is this place, the quietness is getting to me."

"It gets under my skin, too," said Ulfgar. "When these bastards aren't busy eating me." He swung his torch at a cloud of insects, and then beckoned to the other shield-maiden. "I'll try some of your poison now, I think."

Inge grinned and handed him the flask. "It gets better after the first sip, promise."

Ulfgar raised a sceptical brow and took a hesitant sip. His face paled and his brow creased as the liquor passed his lips. "This is what Baht calls a drink?" He spat on the forest floor and groaned. "No wonder he always stinks of cat piss."

Inge grinned and took back the flask. "It has kept me warm through many a cold night, and it's better than being eaten alive."

"That it is," said Ulfgar pressing on ahead. He waved an arm towards the thinning trees as a pale moon emerged from behind the diminishing canopy. "It looks like this dark forest has finally come to an end. Now we will see what wolfish murderers and serpent spines haunt this island."

The forest opened up into a wide valley nestled between steep, windswept hills. A thin strip of silver hinted at the existence of a river not far ahead. Its snaking path ran the length of the valley, and then disappeared beyond the grey walls of the mountain range in the distance.

Halvor ordered the company forward, beyond the shelter of the forest, towards the river. The warriors were relieved to find themselves with empty skies above their heads once more, and moved with purpose.

As they moved out from the undergrowth, Thoril couldn't help but notice the lack of stars. Even without the cover of clouds, the sky was like a black sheet, with only the wan light of the moon guiding their way.

"We will camp by the river." Halvor led the company himself, setting a gruelling pace that soon saw them all wet with sweat and breathing heavily. He waved his axe at his chief scout and motioned to the grey peaks.

"Bjarki and Sigurd will move into the mountains while we rest." He turned to his warriors, walking backward as he took them all in. "Do not sip too heavily on your mead this night. I think we will all need to be sharp come the morning."

His warriors grumbled to themselves, but accepted his warning without rebuke. Most were too tired for thoughts of drink, and the idea of a proper night's sleep was enough to keep them motivated.

Inge had gone off to see if she could not join Bjarki and his scouts, and Thoril found herself walking between Ove and Ulfgar. The moon had not yet reached its zenith, and its pale light made everything look a shade of grey.

"There is no sign of that fool or his company," said Ulfgar. "No tracks, no fires, nothing of our friends. Halvor leads us on a merry chase." He spat at the ground and shook his head. "This place is empty."

Ove snorted from beneath his hood. "It is not empty, Ulfgar. You are just blind to what occupies this land." He waved a hand at the mountains before them and smiled. "We walk where few have walked before, in the place between the living and the dead."

It was Thoril's turn to snort now. "Old Ove, you have seen so much, and yet your stories are always the same. The living and the dead, the beasts of *Náströnd*, the serpent that eats the world. Why have we seen none of these things? Every year you cry your tale, and every year we ship back home, alive and richer than before!"

"I only repeat what I have seen, girl." Ove made the sign of the Fe with a gnarled hand,

and then turned to look at her. His skin was weathered by years of salt and sun, but his blue eyes were as piercing as ever.

He stared at her for a moment, and then smiled. "You have seen something, too, I think."

Thoril shrugged, but in her mind's eye she recalled that flicker of silver beneath the waves, that formless shape slipping through the sea.

"It is no blessing to have hold of the sight," Ove continued. "To see one's future played out before one's very eyes has damned many a man to insanity. But you must be better than that."

"What is it that you saw?" asked Ulfgar.

"It was nothing." She shook her head, readjusting her shield on her arm. "Ove is mad, you know that as well as I."

"I have seen it, too, girl," Ove barked. "It is the world's end that slithers behind your eyes!" He retched out a hacking cough and laughed. "Do not be afraid. Soon they will all see!"

Thoril snarled at the old warrior and picked up her pace, leaving the pair of them behind. It was only when she was at the head of the company, and Ove's choking laughter had faded away, that she felt her mind settle.

He is mad, she thought to herself. *Him and Bjarki both*. Still, there was something in the way he had looked at her that made her think otherwise. The old man had seen more years than any of them, and his words, though often veiled by myth, were rarely false.

She sighed to herself and tightened her grip on her shield. Either way, she would meet her fate head on.

The first night on the island was cold, and Halvor ordered massive fires to fend off the chill. He cared not that someone might see them. After all, who would dare attack Halvor and his company of bloodied? The warriors drew lots for sentry duty, and those that could, tried to slip in a few hours sleep before dawn.

Thoril and the other shield-maiden had laid their kit out beside one of the bonfires, and sipped from Inge's bitter liquor while Ove told stories of the night, and of the first fires.

"When Loki, Odin, and Haenir crossed the vast mountains, they came across a herd of oxen!" The old warrior took a bite from his dried meat and crinkled his nose. "Fresh meat, not like what we've been nibbling on, eh, Ulfgard?"

Ulfgard blinked into wakefulness at the sound of his name and stared across the fire at the old warrior. "What now?" he said.

"Come, come," Inge rolled across the grass and extended her flask towards him. "Don't be boring, Ulfgar. Sit with us."

He shook his shaven head and pulled his blanket tighter about his chest. "I have the next watch. It would look poor for me if Halvor caught me drunk. You heard what he said."

She stuck out her tongue and took a steady draught from the bottle. "You will be sad when there is none left."

He shrugged and closed his eyes. "As long as I get my sleep, I do not care."

"What about you, Ove?" Inge turned to the veteran. "Something to fend off the cold and make your heart kick like a newborn's?"

"I already see things that are not there," said Ove, chewing on his meat. "I rather not tempt fate with your fire water."

"More for me and Thoril, then," she said as the others laughed. She took another sip from her flask and squinted into the darkness surrounding the camp.

The mountains were mere silhouettes in the distance, looming over the sides of the valley like the bastions of some great castle. The river they'd seen from afar was, in fact, two concurrent streams racing beside one another towards the sea. They'd bathed in its water, and even fished, but there was no life to be found in it, and the warriors had made do with dried meats once more.

For a moment, she thought she spotted a movement on the ridge above their camp—a single figure stepping into the moonlight. She squinted up at the hill, trying to bring it into focus, but whatever it was she'd seen had gone.

"You alright, girl?" Ove cocked his head, a strange look on his face.

"It's nothing," said Inge, shaking her head, and then bringing her eyes back down to the fire. "It is only shadows."

"Is it nothing, or is it shadows?" Ove showed his teeth before winking at Inge. "They are not the same."

The shield-maiden rolled her eyes and leaned back on her bedroll. She was tired of Ove and his riddles. "It was both and neither," she said, turning her back to him and the fire. He could figure that one out for himself. She closed her eyes and let the warmth of the fire, and the soft hum of her friends chatter, lull her to sleep.

In the morning, Ulfgar was gone.

Bjarki shook his head as he walked over to Thoril and the others. "There is no sign of him. Sigurd saw him take the watch, but after that, he did not return."

"Where did he stand sentry?" Thoril had been the first to wake, and to find his bedroll empty.

"Not far from here," Bjarki said. He pointed to the base of the ridge, on the other side of the river. "He took over from Eyva and left camp well after midnight. His watch was to end a few hours before dawn, but no one has seen him."

"He can't have gotten far," said Inge, staring at the ridge.

"But why would he have left us in the first place?" Thoril licked her lips and followed Inge's gaze. The drink had given her a splitting headache, and she was finding it hard to concentrate. "It makes no sense," she concluded.

"I am inclined to agree," came a deep voice from behind her.

Halvor stood next to Bjarki and nodded to them each in turn. His mane of hair was wet from the river, and his beard had grown out. Flecks of white and grey dotted the scruff, making him appear even more distinguished.

"It is not like Ulfgar to disappear like this." Thin lines creased his forehead as he frowned. "I suspect he has been taken by whoever has been tracking us this last day."

Thoril and Inge's immediate questions were ignored, and Halvor silenced them with a wave of his hand. "Bjarki spotted them when we landed. A small band, maybe three or four in total. They have been shadowing us since we moved inland, but I had not expected them to act so boldly. Not against our numbers."

Inge shivered, remembering the silhouette she'd seen on the ridge. "Who are they?"

"I cannot be sure. Locals, perhaps. Or other folk like us who've been washed up by the storm. The pathfinders have been instructed to catch one of them, if possible. Then we will see."

"And what of Ulfgar?" Thoril's eyes narrowed as she watched her jarl. She already suspected the answer.

"There is nothing that can be done. We don't know the land, and Bjarki says the surrounds turn into more gulleys and ravines than he can count—too many places to disappear. We will find what has happened to him when we catch one of his captors."

Thoril nodded. She knew Halvor did not allow for dissent. What was done was done, and she'd just have to hope Bjarki and his trackers were as good as they thought they were.

"None of this to the others." Halvor met her eyes, and then stared down Inge and Ove. "I would not have fears of shadow-men spread through the company. They will learn of this when the time is right."

"We will keep your secret, Ironnson." Ove smiled. "But do not think to catch these spectres, or to harm them. They cannot be hurt. They walk between the worlds. This I know, Ulgfar knows it, too."

"We will see, old man," said Halvor, already turning to leave. "There is little that walks in this world that does not fear the sharp end of my axe."

They walked for half a day before someone spotted smoke rising behind them, and Halvor called them to a halt. He signalled to Sigurd and those scouts not out searching for Ulfgar and his mysterious captors. They quickly moved up the ridge to get an eye on where the smoke was coming from.

"Could be Fritjof and his lot," said Inge. She dropped her kit on the ground and placed a foot on one of the larger rocks around them. The valley had started to narrow as they closed in on the crags, and rocky debris littered the floor around them.

"Could be, could be." Ove sucked on his teeth and tracked the scouts up the hill. "Could be a funeral pyre."

"Best not to wonder on such things until we can be sure." Thoril shielded her eyes from the sun with a hand and stared at the rising plumes of black smoke.

"There is another," she said, pointing a little ways away from the first cloud. "It is smaller, but it is the same."

Inge clambered atop the rock and leaned against Thoril as she tried to get a better look. "She's right, there is more smoke from somewhere further back."

"We will find out just now," said Ove, gesturing to the ridge. Halvor's scouts were racing down the incline, trying their best to remain sure-footed as they hurtled down towards them.

"It's the boats!"

The cry went up like wildfire, and Thoril felt a familiar feeling of uncertainty crowd out her other thoughts. *We are trapped here*, she thought as she joined the milling mass of norsemen crowding around Halvor.

"It is true," said the jarl plainly. "Our ships have been set afire. Both *Varúlfr* and Fritjof's ship, though it does not look like the fire on *Kveldúlfr* has taken so well. She may still be salvageable."

"What are we to do?" A voice called from the amassed warriors.

Thoril could see the company was close to panic. Tired men and women, stranded far from home on an island they'd never seen before... It would not take much to push them over the edge. To his credit, Halvor did not seem perturbed by the situation. He rolled his shoulders and turned to Sigurd. The two engaged in quiet conversation, both of them glancing up at the clouds of smoke in the distance, before Halvor raised a hand to silence the company.

"We have no choice but to return to the ships and to see what we can salvage from the fires." He nodded to Sigurd, who moved to gather the remaining pathfinders. "We will wait for Bjarki's return, and then we shall make with haste for the coast."

"And of Fritjof?"

It was Inge's voice that Thoril heard. She turned to see the other shield-maiden standing beside two of Halvor's largest warriors, Theodaric and Henrik. "What happens to Fritjof and his company, and what of Ulfgar? Are we to leave them here, to this island and its people?"

Halvor gave her a look of warning, and then rolled the handle of his axe with his wrists. "There is nothing that can be done. We must look to our own preservation now."

His words were met with agreement by the gathered company, but Inge was not yet done.

"If it were you, we would stay until we found you, or we were all dead."

Halvor smiled, revealing a row of straight, white teeth. "But it is not me, shield-maiden. And I say we go."

Before Inge could continue her protest, Halvor whistled and waved at the remaining pathfinders. "You have until nightfall, and then we are gone."

Inge gritted her teeth, but looked up at Thoril's approach. "Just like that."

"Maybe Bjarki will find something, perhaps of Ulfgar or Fritjof, or both?"

Inge shook her head and wiped at her eyes. She was tired and she was hungover, and she wanted to see her friends again. "It might already be too late. There is something wrong about this place. There is no life here, not even a bird, just these pests that want to drain us of our blood." She swiped at the air, as if to make her point. "Halvor must know it, if we leave now we may seal their fates."

Thoril nodded, but there was nothing more she could say. Halvor had spoken, and his word was law.

Night had long since fallen when the first of Bjarki's scouts returned. Tired eyed and weary limbed, they slowly streamed in. They spoke of a great ravine, guarded by the walls of ancient pillars. Of figures cut from stone and strange sounds in the trees. They spoke of an uneasiness that settled upon them, and a feeling of being watched, of being stalked, hunted. But of Fritjof and Ulfgar, there was no sign.

"We wait on Bjarki," Halvor told the company. "When he returns, we will make for the coast, for our ships."

They waited until the night grew cold, when even fire barely kept the chill from their bones. The camp sat in a state of frozen anticipation, with each warrior ready to move at a moment's notice. But that notice never came. Halvor grew restless and took to pacing around the perimeter, harassing his sentries and forcing them to take deeper forays into the night, to search for the pathfinder. It wasn't long before Thoril and Inge were sent out with a party, into the black of night with only their torches to guide them.

"We will find nothing like this," said Inge. "Stomping around in the night like fools, hoping to fall upon Bjarki by luck."

Thoril lifted the torch above her head and watched the flickering shadows around them. They had been walking for hours now, with still no sign of the pathfinder. What hope she'd had of finding him had diminished, and she just wanted to return to the camp and to the warmth of the fires. She sighed as she stared up at the hills that loomed above them. The peaks were hidden by the night, and what little light the moon shone down on them failed to illuminate the darkest corners of the valley.

"What else would you have us do?" Thoril lowered her torch. "You heard Halvor, we must look to ourselves now. If we don't find Bjarki, we have to leave without him."

Inge shook her head. "Halvor will not leave his precious pathfinder behind."

"Then we must do as he says, and search every crevice of this valley before dawn."

The other shield-maiden rubbed a hand over her scalp. She had not shaved it in weeks, and stubble now covered the tattoos that spiralled across her head.

"Ove has taken it well," she said. "Ulfgar is like a son to him."

Thoril took a swig from her flask and wiped her mouth. "He said he *knew* what was coming. Him and Ulfgar both."

"How could they know?"

"You know what they are like." Thoril turned to her friend and waved at the sky. "The gods tell them stories, or plant ideas in their heads... At least, that is what Ove wants us to think. It is either true, or he is mad. Sometimes I think it is both."

They walked in silence for a moment, keeping within hailing distance of the rest of the party. Arvid and Dagfinn were barely a dozen yards from them, while Uskar and Tommen ranged ahead, their torches appearing like mini stars in the distance.

But, of course, there were no stars here. Thoril hadn't seen one since they'd arrived. She looked up at the sky, careful to keep her footing on the uneven rocks that surrounded the gully.

"It is like Ove says." Inge came to a standstill beside her. "This island is of another place."

They were still standing together, staring at the emptiness above them, when Uskar's horn rung out in the darkness. It blew once, then twice, and then there was silence.

"He's found something," said Thoril as she skipped down from the rocks. More torches were moving through the valley now, heading towards where Uskar's horn had sounded from.

"If it's Ulfgar, I'll box his nose in for leading us on this merry chase." Inge's face shone with hope, and she jogged ahead of Thoril towards the gathering torches. "Then we will see if Ove saw that coming, too," she called over her shoulder.

Thoril smiled at the thought and picked up her pace.

THE DESTROYING FLAME

There were no smiling faces to greet them when they reached Uskar. A band of norsemen stood around three indistinct bodies, bound and gagged with rope.

"It is the Christians," said Tommen at their approach. His eyes were wide, and a sheen of sweat covered his upper lip. The other warriors looked similarly spooked, and fidgeted with their blades as they waited.

"How is this possible?" Thoril stared down at her own slave, who'd been left back on their longship when the company moved inland.

The man's greasy black hair hung over eyes that flickered back and forth across the gathered warriors. His beard was covered in spittle where the gag was loose, and welts had already formed upon his hands.

"It is a trick," said Sigurd, stepping towards the slaves. "Fritjof is playing with us, it is one of his games."

His words were met with silence, and Thoril found herself thumbing her own sword nervously. How had they gotten ahead of them? Who had left them out here to be found?

She knelt down beside her slave and gripped his jaw with a hand. The man bit harder into his gag, and his eyes darted inside his skull, averting her gaze.

"What happened to you?" she asked, tilting his head towards her own. Even if he could understand her, she doubted he would have responded. Something had scared him, and the other slaves, too.

She rose from the floor and nodded to Sigurd. "Let's get them back to camp, see if Ove can make sense of what's happened here. He's spent more time with the Christians than any of us."

Sigurd pulled the nearest slave to his feet and prodded him forward. The wiry blond man gargled from behind his gag, but stumbled forward without resisting.

"Where are their guards?" said Sigurd as he pushed the last captive to his feet. He yanked the man by the collar and drew him close. "Where are the others?" Spit sprayed from his mouth, and his face reddened. The Christian tried to make himself small, cowering away from the massive norseman, but his grip was too tight.

Thoril placed a hand on the warrior's shoulder and shook her head. "It is no use, Sigurd. They cannot speak our tongue. All they know is our rage and the sharpness of our blades."

"You are right," he said, releasing the man. "They are a weak people, made weaker by their god who dies." He kicked at the slave lazily with his foot, and then strode forward, in the direction of camp.

"Ove will know what to do." Inge helped Thoril guide her slave forward. The man was surprisingly strong beneath his rags, and Thoril felt the bulge of muscle on his arms as she directed him back towards the camp. It was his eyes that held her, though. They rolled madly in his head, and did not stop, not even when they'd reached the safety of the encampment.

"It is useless," said Ove, scratching his head. "I cannot make sense of anything they say." The slaves had had their gags removed, though their hands were still securely bound, and were sitting in the centre of the camp. Ove circled them slowly, nodding and shaking his head as he asked them question after question in their native tongue. The responses were hurried and garbled, though the Bretlander tongue always sounded that way to Thoril.

"Ask them how they found themselves inland," Halvor's voice boomed above the confused chattering of the Christians. "Was it Fritjof? Is this some game he is playing with us?"

Ove translated the words and then waited as the leanest of the three replied. After a moment, the veteran turned to Halvor and shrugged.

"He says they came through the earth."

"What foolishness is this?" Halvor stopped his pacing and turned to the captives. His axe rested in the crook of his arm, and his eyes shone red in the firelight. "Do they mock me, Ove?"

The old man raised a brow and met the jarl's stare. "I think, given their position, they would not dare, Ironsson."

Halvor glanced at the slaves, his eyes narrowed into slits, then he spat at the fire. "Find out what happened here, Ove. And no more of these stories, I will have the truth."

"I will do what I can, but I am not familiar with all of their language. There are words that do not make sense to me."

"See that it is done." Halvor spared one last look at the captives, and then stormed off into the night.

Once the jarl was gone, Thoril sat down beside Ove and watched as the slaves chattered amongst themselves. Much of their panic seemed to have receded, but they still flinched when she arrived.

"They are scared." Ove scratched his nose with a thumb and looked to Thoril. "They were asleep on the ship, and woke up to screaming— probably Eluf and his men."

"What, then?"

"I am not sure. The language they speak is strange, littered with metaphor... So, I cannot tell quite what is true and what is an allusion to fact. Why they were spared I cannot tell, but it has something to do with the blood of their three-faced god—it is not pure, or it is too pure, I do not know."

"What of Eluf and the other's guarding *Varúlfr*?"

"Nothing. Only their screams."

Thoril frowned at the old warrior. He was right, it sounded like nothing more than the mutterings of madmen. Hardly enough to satisfy Halvor or the others.

"Did you not see this," she asked. "In your dreams?"

"There was nothing of the Christians, nor of the burning ships." Ove turned his hands over, mapping the scars on his knuckles with a finger. "This place blinds me to our fate. I only see fragments, but it is not enough. It is worse with the Christians. What I do see is blurred, as if from a great distance."

Thoril leaned back, resting on her hands. "What are we to do? No Fritjof, no Ulfgar, and now no Bjarki."

"Halvor will want us to stay. He owes Bjarki a debt of blood, and will not leave this place without him. Even if it means he risks us all."

That night they caught their first glimpse of the strange people who had been tracking them. Sigurd saw them first, standing upon the ridge above them. But then more were spotted, until the hills seemed filled by their presence. Dozens of figures moved silently across the forsaken landscape, torches raised to the starless sky. Halvor ordered the company to battle-readiness, but the observers seemed uninterested in an open fight.

"I do not see a blade among them," said Sigurd as he strode between the massed ranks of norsemen. "Catch one alive if they come at us."

But the onlookers seemed content to simply watch from a distance. They moved away if any of Halvor's party got too close, only to reappear further along a moment later. The warriors grew frustrated, and some of them lobbed stones at the figures, to little effect.

"They are testing us." Thoril moved up beside Inge and Ove, taking her place in the shield wall. "Probing for a weakness, or trying to bait us into chasing after them."

"It might work," said Inge. She nodded to a band of younger warriors at the foot of the hills. The men were slowly hyping themselves up, and only the appearance of some of the company's veterans stopped them from racing headlong at the watchers.

Ove lowered his shield and rubbed his eyes with an arm. "They are young and foolish, but we were all like that once. Halvor will see them in line." His words were soon followed by the hoarse bark of the jarl, and the offending warriors quickly fell back into place.

"You see," said Ove, staring back up the walls of the valley. "Not even youthful vigour ignores the will of the jarl." He squinted into the darkness and blinked before turning to Thoril and Inge. "I fear we will need his strength before long, both of his mind and his axe."

The three stood together until the early hours, watching the watchers. It was only when the sun rose, and the figures retreated into the many caverns and ravines that splintered off from the valley, that the band finally found rest.

That morning, they found Fritjof and the crew of *Kveldúlfr*.

Their bodies, over thirty of them, had been nailed to stakes and hung rotting beneath the sun. The forest of corpses was found by one of Bjarki's pathfinders, upon the ridge nearest the grey walls of the ravine. Halvor had led the party up the hill as soon as he'd heard the news.

Swarms of gnats clung to the dead in such numbers that it was impossible to make out the features of the deceased. By the smell, it was clear that they had been here for some time. Longer, perhaps, than was possible.

"We must burn them," Halvor declared. "This is no way for a viking to enter Valhalla." He pointed towards the thin line of trees that ringed the hill. "A mighty pyre for the fallen, to usher their spirits on to the next life. Then we will deal with those who dared take up swords against our brothers."

The norsemen took to the task with vigor, while others set to removing the crew of their sister ship from the wooden stakes. It was a gruesome task, and Thoril found herself retching as she cut the bonds holding an elderly warrior to the post. Removing the nails from his wrists proved to be more horrid, and she was forced to step away from the corpse for a moment.

"They will thank you for it," said Ove, walking towards her. "Once they find rest in the great halls of our fathers."

Thoril nodded and wiped her brow. Braziers had been lit alongside the dead, and the smoke fended off the worst of the insects, but the heat wasn't helping with the smell.

"If we had not come upon them, the dead might have returned." Ove drew a blade from the folds of his sleeves and approached the stake. "To leave a body like this, with the head towards the heavens, is to encourage the becoming of draugr. You can see here"—he tapped the swollen leg of the corpse with the knife—"even now, the corruption has begun. These bodies will soon welcome unlife, and then we will have to kill our brothers and sisters, even if it is no longer truly them." He shook his head sadly and began the grisly task of removing the nails from the warriors hands and feet.

Thoril watched quietly, and then helped Ove take the body down and place it on the floor, beside the others. Behind them, the pyre had grown, and now covered much of the surface of the hill.

"They will see this fire from Tronde." Ove smiled sadly and patted her shoulder. "And when we return home, we shall feast to the memory of those we lost here."

Thoril wiped her hands on her breeches and stared down the line of posts. "Any sign of Bjarki or Ulfgar amongst the dead?"

"Inge searches now for them, but she will not find them here, I think."

She looked quizzically at the old warrior, but Ove simply shrugged. "This is not the fate reserved for Ulfgar. As for Bjarki, I suspect he would not let his body be caught like this, not by whoever haunts these hills."

"You think he is still out there?"

"It is what the jarl believes, and if anyone can hide himself away in a place like this, it's Bjarki."

"Then why not return to us, if he is still alive and free?"

Ove sighed. "I do not have all the answers, girl. And in this place, I can see as much as you. It is just a feeling, that is all. Perhaps Inge will come upon their bodies both, and then we can mourn their passing with the rest of them. But until then, I sense there is more to come for both Bjarki and Ulfgar."

"Halvor will want us to continue on, won't he?" Thoril said the words softly, so that only Ove could hear.

"He will not let this go unpunished, and he will not leave Bjarki to suffer this same fate." Ove raised a hand and gestured to the bodies still bound to the poles. "There must be a bloodening now, and vengeance for our fallen. Halvor will bring violence to those who have done this."

Thoril nodded, and watched as another body was removed from its stake. "Good," she said, gripping the hilt of her sword. "Vengeance it shall be."

They watched from the hills as the pyre was lit, and great plumes of smoke blew across the valley, aiding the dead in their journey beyond. It was Inge that first recited the words of Hialmar's Song. She had found Akes' body with the rest of them, and the words rung out cold from her mouth.

Flies from the South
The famished Raven
Fly with him
The fallow Eagle
On the flesh of the fallen
I shall feed them no more
On my body both
Will batten now

The sad notes of a tagelharpa joined her voice, and then the soft, rhythmic beat of a drum, too. Thoril watched as the flames roared across the hastily built pyre, and felt her heart go hard at the thought of her fallen raid-mates. To survive the swords of the Bretons and Njord's angry seas, only to be slaughtered on a strange island, far from home. She scowled. Ove's predictions be damned, she would see her kin avenged, and she would see Tronde again.

When the last note of Hialmar's Song faded, the company put the funeral pyre behind them and set off towards the mountain pass. Sigurd made sure there was always a sword and shield between Halvor and the empty hills, but the jarl ignored his mothering and moved speedily to the front of the band.

The remaining pathfinders fanned out, occupying both the high and low ground surrounding the norsemen. They would not be caught out by those who had butchered Fritjof and his crew.

It was sometime after noon that one of the scouts returned, in a state of nervous excitement. He was quickly taken aside by Halvor, who questioned him intensely, before being sent back out into the hills.

"Something is afoot." Inge shifted her shield over her shoulder and watched as the pathfinder disappeared up a rocky outcrop.

Halvor signalled to a band of veterans, and soon had them following in the scout's footsteps. The warriors were less light of step, and smaller rocks and stones rolled down the side of the hill, causing a groan from the disgruntled warriors closest.

When the scout returned, with his escort of veterans in tow, he was carrying a small object in his hands. Thoril tried to get a proper look at it, but whatever it was lay hidden beneath a bundle of rags.

"Let's see what he's found," said Inge, pushing her way to the front of the company. Thoril and Ove followed, ignoring the cursed complaints of the other norsemen as they navigated through the press.

Halvor was standing with Sigurd and Tommen, staring down into the bundle, a strange look on his face. The scout was talking rapidly into his ear, but it was clear that Halvor wasn't listening. He placed a hand into the rags and retrieved the object, lifting it above his head for all to see.

"This is what we face in this Gods' forsaken place." He spat at the ground and rotated his hand so all the gathered warriors could get a proper look. "Truly, it is a being cursed."

The jarl's fingers were wrapped around the pale white surface of a skull. Though distinctly human, the shape was warped, and the cranium jutted out unevenly. The forehead was sloped and smooth, and elongated in a manner that seemed almost serpentine. Thoril felt her stomach churn as she gazed into its empty sockets.

Behind her, she heard the Christians praying frantically to their dying God, before they were forced into silence by their captors.

"Behold the beast." Halvor turned the skull in his hands and stared into its ever-smiling face, before letting it fall from his grasp. "And what awaits it." He stomped a foot down hard, smashing the skull to pieces, and then rolled his shoulders. "Only the godless could do this to themselves. Only the godless could force their skulls to such a shape, to mimic the unfit and deformed…" He sneered in disgust, then pointed at what remained of the white bones. "We will see the same thing repeated, a thousand times, if needed." With that, he turned his back on the company and strode towards the crags.

The warriors followed him without hesitation, and two dozen norsemen jogged up the last hill before the opening of the ravine. But when they reached the summit, even Halvor was forced to take pause. A low muttering spread amongst the ranks as more of the company came into view of the grey walls of the mountain pass.

"This I did not see," said Ove as he stared at the opening. "How did I not see this?"

Before them, on either side of the mouth of the ravine, the rock walls had been cut and chiselled. Two great carvings looked down upon them. Hewn from the surface of the rock itself, the shapes formed were almost as tall as the crag itself. The artist evidently had some skill, and the representations were almost lifelike.

Thoril felt her skin crawl as she gazed upon the first of the two carvings. On the left of the passage, a great snake stretched out across the length of the wall. Its coils were wrapped around a depiction of the mountain itself, while its angular head stared down on the entrance to the passage, its massive fangs exposed. The carver had somehow managed to create the impression of colour without its use, and Thoril could almost see the silver scales of the beast beneath the sea once more.

In contrast, the other engraving seemed more primitive. Rather than the smooth corners of the serpent's depiction, the angles used were all sharp and rough, at times obscuring parts of the carving entirely. Despite that, Thoril could still make out most of the piece. It depicted a man sitting on his haunches, with his legs crossed. His one hand was raised, with two fingers extended to the heavens, while the other was pointed downward, towards the ground beneath his feet. As Thoril got closer, she could just make out the poorly hewn shapes of more serpentine bodies wrapped around his own.

"Eels," said Ove as they approached. He was right. What she'd mistaken for snakes were, in fact, dozens of eels covering his skin like armour.

"This is an old faith." Ove made the mark of the Fe with his one hand, and pulled his axe from his belt with the other.

"You have encountered these images before?" Thoril frowned at the veteran, and then stared back up at the carvings as they walked beside them.

"This one, yes." Bjarki pointed to the man and his armour of eels. "But this." He screwed up his eyes and stared at the snake. "I have not seen something like this before, not even on my journeys to the land in the West."

"Who is the man?" The shield-maiden stepped onto the sand that made up the floor of the ravine and helped Ove down from the rocky ledge beside her.

"He is a figure from pre-history. Neruk, Elil, Nergal, The Destroying Flame, he has gone by many names, and has had many worshippers. His time has passed though, with the coming of the Christians, and the worshippers of Allah."

"The Destroying Flame." Thoril clenched her jaw and took one last look at the carving of Neruk. His eyes seemed to follow her, and she felt she was being watched even when it was finally gone from sight.

A shout from behind her stopped her in her tracks, and the whole company turned to see what had caused the commotion.

Henrik and Eyva were trying to pull the Christians into the ravine, but they had dug their heels in and wouldn't go any further.

Thoril saw her own slave pulling at Henrik, sheer panic in his eyes, while the others had fallen to their knees and were begging their captors not to force them to continue.

"On your feet!" Henrik shouted. He smashed a meaty palm into her slave's face and dragged him through the sand. The others grabbed onto the viking's legs, slowing him to a halt, and giving her own slave enough time to get back to his feet.

"They will kill them," said Ove, but Thoril was already moving towards the huddle of bodies.

"Enough," she called as Henrik kicked his knee into the lanky Christian's face. The man sputtered blood and grabbed his nose as a moan erupted from his throat. She lifted her sword threateningly when Henrik caught her eyes. "He is mine." She pointed her blade towards her slave and nodded. "I will not have you kill him because he has slowed you down."

He shrugged. "They will not go any further."

"I will take him," she said, lowering her sword. "If he does not come, then I will punish him as I see fit, with blade or fist, but it will be *my* blade or fist."

Henrik shrugged again, but let go of her slave and took a step back. "Be it on you," he said, finally.

Thoril nodded and grabbed the slave by his collar. Understanding seemed to have dawned on him and he did not resist, knowing that his life was truly at risk. She prodded him forward with her shield and walked him back towards Ove.

"What's gotten into them?" Inge joined her as she guided her slave. She stank like spirits and smoke.

"I don't know," she replied. "They are scared easily, these Christians."

"Or they know something we do not." Inge cackled, and swigged deeply from her flask. Thoril couldn't see where she'd placed her sword or shield, but she wasn't in the mood for a fight.

Her slave seemed to have calmed, and the other prisoners had followed after him, preferring to face their fears than face a beating from an angry norseman. She watched him carefully as they walked through the opening to the ravine, and saw that he was talking softly to himself, reciting what seemed to be the same words over and over. He was at prayer, she realised. She glanced at the other Christians and saw that they were doing the same thing. She didn't know why, but it made a shiver run down her spine.

HELVEGEN

The ravine opened up until there was enough space for the company to walk side by side, without touching the walls. Halvor stayed at the front, and sent roving bands of warriors forward, sometimes joining them himself. His voice became a near constant feature as noon turned to late afternoon. He shouted reassurances and words of praise, of vengeance and anger. It was only when dusk fell, and his voice grew hoarse, that silence fell over the warriors.

"That skull," said Thoril as Halvor called them to a halt for the day. "How did it come to be shaped in such a way?"

Ove clicked his teeth, and dropped his shield and bedroll to the ground. "It is through binding that such deformities occur. I have seen it once before, though not to such an extent. As an infant, the skull is bound with rope and cloth. The pressure forces the head to grow in such a way, or the child dies. One or the other."

"Why would anyone do such a thing?" Inge slumped down on the ground beside Thoril and made a face. "To risk death, only to be rewarded with deformity. It is madness."

Ove stretched his back out and yawned. "It is beyond me. It was a long time ago that I last saw it, and the man I had seen was already dead, so he could not answer my questions."

Inge chuckled and rolled onto her side to stare at Thoril. "The Christians seemed troubled by it. Go on, ask yours what he fears."

Thoril turned her head to her slave and watched as he chewed on the dry meats she'd provided. The man's eyes met her own for a second, before he lowered his head and focused on his meagre dinner.

"Ask him, Ove." Thoril rubbed her hands together and nodded to the old warrior. "Maybe it will help us figure out where we find ourselves."

"It is not so easy." Ove frowned. "These Bretlanders speak in dialects I am not familiar with."

"Try." Thoril took a bite from her own supper and chewed it slowly, gesturing to Ove as she swallowed.

Ove sighed and walked towards her slave, who ignored him until he felt a boot prod him gently in the side. The veteran knelt down on his haunches and started speaking in the Bretlander tongue, using his hands to articulate and emphasise points when communication seemed to break down. After a while, once the first fires had been built, Ove rose from his knees and wandered back over to them.

"And?"

Ove eased onto his haunches and palmed his hands. "Neruk, the old god carved into the mountain... The Christians think he is someone else."

Inge rolled her eyes. "Who do they say he is? Another god who dies?"

"Addir-Melek," said Ove. "The blasphemer. I had not heard of him until now, but they believe he is a servant of the devil, and that this is the way to hell."

"Servants of the devil, ancient gods, and the path to Náströnd itself." Inge lay on her back. "What are we to believe, Ove?"

"Perhaps they are the same thing," said Thoril.

"Not you, too." Inge kicked dirt towards her and laughed. "You are always the one telling Ove and Ulfgar off for their stories, Troubled Thoril! Now you believe them?"

"I do not say that they are real, just that they represent the same thing." She crossed her legs and put her hands between them. The night air was bringing with it a chill, and smaller fires would soon be lit all around the camp.

Inge rolled onto her stomach and stared out into night. They had stopped where the ravine grew widest, and the towering walls were less imposing. Inge traced the movement of their scouts, following their torches as they moved alongside the edge of the ravine. Great shadows hung to the sides of the incline, and it was only when one of the torches grew closer to one that she saw it was not a shadow but a gaping hole in the side of the rock. There were dozens of them, scattered all about the valley. She squinted against the darkness and watched as one of the torches disappeared down a tunnel, only to reappear moments later at another tunnel further along.

"This place is a never-ending maze," she said, turning back to her friends. "I will be glad to see it behind us, if we ever make it off this island."

Thoril nodded, but Ove remained quiet, deep in thought. He remained like that even when the smaller fires were lit, even when Inge and Thoril were wrapped up in their bedrolls, fast asleep.

"Wake up, Thoril! Get up!"

Thoril awoke with a jerk, and instinctively went for her sword. Her eyes adjusted to the darkness, and she saw Inge sitting over her, her eyes wide and a nervous look on her face.

"What is it?" She wiped the sleep from her own eyes and rested on her elbows. Ove was nowhere to be seen, but the rest of the camp was being woken up by sentries and those who couldn't sleep.

"Listen," said Inge, holding a finger to her lips.

She listened. It was soft at first, barely a sound on the edge of hearing, but as she focused it grew louder, until it was all she could hear. A low moan, punctuated by silence, carried itself across the camp, repeating itself over and over.

"What is that?" She moved into a sitting position and stared into the night.

"At first I thought it was the wind echoing through those tunnels, but then it got clearer." Inge shifted until she was kneeling beside her, and touched her arm with a hand. "Thoril, it is a person. Someone in great pain, calling out."

"Where is Ove?" Thoril dragged herself up from the ground, her tiredness forgotten.

"He is with Halvor. He thinks it might be Ulfgar, but who is to say." Inge joined her standing, and the two started walking towards the camp's perimeter.

The rest of the company was wide awake by the time Halvor had planned on a course of action. His scouts had moved out the moment the voice on the wind made itself heard, and had identified one of the tunnels as the source. Sigurd and a band had already moved into the tunnel, and the rest of the company would follow.

"It is Bjarki or Ulfgar, or both." The jarl stood by the fire in the centre of the camp and stared into the gathered faces. "It does not matter. It is one of us, and we will not let his cries go unanswered."

The gathered norsemen were in full battle-gear, their shields held at the ready. Many of them had applied ochres and paints to their faces, and only their eyes shone out beneath blood-red visages.

"Sigurd leads the vanguard. His veterans will mark a trail for us to follow. Then we will have our vengeance, and these vile beings will know that Halvor and his Bloodied have fallen upon them!" He raised his axe and let out a guttural howl, thumping his shield as the rest of the band joined him.

Thoril found herself howling with the rest of the party, and the weight of days fell from her shoulders. Finally, they would confront the enemy face-to-face. Finally, they would bring steel to flesh, and release the frustration that had followed them since landing on the island. She would follow Halvor into the tunnels, and she would bloody her blade once more.

She accepted the torch offered to her as she walked past the fire, in Halvor's wake, and moved into a jog beside Inge and Ove. The other shield-maiden had a look of glee on her face. No doubt she was running through the same emotions she was. But Ove only smiled sadly when she glanced at him. He was too caught up in his stories, in his games of fate, and the will of the gods. The will of the gods was with them, and with their hero Halvor! How else could they perform such feats of strength and courage against the Bretlanders? How else could they survive the storms thrown at them. Even the Christians, with their miracles, could not compete with the chosen Bloodied of Halvor.

The entire company moved towards the tunnels, and Thoril even saw the slaves being pushed along in the direction of the entrance. They would all bear witness to the wetting of her sword.

She gripped her shield closer to her chest as the warriors were forced to press together. The tunnel entrance was narrower than it looked, and she smelt burnt hair as the norsemen bunched up.

The air grew hot, and sweat quickly soaked her undershirt. Beneath her feet, the rock was smooth, and she could feel a slight incline. They were heading underground.

The tunnel grew wider the deeper they went, and soon there was enough space for the band to move unhindered by one another. Halvor waved the norsemen forward and took stock of his surrounds.

The walls around them were smooth, as though the result of a current or stream. Small passages ran along the side of the main tunnel, but none of them were foolish enough to explore lest they lose the main party.

Sigurd had been true to his word. Red paint stained the walls, marking out his path ever downward.

The sound of suffering continued as they mapped out the tunnels, growing louder as they explored its depths. It wasn't long before Thoril wanted to cover her ears, or to scream loudly, anything to block out the noise. She could see the others were growing uncomfortable with it, too, but with Halvor in the lead, they plodded on regardless.

By the time the tunnel ended, becoming one great cavernous chamber, the groaning voice was all anyone could hear. Thoril ground her teeth as they emerged from the passageway and lifted her torch up to fully see the hall. The light flickered as a cold current blew through the gallery, and she turned to see about a dozen other tunnels lined up beside the one they'd just come from. They'd have openings all across the island, she had no doubt about it.

She spotted another of Sigurd's red spots of paint, marking out their route so that they did not get lost, and then turned to take in the chamber.

The light of their torches barely illuminated the walls closest to them, let alone the hall itself, and Thoril found herself staring into pitch black on all sides.

"Where is Sigurd?" Inge had to shout above the reverberating groan that seemed to come from every passageway at once.

"He must be here!" Her own voice sounded thin and soft, but her friend nodded anyway. Rather than shout again, Thoril pointed towards Jarl Halvor, and they both started to walk towards him.

Before they reached him, Inge raised a hand and turned to Thoril. She pointed to an ear and frowned. Almost as quickly as it had begun, the groaning voice on the wind had gone quiet.

"Is that a good thing?" Inge bit her lower lip and watched to see how the jarl would respond.

Halvor raised a hand, bringing the company to a halt, and tilted his head. He stood like that for a moment, listening to the darkness. It was only then that Thoril saw a flicker of movement amongst the shadows made by their torches.

She squinted and lifted her own torch higher to dispel the void that surrounded them. Her breath caught in her mouth as another figure moved within the shadows, and then another.

Just beyond the orange glow, shapes had begun to emerge, dozens of them, until the whole cavern seemed filled with darting forms, moving in and out of the light. Thoril could make out faces now, as the inhabitants of the cave grew more brazen. Wrapped in cloth and bound by rope, the leering visages that greeted her were misshapen and deformed, like the skull they'd uncovered in the valley. To see such disfigurement brought to life made her stomach churn, and she felt herself shrink back behind her shield.

"They carry no weapons," said Inge from beside her. Thoril looked, and watched as one of the figures stepped into the light, before disappearing once again. Inge was right. The man was unarmed and unarmoured. Aside from the rags he wore, and the head bindings, he carried nothing.

"We will make short work of this." The shield-maiden grinned beneath her own torch and strode forward more confidently than before.

Despite the appearance of the watchers, they made little attempt to attack or slow the war party. They kept to the edges of the light and tracked them as they moved deeper and deeper into the cavern. Thoril noticed more tunnels on the walls, and some even on the floor beneath them. She was sure there were more above their heads, but the ceiling was shrouded in a darkness not even the light of their fires could push back. More of the deformed figures appeared from these passages, but they kept their distance, content to watch Halvor and his Bloodied move through the cavern.

Thoril felt her foot step in something wet and stared down at a small pool of water, then dragged her boot out and tried to kick it dry. Ove was knelt down beside another of the puddles, his brow furrowed.

"It is salt water," he said, when Thoril turned to him.

"But we are days from the sea."

"Maybe, but these tunnels… We do not know how deep they go, or what lies beneath the island. They may be flooded by the sea when it storms."

Thoril shrugged. She cared little about the comings and goings of the tide, or for flooding tunnels, provided she was not there when next it happened.

The puddles of water grew more numerous and larger. She was sure she saw movement within some of the black pools—silver shapes writhing within their depths, but when she looked closer, there was nothing.

Inge was the first to notice a change in the ground beneath their feet. She let out a groan and pointed her torch at the floor. Thoril felt her hackles raise as something broke under her boots. The others were noticing it, too, and even Halvor spat in disgust.

The floor was littered with hundreds of bones, and one could hardly make out the ground beneath them. It was like staring at some macabre shoreline. Thoril saw more of the warped skulls, elongated and serpentine in shape, but there were others, too. The skeletons of all manner of beasts blanketed the chamber, and cracked beneath their feet as they moved over them.

The watchers maintained their distance, but seemed less rushed to get out of the norsemen's way, and Halvor nearly caught one with the side of his axe. Others darted back into the tunnels whenever the band made to attack them, but it was clear they were readying for a fight.

When they had walked for some time over the bone carpet, Halvor called the party to a halt.

"Listen," he said as his warriors sipped from their flasks and wiped the sweat from their brows. Deep inside the cavernous chamber, Thoril could hear the sound of a drum ringing out. It beat a slow rhythm, but the sound was unmistakable. Another sound joined that of the percussion, a low hum that seemed to echo through the tunnels.

"Where did they go?" Uskar turned to the gathered warriors and waved a hand at the empty tunnels. He was right: the watchers had disappeared, leaving only the vikings in the chamber.

The drumbeat upped its tempo, and Thoril felt the hair on the back of her neck rise as a fell voice joined it. It droned out words she could not understand, but the meaning was clear: Death. The End.

Other voices joined it, singing out from a great distance, but closing in with every chanted note.

"Shield wall!" Halvor called, dropping his own flask and lifting his axe. His warriors rushed to obey, and wood clashed against wood as the vikings joined in a defensive formation.

The shadows around them started to move, but this time, the figures were not content to hide away. They raced towards the band, charging across the bone floor, even as their feet were cut to shreds by the jagged remains.

The voice in the chamber reached a sickening crescendo, and suddenly hundreds of torches were lit all around them, finally illuminating the chamber entirely. Thoril nearly baulked at the sight. The bone floor stretched out as far as she could see, and there was no visible end to the cavern itself. She'd been right about the tunnels above their heads: the ceiling was covered by them, as was large swathes of the floor.

What caused her to flinch, however, was the sheer number of figures that were bearing down on them. There were *hundreds*. Some were hunched over, their deformities afflicting more than just their skulls, while others seemed small and ungainly on their feet. It didn't matter. Unarmed or not, she didn't know if they could be beaten.

Halvor beat his axe against his shield in a steady tempo, over the sound of the drum in the depths. He glanced at his warriors and grinned. This was what Halvor was made for: overcoming the odds and proving the gods favoured him.

Thoril felt her nerves calm, even as the cave dwellers bore down on them. She dropped her torch, no longer needing it, and drew her sword.

"Brace!" Halvor leaned into his shield, as did the rest of the company.

When the horde of deformed monstrosities met the shield wall, it was with a blood-curdling scream, followed by the crump of bones breaking and flesh being torn. Thoril threw her weight behind her shield and stabbed out between a narrow gap formed between her and Inge's shield. She was rewarded with a garbled cry, and the pressure against her arm was relieved, before another body flung itself at her.

She repeated the process again and again, until her arm grew tired, but still she carried on. Blood covered the floor, running in a steady stream across the bones, and still they carried on. Jarl Hover shouted out orders, pushing the press ever forward as they butchered their way through Fritjof's murderers.

The savage people that inhabited the cave were unrelenting, despite their losses, despite their lack of weapons. They used their numbers against the norse, and Thoril saw more than one of her brothers pulled down by their sheer weight, before the shield wall closed around the gap again.

When she felt she could not lift her sword again, and the sweat in her eyes was blurring her vision, the attack finally faltered. The steady beat of the drum in the distance finally fell silent, and the only sound was the bark of Halvor and the screams of those who fell beneath their blades.

"Finish!" Halvor cried, breaking from the shield wall. He swung his axe in a vicious arc, dispatching two foes in as many seconds, then catching another with the back of his boot. He smashed his shield down into the mutants skull until it stopped moving.

"With the jarl!" a voice cried, and the shield wall broke, releasing twenty angry norsemen upon the thinning ranks of the cave dwellers.

Thoril charged out with Inge, leaving Ove to deal with the wounded abhorrents strewn across the battleground.

Tired as she was, she felt her strength renewed at the thought of avenging her fallen raid-mates, and of bringing this cult of death to an end. Her sword slashed at exposed necks and chests, arms and legs, until all she saw was blood. It was only when the last of the death worshippers had disappeared down the tunnels, and the beating drum had faded for good, that she heard the soft, sibilant whisper.

She glanced around her, and saw that others had noticed it, too. Most of the warriors were standing still now, listening to the wind, and Thoril was gladdened to see so many of their number left. She flinched as the hissing sound grew louder and turned back to the tunnels that surrounded the chamber.

Theodoric was walking towards the nearest opening, his head cocked to the side as he sought out the source, while the rest of the company slowly edged back towards Halvor.

"Any ideas?" Thoril asked of Ove as they rejoined the shield wall.

"You have already seen it. You know what lurks beneath the tide." Ove closed his eyes and shrugged. "Now we must meet it."

Thoril crinkled her brow and held back a snarl at the old man's words. "It is—"

Her words were cut off by a cry of alarm, and then a high-pitched scream. She turned towards the tunnels in time to see a flicker of silver, and the smooth scales of a gigantic form as it moved past the nearest opening. A giant tail appeared for a moment, and then it was gone, leaving an opening as empty as it was a moment before.

Thoril felt her heart pounding in her chest, and her legs started to shake beneath her. Theodoric was running back towards them, a look of primal fear on his usually stoic features.

"It is Jörmungandr!" he cried, smashing past the now reformed shield-wall. "The Midgard Serpent is here."

Halvor shook his head, but gripped his axe tight in his hand. "Stand fast," he cried, but his voice wavered and his face was pale. "We are Odin's kin, and we do not run."

From the tunnels all around them, another wave of figures appeared. They started to sing in that strange tongue of theirs, and Thoril could hear the drum pick up its beat in the distance again. Her whole body was shaking now, as fear gripped her heart. She thought it would stop entirely, but a hand clutched her shoulder gently, and she turned to find Ove smiling at her.

"We must not fear this," he said, nodding to the tunnels. The hiss was growing louder, and it seemed to come from all the passages at once. "Soon, we will either feast in the halls of our fathers, or we will kill this thing and become like gods ourselves."

She took a deep breath and nodded, somehow conjuring up a smile for Ove. The old warrior patted her on the shoulder again, and then joined the shield wall beside her.

When the great serpent finally appeared, it was from one of the holes above the gathered norsemen. The beast pushed through debris, sprinkling them all with stone and dust, before it thrust its head out into the open. Thoril nearly cried out, but kept her fears in check as the giant snake slithered out into the cavern. The creature was impossibly large, its head the length and breadth of a longship, while its body seemed without end. Row upon row of fangs emerged from behind black gums, and massive red orbs stared out from its arrowhead-like face. Two muscular appendages hung from the beast's sides, and ended in sharp claws the size of a man. The silver scales that covered it were a mess of scars, and massive cuts long since healed. What creature could do such a thing to such a beast, Thoril wondered as it lowered itself to the ground.

All around them, the snake-worshippers were emerging, chanting and cheering as the serpent moved closer to the norsemen. Some were foolish enough to get too close to the snake, and were crushed beneath its coils. Others moved to flank the serpent, and encircled the vikings so that there was no clear route of escape. Though, by the look on Halvor's face, escape was not on his mind.

The norseman rolled his shoulders and tested the sharpness of his blade against his forearm.

"You see this," he said, turning to face his warriors. He raised his arm and nodded to the thin stream of blood running along it. "This blood is the blood of norse, of Odin's son. It is the blood of Freyja and of Vali. It is the blood of Balder. This blood is the same blood that will course through Thor when Ragnarok comes, and Fenris and Jörmungandr light fire to the world. It is like poison to the beast." He looked over his shoulder at the approaching serpent and the gathering cultists. "Now help me kill it."

His warriors moved in behind him, still in shock at the sight of the serpent, but emboldened by his words. Halvor seemed to grow before them, his size and strength swelling to match his words.

For a moment, it seemed that they could perform this impossible task. That they could slay this beast with axe and sword, with spear and shield. Indeed, when Halvor moved into a loping run, his axe raised and a war cry on his lips, it seemed an inevitability.

Thoril chased after him, her own sword raised, howling and cursing with the rest of the band as they closed on the serpent. The creature hesitated, unused to being attacked, unused to anything but fear. It gave Halvor the time he needed to make the last few meters. He leapt into the air, pushing aside the cultists who scrambled into his way, and embedded his axe in the serpent's side. The beast lashed out, but Halvor had already rolled out of the way and retrieved a short blade from his belt.

Then the rest of them were on it. Thoril stabbed deep into the creature's quivering flesh, yanking her sword back and vomiting as the stench of rotten fish erupted from the wound. She wiped her mouth and fell back before the thing could slam its tail down on where she'd just been. Others thrust their blades into the creature's flank, while the rest took to clearing up the horde of deformed that were still biting at their heels. She caught sight of Halvor crawling up the snake's flank, using his stabbing blade like a climbing tool, and then he was gone, hidden behind the beasts lashing body.

Inge crashed in beside her and cut down with her blade, piercing through flesh and bone. She grinned madly at Thoril, and then rolled out of the way, before the serpent could react. The norsemen were clinical in their approach, and dozens of the snake worshippers were killed, even as the serpent itself was cut to a bloody mess. Still, the beast's skin was thick, and its scales deflected much of the damage done.

Uskar was the first to fall. He lingered too long, trying to retrieve his spear from the snake's chest. The beast didn't even use its fangs to kill him, it simply smashed its head down against the ground he was standing on, leaving nothing but a red paste behind. The next to fall was Theodoric. Encouraged by the jarl's actions, he tried to clamber up the side of the snake in order to get close to its head. His hand slipped against the smooth scales and he tumbled to the ground, only to be crushed beneath the serpent's coils.

For a while, they fought like heroes, battling back both serpent and cultist. Blood ran like rivers from the creatures flanks, and great welts had formed all along its chest. The warriors learnt to move and duck out of the way whenever it slammed its body against the ground, and roll out of range of its massive coils. Thoril fought harder than she'd ever fought before, and was rewarded time and time again as blood spewed out from the creature's wounds. Even the serpent's worshippers began to doubt the strength of their god, and a great cry went up each time one of the viking's impaled the beast.

But the creature was old, and it had fought many battles. When it finally caught sight of Halvor climbing between its scales, the serpent struck with blinding speed. The jarl let out a cry as the creature caught him between its jaws, and a massive fang penetrated his chest. Thoril nearly dropped her sword and fled, but anger coursed through her at the last second and she found herself slashing out at the beast violently.

To his credit, when Halvor died, it was with a sword in his hands and a howl on his lips. Even as the serpent tore the life from him, he sunk his knife deep into the creatures gums, causing it to thrash madly, before it flung the lifeless corpse across the bone fields.

Halvor's Bloodied fought on for a while longer, but with each moment that passed, another of their number fell. Norsemen were consumed whole by the creature's gaping maw, crushed beneath its coils, or swarmed by the cultists. Tommen, then Eyva, Henrik, and then Ove and Inge—all of them were butchered.

Thoril screamed in rage as the serpent killed them, until a hand pulled her away from the fight and she was running. Fleeing from the end of the world, back the way she'd come.

She didn't know where the torch had come from, but she held it out before her as she ran. The sounds of battle had long since faded, and all she could hear were her feet sloshing through puddles and cracking old bones. Those who had fled with her were dead. Caught by ambush after ambush of the serpent worshippers, only Thoril remained. She had to survive—only she could tell the saga of Halvor and his band of Bloodied. She paused at the entrance to one of the tunnels and saw that a red mark had been painted on the wall. *Sigurd*, she thought as she moved towards the entrance. She frowned and looked at the floor. She didn't remember there being bones at the entrance to the tunnel. Her torch still raised, she walked over to the next tunnel and saw that the same mark had been painted on its walls, and on the next, and the next. Thoril shivered as the torch began to flicker. She didn't have long before it went out. Gritting her teeth to hold back the fear that threatened to overwhelm her, she moved on. If she could just find the right tunnel, she had a chance.

In the depths of the cavern, a drum began to beat.

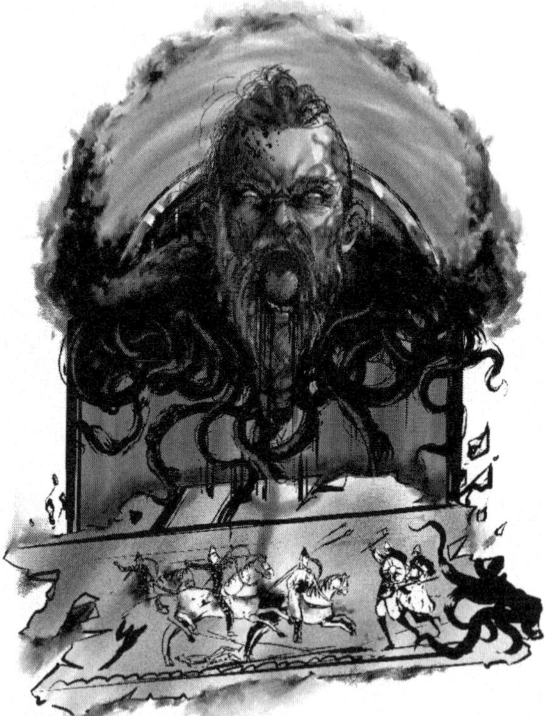

The Knights of the Non-Euclidian Table

THE ROT OF CAMLANN

"That's the last of them," said Theodoric, wiping the edge of his axe against his breeches. The stocky Saxon prodded the nearest body with the tip of his boot and looked up at Gawain. "Next time, leave some for me, eh?"

"Next time, be quicker." Gawain moved through the room, listening to the stiff floorboards creak beneath the weight of his armour. There was a muffled thump from one of the rooms above, followed by the distinctive crack of Sir Garin's laughter and Raaf's whiny chattering.

"At least the lads are having fun," said Theodoric, grinning. "Nothing like butchering a nest full of devil worshippers to lighten the soul."

Gawain nodded, kneeling beside one of the woodsmen splayed out across the floor. He dragged his sword across the man's homespun tunic, cleaning the lifeblood from his weapon before sheathing it and getting back to his feet. He knew better than to linger for too long.

"Come on," he said, walking out of the room. They'd have to torch the place.

Raaf had spotted the cabin nestled between the trees of Hatfield Forest just as dusk was starting to settle. It'd taken another quarter mile before Gawain could see it. Damnit, but the boy's eyes were good.

Sir Garin and Theodoric had ridden on ahead to scout the place out, but he'd known the truth of it before they'd returned. A thin wisp of smoke had curled up into the reddening sky, confirming it wasn't abandoned. And the rest had been obvious. No god-fearing Christians remained in this part of Britain, only their graves.

There had been five of them, and however many more Garin and Raaf had dispensed with upstairs. Black-gummed and red-eyed, they'd met Sir Gawain and his men with curses on their lips, only to be cut down like the dogs they were. He'd have left their bodies in the dust and mud and shit if it wasn't for the rot.

"How many?" asked Gawain as Raaf and the hedge knight emerged from the bottom of the stairs.

"Three," said Garin, stepping into the small lobby. He was taller than Gawain and heavier. The floorboards squealed beneath his weight, and his sabatons cut into the wooden panels. "Raaf put an arrow through the first and let me do the rest."

Gawain grunted, meeting the hedge knight's eyes. Garin wore his hair long, tied behind his head in a knot. His armour was well-worn but well-kept, and he wielded his two-hander more nimbly than most did their side-swords. The Listenoisean had answered Bedivere's call to muster after Camlann… where everything had changed.

"We still have a little light," said Gawain, pushing back the memory. "Another hour before nightfall, at the least."

"And then the comet will guide our way," said Theodoric, lumbering up beside him. The Teuton crossed himself, a toothy grin appearing from within his black beard. "The Devil's Eye."

"Aye," said Gawain. "So it is."

The small company left the cabin behind them, moving deeper into Hatfield Forest as white tufts of smoke began to bloom from the dwelling. Fire was the only way to deal with the rot, the only means by which to purify the soil of Mordred's spawn. Arthur had discovered that, after cleaving through the ichor-covered skin of a great, tentacled serpent that had set upon him when they had returned from France. The ground around the beast had started to warp and twist until not even holy water could cleanse it. The King had thrown a torch upon the carcass, his brow furrowed and dark as the beast screeched and writhed and twisted beneath the flames. That had been but the beginning.

Bedivere and his host would see the smoke from the King's Road and hasten towards it, of that Gawain had no doubt. He wished nothing more than to wait for them, to find some solace and solidarity in their numbers. But he had a charge to fulfil, and honour demanded he complete the task at hand.

He clicked beneath his breath, guiding Gringolet with his knees as the sturdy charger picked its way deeper into the woods. He rode behind Theodoric and Garin, with his squire, Raaf, taking up the rear.

The forest was silent, with no sound of bird nor beast—not even the wind. Tall trees grew around the narrow path they rode, their roots digging deep into the earth. The woods were old—older than Camelot, than Lady Britain herself.

Tangled rose vines grew across their boughs, forming tapestries of colour, set on looms of wood and green ivy. Shards of light pierced the dense canopy, giving life to the dense shrubbery that surrounded them. Gawain saw plants that he'd never seen before: flowers that blossomed like scabby wounds, orchids that recoiled away from the pale light.

There was a smell, too, a sort of musk that grew more pungent the further they went. It reminded him of turned meat, and he lowered his visor to try and limit the stench.

They crossed a babbling brook as the last rays of the day began to fade, turning at first a shade of orange and then red. Gawain could see little slivers of sky above, between the leaves and branches. Thick clouds sprawled across the heavens, their dark bellies heavy with rain. To the north, he could just make out the tail of the comet. *Arall Myrddin*, Merlyn had called it the night it had appeared. They had been in France, hunting down Sir Lancelot and his allies when the fiery comet had first split the night sky.

Not so long ago, Gawain thought as he ushered Gringolet up the opposite banks of the stream. It felt like a lifetime had passed since they'd returned home, only to find Mordred upon the throne of Logres. The little rat bastard. His own brother, by blood, if not in spirit. Gawain had vowed then and there that he would be the one to kill him, but the chance had never come, not even at Camlann, where Arthur and that godless thing that had once been Mordred battled for the kingdom.

They rode on a little while further before the trees began to thin out, stripped away like old King Pellinore's hair, and came to a stop before a shaded glen that opened up upon a wide valley.

"This looks like the place," said Sir Garin over his shoulder. The hedge knight twisted in his saddle, nodding to Theodoric and the other knight. "This is what Sir Bedivere wanted. A place to meet the traitor. A burial ground."

Gawain lifted his visor, breathing in the air. It was fresh, with the taste of rain and grass. A pair of rolling hills crowded in the valley, the hunched backs of giants resting beneath the earth. To the east, the black trees of the forest disappeared into the hills while a thundering river coursed along its western boundaries. The field was flat and long, perfect for the bristling charge of knights in armour.

"Aye," he agreed. "This is the place."

Theodoric rode up beside him, coming to a stop on the edge of the woods before breathing out deeply. "A bloody fine field," he said with a blink of his hooded brown eyes. He rapped his hairy knuckles against the shield hanging from his horse's flank and nodded solemnly. "Couldn't have picked one better if the Lady herself had appeared to show us the way."

Gawain gave the Saxon a thin smile and then turned to Raaf. "It's time you earned your keep, son. Go and fetch Sir Bedivere and his men. Lead them back the way we came, and don't tarry about. He'll want to see this place before the last light."

"Hold on, lad." Theodoric pulled at his reins, turning his horse as the squire made to head off. "I think I've spotted our supper."

Gawain followed his gaze, staring into the thicket on the other side of the churning river. A silver stag had emerged from the forest and was cautiously making its way to the water's edge. A thick mane of velvet hung around its neck—the remnants of its winter fur—and its white-tufted tail swept from side to side as it made its approach.

"Look at the horns on that one," said Theodoric, gesturing at the boy to unshoulder his bow.

Raaf looked uncertain for a moment, caught between the instructions of his master and Theodoric's motioning, but at a nod from Gawain, he shrugged off the bow and drew an arrow from the quiver at his side.

"That's a fourteen-pointer, that is," said the Saxon, nudging his own horse forward.

"Careful," said Garin. "You don't want to spook it."

"Careful yourself." Theodoric grinned. "I'm not about to have porridge for supper and breakfast again, knight. I'll run it down if needs be."

Gawain leaned forward in his saddle, watching Raaf as he edged closer to the stag. The boy was good with a bow and could knock a moorhen out of the sky at two hundred yards, but the buck was still too far away. It'd have to be a clean kill. They couldn't waste time scouring the forest for a wounded stag—not after nightfall.

When Raaf was closer, just on the edge of the treeline, he notched an arrow to the string and drew it taught against his chin. His form was perfect, and Gawain knew the arrow would fly true.

A gentle wind blew through the trees, rustling the grass and sending woody seeds and spores swirling towards the field. Gringolet shifted beneath him, stomping its hooves against the ground, and Gawain felt a sense of unease settle upon his shoulders.

Now, boy, he thought, before it smells our scent.

The stag looked up from the stream, turning its head towards the forest. Its velvet pelt was matted and dirty. Scars and blisters covered the creature's neck, festering wounds that seemed to pulse, even as the creature stared at them. A dark substance, too black to be blood, was splattered across the stag's fur. It had been attacked, and recently, by the looks of it.

The knight rested a hand on the pommel of his sword, his eyes flicking to the shadowed thickets that surrounded the river. Perhaps a lion hunted these woods, or something worse? Had they stumbled upon a victim of Palamedes's Questing Beast? There was something wrong about the way the animal stood, its shoulders hunched, its muscles bunched up like a predator, ready to spring upon its prey.

Gawain blinked, the breath leaving his body as an icy cold hand clutched at his heart and crawled along his skin.

The stag had three eyes.

IDYLLS OF THE KNIGHT

"Merlyn was right. This land is cursed." Theodoric spat into the fire before taking another swig from his flask and passing it on to Garin. "Not even the beasts have been spared, and that was to be my dinner."

Gawain nodded solemnly. After Raaf had put an arrow in the wretched stag's heart, they'd doused the corpse in sesame oil and burned it. Bedivere and his host had arrived not long after, drawn to the flickering flames like bloodhounds. They'd set up camp along the river, beneath the trees before the clearing. Over ten thousand men, the heart and spirit of what remained of Arthur's armies, now rested within the shadow of Hatfield Forest.

Gawain waved away Garin's proffered flask, leaning back against his riding saddle and the rolled-up blanket he was using as a cushion. "The roots of darkness are deep here. It's true. But the land shall be cleansed and born anew."

"The words of a priest." Garin laughed, wiping his lips with the back of his hand. "Between you and Father Tawly, I don't know who is more serious."

"It's the Father, for sure." Theodoric snorted, scratching at his beard. "I haven't seen the man laugh nor smile. And they say us Saxons are without humour."

Gawain stifled a smile at the thought of Father Tawly and his sermons. The man could spit fire and brimstone when his ire was raised, and even the hardiest of knights baulked at his admonishments.

"Where is that old fart?" Garin sat up on his haunches, gazing around the camp for a sign of the white-robed preacher. The hedge knight was dressed in just his padded gambeson and breeches. The quilted doublet he wore was stained with sweat and grime, and Gawain felt a moment's sympathy for the knight errant. Since Camlann, the lives of all had changed, but questing knights had felt it more than most. There was no keep to return to, no round table to aspire to. Gone were the heroic adventures, the swooning damsels, and golden trinkets. The spark was gone, and now there was only survival—mere survival.

"He'll be around," said Gawain, tracking Garin's eyes as he looked about the camp. "Likely filling his censers for the morrow."

A dull glow hung over the rows of tents, casting shadows that stretched as tall as the trees they rested beneath. The light of Arall Myrddin was growing stronger, a red hue that seemed to pervade all corners of the night, like the sun itself. The comet was barely visible during the day, but when darkness fell, it was like a scar upon the heavens. It hardly moved when you watched it, but each night, it was just a little bit closer, just a little bit bigger.

Gawain spared it a moment's scrutiny and then glanced about the camp. There were no grand pavilions and lofty gazebos beneath the trees, not even for Sir Bedivere and the remaining Knights of the Round Table. Like the days of questing, that, too, had passed. Now each man slept in what he could carry or strap to the back of his horse.

Footmen and knights shared fires in front of their tents, more equal now than any knight of the table had ever been. They engaged in muted conversation or exchanged mead and watered-down wine. There was some laughter, but it was nervous and forced, hardly the hearty roar of men celebrating the night before a battle.

"I see Bedivere is fulfilling his duties." Garin nodded his chin towards a line of red and yellow tents on the edge of the treeline. Arthur's French allies had answered his call when news of Mordred's treachery had crossed the channel. Knights from Fécamp and Bodoual had taken up arms in his name. Men as far east as Auvergne had come, knowing him to be valorous and true and his cause worthy.

Sir Bedivere walked among their tents, offering words of reassurance and exchanging jokes in the smattering of French he'd picked up at Court. He wore a light tunic of red and gold—the colours of Camelot—and walked beside a towering figure Gawain recognised as Sir Kay.

"He's no Arthur," said Garin, watching Bedivere as he knelt beside a gruff-looking chevalier. The two men exchanged a few words before Bedivere clasped him on the shoulder awkwardly and got back to his feet.

Gawain was hesitant to agree, but Garin was right. Bedivere, for all his strengths, was not like Arthur. He was stiff around men he didn't know and lacked the charm and openness of a true leader. Lancelot should have been here, leading them—they all knew it. But fate had decided otherwise. Or rather, Lancelot's betrayal had.

Gawain had written to him, even offered him forgiveness if he would just return to Arthur's side to destroy the usurper and cleanse the land of the poison that had taken root. Lancelot's crimes were but those of a child's compared to Mordred's blasphemies. But there had been no reply, and now it was too late.

Sir Bedivere had done the best he could. There was no denying it. Better than any man still standing could have done. He'd taken Arthur's words to heart and scraped together what was left of Britain's armies after the battle of Camlann. They stood united now, ready and willing to give battle, to avenge the fallen—to avenge the King.

"He is a good man," said Theodoric, "but he bears a heavy burden. Too heavy, I think."

"We shall see." Gawain turned away from the camp and stared over the fire at the bulky Teuton. "What of you, Theodoric? Will you return home when this is done? There is a place here for you, I think, once we have undone Mordred's grip on the land."

The Saxon let out a heavy sigh and stared up at the night sky. He was quiet for a moment, his eyes fixed on the comet before he blinked and turned back to Gawain. "I have been away for too long already. I will need to return to Domburg when... if we defeat Mordred. It seems we Saxons have our own monsters to deal with."

Gawain raised a brow. "What have you heard?"

"Little from across the Elbe, but there are stories..." Theodoric shrugged. "Since the comet, the forests have become treacherous. More than that, there is talk of creatures lurking in the old towns, feasting upon anyone foolish enough to wander out at night. My lord had gathered a host to investigate further, but I have not heard from him since."

"Bandits and cutthroats," said Garin. "There is no reason to think Mordred's corruption has spread."

"Aye," Gawain grunted. "This devil's pact is one brought to bear by the traitor. It will not have crossed the shores to affect your countrymen."

Theodoric nodded but looked unconvinced. "All the same, I must return to Hamburg once we cut the rot from Logres."

Garin took another swig from the flask and stared deeply into the fire. "I would like to see this Domburg for myself," he said after a while, "and compare it to our own keeps. Perhaps I will join you, if you'll have me?"

Theodoric grinned, slapping the hedge knight on the shoulder with a meaty palm. "Aye, I'd be grateful to have your sword and company. Maybe you'll get a taste for real ale while we're there, too. Not this piss-poor Logrean stuff."

"You don't like our drink?" Bedivere appeared beside the fire, Sir Kay, like a shadow, beside him.

Theodoric chuckled, nodding up at the knights. "It's not so bad as the swill they drink in France, but it's no Saxon brew."

"I shall pass on your complaints," said Bedivere with a thin smile. He looked tired, Gawain thought. His face was scarred from where a mace had caught him on the continent, and his hair flecked with grey. Still, there was a resilience about him—a dogged spark behind his pale eyes.

"Maybe you Saxons would fight better if your drink wasn't so strong," said Sir Garin with a chortle. He moved out of reach of Theodoric, just as the chuckling Teuton swiped at him with his hand. "A joke, a joke!"

"Speak for yourself, lad. You wave that zweihänder of yours around like a drunk. It's a miracle you haven't knocked all our heads off."

Gawain rolled out of the way of the tumbling forms, getting to his knees as

Theodoric tried to pin the younger knight. A smile spread across his face as he watched them jostle with each other, his laughter joining theirs.

"It is good to hear you laugh again."

Gawain turned to meet Bedivere's eyes and nodded, feeling his smile fade. They hadn't spoken much in recent weeks. None of the knights that had sat with Arthur had. The memory was still too fresh.

"You picked well," said Bedivere, nodding out towards the valley. "A worthy place to decide Britain's fate. What do they call it?"

"I do not know that it has a name." Gawain stared across the tents, at the field. Grass grew in clumps nearest the river, but it gradually began to thin until it was no higher than his ankles. The light of Arall Myrddin glowed like a beacon above it, giving the field a rubicund tinge, the grass blushing like embers at the bottom of a hearth.

"It'll need a name if the bards are to sing of it in the years to come." Bedivere shrugged. "But... perhaps that is better left to someone more poetic than I."

Songs and poetry, thought Gawain. As if mere words could ever capture what they had all seen—what they had fought. His thoughts turned to Mordred, his cousin no more. "You think he will come?"

"He will come." Bedivere stroked the pommel of the sword at his side with the palm of his remaining hand. He'd lost the other in battle many years ago but had been no lesser for it. Some had said he would have been the equal to Gawain with the use of both hands, maybe even Lancelot himself. "And then I will put him down like the lecherous cur he is."

Gawain nodded, looking down at the sword. Excalibur. It rested awkwardly at Bedivere's side, a little too long for the knight, unwieldy. But Bedivere wore it all the same. There had been those who had questioned by what right he now wielded the Sword of Kings. Those questions had been silenced with a wave of Merlyn's wrinkled hand, and a word barked out in anger. Then the old man had left, striding out of the keep bare minutes after Arthur had been buried. Gawain had never seen such a look of pure despair on any man's face before that moment.

"What of Merlyn?" he asked, voicing his thoughts. "Will he join us on the field?"

Bedivere pursed his lips, the scars around his mouth twisting with the movement. "I have not seen or heard of him since he left Tintagel Castle. And I do not expect to hear from him again. For a man of prophecy, Arthur's death left him... shaken... unhinged. I think he might have gone mad from it."

"He was changed, even before Camlann." Sir Kay's voice was deep and resonant, commanding attention. The knight shook his head, breathing out as he stared up into the night. "It started when the Devil's Eye appeared. It took him unawares. I do not think he foresaw it or what followed."

"He failed Arthur," said Bedivere. "As did we all."

"Aye," said Gawain. He felt it more than most. He had been there when Mordred struck. He had seen the lifeblood seep from Arthur's breast, and known then that all the goodness in the world was no more.

"Come on," said Theodoric from beside the fire. He'd given up tussling with Sir Garin and was nestled down beneath a blanket with his flask. "Enough talk of prophecy and death. There will be plenty of that tomorrow. Where's the boy? Raaf! Give us a song, before your voice breaks and you sound like the rest of us ugly bastards."

Gawain's squire appeared from within one of the tents, rubbing sleep from his eyes. He shook the curls from his face and squinted at the men sat about the fire, before glancing at Gawain.

The knight shrugged. If the boy wanted to sing, that was his business, and he wouldn't stop him.

"Give us a song, lad!" Theodoric clapped his hands together and grinned.

"What shall we have?" asked Garin, warming to the idea. "Do you know Can vei la Lauzeta? What about Redit Aetas Aurea?"

Raaf shook his head, looking out of his depth. "I am no troubadour, sir. I know The Lady and the Fox and a few tavern ditties, but not much else."

Theodoric pushed Garin by the shoulder, wagging his finger. "If you want to listen to French songs, go sit with the French, eh? Don't bother the lad with them."

"They are good songs," Garin said, rolling his eyes. "Songs worth singing."

"There are no more songs worth singing." Gawain sat back down beside the fire, gesturing to Sir Bedivere and Sir Kay to join them. The two knights looked hesitant for a moment but eventually sat down stiffly before accepting Garin's flask.

"Aye," Theodoric grunted, his smile fading. "Still, I'd like to hear the boy sing. Something to raise the spirits, eh?"

Gawain sighed. The words had come out darker than he intended. The eve of battle was no place for his morose comments, no matter the truth of them. He scratched at his chin, thinking, and then nodded to his squire. "How about the Idylls of the Knight?"

"I know that one," said Raaf, smiling faintly. "Though I cannot do it justice."

"Try," said Sir Bedivere. He'd crossed his legs and was leaning forward against them. The light of the fire flickered across his scarred face, adding to the glow in his eyes.

The squire nodded again and pushed Theodoric's legs out of the way so that he could stand amongst them. He stared at the faces around him one last time and then took a deep breath before beginning.

His words were soft and clear, to start, but grew louder as the boy found his voice. Gawain caught himself smiling as he listened to the old song. He had heard it often at the King's court, the tune a particular favourite of Arthur's.

There was a knight most chivalrous, the fairest in all the land

He wore his lady's favours, wrapped around his hand

Oh, King! He was a beauty, a hero to be sure

But he fought the Devil's hubris, and his heart remained pure

When there came a call to battle, he rode from far and wide

Atop his mighty stallion, his sword at his side

He fought with might and fury, a feast for the eyes

And broke the Devil's grip, he cleared those blackened skies

Then he rode back home and kissed his lady

He was the knight most chivalrous, the fairest in all the land

Gawain remained sitting by the fire after the song was sung, after everyone else had gone to their tents. He watched the embers fade, not bothering to get up to add more wood. The night air was cold, and he could feel a little of the remnants of winter's edge against his skin. But he didn't mind.

He stayed like that for a while, remembering old songs sung in old halls, with old friends.

WHAT THE COMET BRINGS

Dawn brought with it a low-hanging fog, streaming in from across the river. It coiled around the ankles of Bedivere's horses and men, covering the ground like steam rising from the earth. The red hue of Arall Myrddin was still visible above, competing for supremacy with the early rays of the sun. Its light reflected off the fog, giving everything an ethereal glow, making the men uncomfortable.

Gawain rode beside Sir Garin and some of the other free knights who had joined their cause. Theodoric had woken late, complaining of a splitting headache. So much for weak Briton ale. He'd left Raaf back at the camp to help the Saxon dress in his plate and told the boy to meet him on the field.

"Not a day I would have picked," said Garin. The hedge knight wore a yellow surcoat over his lobstered-plate armour, his family sigil embroidered upon the fabric. The rounded visor of his bascinet helm was tilted up to reveal his face, and he wiped his eyes as he stared across the field.

"Nor I," Gawain agreed. He tugged at his gauntlets, tightening them until they felt comfortable around his wrists. His own armour put that of the hedge knight's to shame. He wore a gilded cuirass inscribed with the oaths he had made upon attaining knighthood. Golden filigree latticed the edges of his pauldrons while delicately carved symbols had been wrought upon the surface of the burnished steel. Precious stones were embedded in his helm and the grooves of his plate—blessed jewels that warded against evil. The fiery red surcoat he donned over his armour was embroidered with birds and flowers and golden knots.

"I don't know if Grildenshank will be willing to charge through that." Garin ruffled the mane of his horse, patting the stallion's great side with his hand as he stared down at the fog.

"The sun will clear it soon enough," said Gawain, his eyes moving over the ranks of footmen crossing the field. "It's what we find beyond the mist that should be the focus of our concerns."

Garin grunted. "Whatever it is, we will not be caught unawares this time."

This time. Not like Camlann, then.

Bedivere had spread his army out over the field, favouring the left flank and the dark forest that hemmed them in. Tight formations of pikemen edged towards the centre of the clearing, the mist swirling beneath their feet. Behind them strode the burly greatswords who would wade into the fight once the pikemen had blunted whatever blow was to fall upon their lines. Groups of archers hung around the back, chattering amongst themselves as they watched the formations begin to move.

Bedivere and his knights observed the unfolding lines from the treeline, not yet committing themselves to the field. Over four hundred of them were gathered within the shadows of Hatfield Forest, their banners lowered as they waited for the first sign of Mordred. When the traitor came, they would declare themselves and meet him in open battle.

"Still nothing," said Garin as another team of scouts emerged from the undergrowth opposite their position. The men jogged by slowly, unencumbered by any sense of urgency. If they'd spotted anything of Mordred, they would have been breathless, panicked.

"You could have waited for me," came Theodoric's voice from behind. Gawain turned in his saddle, staring back as the Saxon rode up to join them.

"We thought it best to let you sleep in a little." Garin chuckled. "Your drunken snores kept up half the camp."

"Nonsense." Theodoric scoffed. His eyes were red, and there was something sticky in his beard. "I'm a deep sleeper, that's all."

Raaf joined them a moment later, leading his speckled grey horse between the trees and coming to a stop beside Gawain. The boy had donned the chainmail Gawain had given him for his name-day and strapped a short sword to his waist. His longbow hung over his shoulder, beside a quiver full of arrows.

"What have we missed?" asked Theodoric, taking a sip of what Gawain hoped was water from his flask.

"The comings and goings of scouts, mostly," he replied. "The pikes dug up a nest of snakes by the river just after first light. Abhorrent things with extra limbs and snapping fangs. It's a wonder none of them were bitten."

"Cursed," Theodoric grumbled beneath his breath. "This place is cursed."

"Aye. So you keep saying."

"That I keep saying it doesn't make it any less true."

Gawain raised a brow. "Nor any truer."

The Saxon shrugged, thumbing at the handle of the great axe that rested upon his lap. Its blade was sharp, freshly cleaned—either by Theodoric or Raaf—and shone dimly in the morning light. "If he does not come today—"

"He will come."

"But if he doesn't?"

Gawain shifted in his saddle, feeling the weight of his shield resting against his left leg. "Then we will go to him and flush him out of Camelot. Either we will do it now and succeed, or others will come after us and drag that treacherous beast to hell."

Somewhere up ahead, a horn blasted out a single note from within the mist. It hung in the air, a shrill echo rising above the chittering archers in front of Gawain and the waiting knights.

A horseman appeared on the other side of the glen, punching through the undergrowth as he untangled himself from the dense forest. His white charger hissed out steaming air, its flanks heaving as it galloped across the field. The fog seemed to rise up around them, conspiring to slow their mad dash back to the lines, but they pushed on regardless, dispersing the mist, even as it formed before them.

The rider cupped a horn to his mouth, blasting out another high note as he ploughed across the glen.

"He has come," said Gawain. He felt a shiver run down his spine and ground his teeth together. *He has picked his moment, too*, he thought, staring at the red-tinged mist that churned across the glen.

Theodoric swore beneath his breath, letting out such a volley of foul words that Gawain found himself wincing. He exchanged a look with Sir Garin before staring further along the line.

He could hear Bedivere's voice raised, shouting out commands before the rider had even made it back to the treeline. There could only be one thing he'd report: *he has come*. Gawain watched as the one-handed knight waved towards the opposite treeline, spitting out words quicker than he could track them. There was a flurry of movement as the knights around him moved to obey, prompting their restless horses onto the flatland.

Another horn rang out from Bedivere's position within the trees. As the note faded, great banners were unfurled, cloth and canvas bearing the crests of a dozen households. Pendants fluttered above the heads of knights from all across Britain, from across the channel. Gawain saw Arthur's dragon beside Saxon sigils and the emblems of the French aristocracy.

Priests wandered out from the woods in front of the knights, their white robes trailing behind them as they began their chant. Gawain saw Father Tawly amongst their number, swinging a smoking censer before him, a hand raised to the heavens. His long hood was drawn up to his ears, a bronze cross swaying from his neck. The old priest made for the nearest infantry block, scowling out a litany as he joined their ranks.

Sir Garin nudged his horse forward, nodding to the yellow signal flag as it was raised above the banners. "Time to move," he said.

"Aye." Gawain dug his heels into Gringolet's flanks, guiding his charger through the last of the trees, towards the river. He heard the rumble of hooves behind him as two dozen knights and chevaliers followed. Sir Bedivere had given him command of the western flank, while he would lead the bulk of the knights, with Sir Kay, from the east.

He reined Gringolet in just behind a square of greatswords and nodded down at an approaching footman. "What have you seen?"

"Nothin' yet, ser." The man wore a wide-rimmed kettle helm over a leather skullcap. His face was clean-shaven, and a slither of silver mail shone out from beneath his patchy surcoat. He sneered into the fog, his lips curling up around a set of yellowing teeth. "But we'll be ready for them when they come."

"Keep an eye on the river," said Gawain, steering Gringolet towards the muddy banks. "I won't have any surprises."

The sergeant saluted sharply and made his way back to the square, shouting out commands as he went.

"The river?" Theodoric raised a brow as Gawain came to a halt beside him. "There'll be no crossing that, not this time of year."

"You never know," said Gawain. "Mordred is as cunning as he is foul. I won't leave our fates up to chance."

The burly Saxon shrugged, his eyes narrowing as another horn blast rent the air. This one was different, from further away. It came from the forest on the opposite end of the field, a low humming note that seemed to grow with each passing second. Gawain patted Gringolet's side reassuringly as he felt the stallion flinch beneath him and watched the woods for signs of movement. He thought he saw a shape shift within the mist, but it disappeared as the horn's note faded away.

"Look!" Raaf pointed a hand towards the furthermost fringes of the forest, where the trees joined the first mounds that became rolling hills, the giants' backs.

Gawain followed the boy's gesture, staring into the foliage and shadows. It was subtle at first: a coiling wisp of fog displaced, a flicker of movement beneath the branches. But as the seconds trickled by, he began to notice figures emerging from out of the darkness. "Steady now," Gawain whispered, tugging at Gringolet's reins to keep the destrier still.

Theodoric's horse tilted its head, trying to turn away from the growing mass of figures appearing on the other end of the field, churning up grass with its stomping hooves. "Here they come," said the Saxon, forcing his charger around to face the treeline.

Gawain saw banners rising above the gloom, unfurling to reveal the red and black of Mordred's colours. Dawn's dim light flickered off burnished steel and bronze, adding to the tint of vermillion and silver that coloured the low-hanging fog. A drum sounded from somewhere within the haze, beating out a slow, monotonous rhythm as more horns blasted out their heralding notes.

Mordred's allies were many—less since Camlann, but the slaughter of that battle had only diminished their numbers, not their fervour. Men of the old faiths: Picts and Celts; giant, bearded warriors from across the North Sea; all those who had hated Arthur and thrown themselves behind the usurper, the heretic. Gawain recognised some of the banners—those of good Christian households that had gone astray. He spat when he saw Gualan's twin-headed eagle rise amongst their number. He had fought with Tual Gualan on the continent, beat back black bears and savage brutes, shared mead and laughter in the dark forests of Languedoc while they searched for the grail. To see him aligned with Mordred… He clenched his fist as anger coursed through his veins. There would be a reckoning this day.

The shapes beneath the banners turned into formations as they cleared the forest. Rows of spears and poleaxes lined up beside more primitive-looking phalanxes, marching in time to the slow beat of the drum. From a distance, the warriors looked unchanged—simple footmen wading through the mist. But Gawain knew that, up close, their faces would be twisted by rage, their gums blackened by rot, and their eyes blazing with madness. All who had turned to Mordred had turned away from God.

He squinted at the trees, blinking as he tried to focus on the shapes moving beyond the footmen, searching for the tell-tale signs of horsemen, of Mordred and his blasphemous knights. All he saw were the silhouettes of crooked branches, gnarled and twisted, and the flicker of steel and shadows as more men moved out from the forest.

The priests along Bedivere's lines began to sing out their sermon, striding out in front of the ranks of massed pikemen to recite their liturgies and bless the warriors who were about to meet in battle. Gawain spotted Father Tawly on the edge of the riverbank. The old priest had drawn back his hood and was spitting out the words of a prayer with such force that his face had gone a shade of red to match the light of Arall Myrddin. He waved his censer along the ground, the intricately carved vessel billowing clouds of incense to meet with the mist wrapped around his ankles.

A low-pitched whine reverberated across the dale, and Gawain looked up to see Mordred's host begin to move with purpose. At its spearhead, the Norsemen had formed up into a shield wall and were jogging across the field towards them.

"Archers!" came a call, repeated all along the lines. Gawain could see Bedivere moving along the edges of the field, calling out orders as they braced for the coming battle. He wore a surcoat of brilliant blue and gold over his thick plate. The visor of his great helm was already lowered, and a shield strapped to his left arm. He waved the sword, Excalibur, over his head as he barked out commands. The blade seemed radiant in the murky gloom, shining brighter than even the comet from where he stood.

Another voice was raised above the sound of drums and chanting priests, followed by the satisfying twang of a thousand bows being released in unison. Gawain watched the arrows shoot skyward, arcing through the morning air, before plummeting down towards the approaching Norsemen. The pagans raised their shields at the last moment, catching the arrows or buffeting them aside. There were a few screams, sharp yells and cursed words in a cursed tongue, but the bulk of them trudged on without missing a step.

Gawain could see their faces now, expressions frozen in anger and bloodlust. Fresh scars and tattoos covered their exposed flesh—barbaric symbols and putrid markings that made him scowl. Most of the Northmen wore little more than rags, their shields and axes being the only thing worth preserving in their warped minds. Black mouths roared wordless cries, their eyes rolled back to see something only they could see.

Bedivere's pikemen stepped forward, their lines bristling with razor-sharp edges as they braced for the Norse. The squares along the riverbanks pivoted, turning inwards to face the centre as the pagans gathered speed. The greatswords were already moving up behind the pikes, making ready to add their support once battle was met. They carried their heavy two-handed blades across their shoulders and left enough space between one another to swing them unobstructed.

Another twang and a vicious volley of arrows soared over the pikemen's heads, taking the Northmen full in the face. More shouts and cries, more sworn words in a guttural tongue. But it wasn't enough. A horn blasted out three quick notes, and the closest Norsemen broke into a sprint, loping across the field with frightening speed, raising their axes as they closed the gap.

The two lines met with the crump of tearing metal and screaming steel. Bodies and limbs went flying, sprawling across the grass as the Norsemen tried to break into the squares. Giant men, standing three feet taller than the tallest Briton, lashed out with enormous hammers, sending the gathered pikes reeling. Others rolled under the shafts, lunging up to tear into the pikemen's bellies with short stabbing blades. Dozens of Northmen were caught by the polearms, impaled and cast off as Bedivere's men resisted the onslaught. More of them fell beneath the knives and daggers the pikemen wielded in close combat, punctured full of holes the moment they got within range.

Gawain watched on silently as the greatswords joined the fray, swinging their massive weapons in blistering arcs. They matched the Northmen in strength, if not in size, and sliced through shield and flesh and bone alike.

A blur of movement drew his eyes to the curling tendrils of red mist behind the shifting squares of battle. Shadows appeared within them, warped figures beneath twisted banners, crooked shapes of unearthly proportions. He flinched as a chorus of bestial sounds rose above the screams and shouts of warfare. Animalistic grunts and tortured howls blared louder than the horns and drums, louder even than the screams of dying men.

Sir Gawain lowered his visor and drew his sword as he nudged Gringolet forward.

USURPER

Gawain hacked into a howling Northman's face, cleaving it clean in two before deflecting a blow aimed at Gringolet with his shield. The destrier turned on its hooves, sending another pagan warrior spinning into the press, and plunged forward. Years of training and discipline paid dividends as the charger manoeuvred its way between the howling heathens, guided only by the light touch of his knees.

An axe glanced off Gawain's vambrace, numbing his arm but not managing to penetrate the polished steel. A red-faced Northman appeared behind the axe, snarling madly as he tried to scramble up Gringolet's flank. Gawain leaned forward in his saddle and shoved the point of his sword down the man's throat, brushing the still-yowling body aside with his shield.

"Come on," Gawain growled, smashing the pommel of his sword into a bearded giant. The man stood near as tall as he did on his horse and wider still. His face was scarred with black markings, and his eyes shone red and bloodshot from within his immense skull. He let out a throaty roar and lumbered forward, only to fall to his knees when Theodoric planted the beard of his axe into the back of his head.

The Saxon grinned at Gawain, pulling the axe free from the giant's parietal bone with a sickening shloop. He nodded down at the now-prone form of the Northman and smirked. "Big bastards, these Jutlanders."

"Aye," said Gawain, guiding Gringolet towards Theodoric and staring across the field.

His knights had charged in not long after the greatswords, tearing through the flanks of the Norsemen, even as they baulked beneath the combined forces of pikes and footmen. The Celts and Picts in Mordred's army had flung themselves into the fray in support of the pagans, only to find themselves brought to heel by the hooves of Sir Bedivere and the bulk of his knights. The battle had then dissolved into hundreds of fixed skirmishes, flashpoints of violence between groups and individuals, as all strategy and tactical acumen fell away.

"They'll be on the run soon." Theodoric dabbed at his sweaty forehead with the back of his gauntleted hand before giving up on the idea. "I saw the Gaels leaving the field, tails between their legs after Bedivere got in on them with his knights."

Gawain nodded. Even in the chaos of the press, he could see the tide was shifting. It wouldn't be long before the day was won. "Still no sign of Mordred," he said, staring into the fog. He saw a flash of silver as more knights charged past, hunting in packs like wolves. A troupe of pikemen jogged into the haze, disappearing into the red glow as they followed the knights.

"He'll be here," said Theodoric, whistling through his teeth as he spotted another Norse giant appear from within the fog. The man was covered in cuts and wounds—deep, rotting things that seeped rivulets of blood and gore. He lumbered forward, his slow gait picking up when he saw the two knights.

Gawain met Theodoric's grin with a smile of his own and dug his heels into Gringolet's flanks, urging his steed onward to meet the giant.

They found Father Tawly's body in the middle of the dell. What was left of the priest had been hacked and bludgeoned almost beyond recognition, leaving his once-white robes sodden and red. The symbol of his faith, the bronze cross he had borne about his neck, now lay embedded in his stomach. Someone had taken an axe or saw to his limbs, removing them from his body and placing them in a pile beside it, like some grotesque cairn of flesh.

Gawain muttered a prayer to himself as he stared down at the massacre, feeling his gorge rise. This was no way for a good Christian to die, torn apart by blasphemers and devil worshippers. The priest had deserved better—they all did.

"Bastards," Theodoric spat, twisting in his saddle to stare down at the corpse. "Accursed heathen bastards."

"How did Father Tawly get ahead of us?" Gawain frowned, staring back the way they'd come. They had fought their way through Picts, Norsemen, Celts, and treacherous Englishmen, sending them all reeling into the afterlife. The priest should have been well behind their lines, mingling with the archers at best.

"I don't know," said Theodoric with a shrug. "Must have gotten caught or something."

Gawain shifted in his saddle, sparing the Father one last glance. They'd have to give him a proper burial once the field was cleared.

He looked up towards the opposite tree line, feeling his eyes drawn to its shadowed confines.

Sir Bedivere was riding up ahead, surrounded by an entourage of knights beneath Camelot's banner. They had ridden unopposed, barrelling through Mordred's forces with ease. His own men had waded up along the western flanks, rolling up what remained of the opposition, putting them to flight or the sword.

His eyes narrowed as he saw a shadow detach itself from the treeline, followed by another and another.

"Uh, Gawain." Theodoric was pointing towards the forest, his brow knitted tightly as a strange look crossed his face.

"I see them."

The air seemed to shimmer as the shadows took shape, black hooves pounding against the earth, churning up soil and grass beneath them. The fog grew thicker around their forms as if the great gusts of air from their heaving chests was its cause. Huge slabs of muscle rippled beneath sheets of barding, as black as pitch. The mounts were the match of any sired in Camelot, larger even. But it was not the monstrous steeds that drew his eye—it was their riders.

He had seen them before, from a distance on the fields of Camlann. Mordred's fell knights. Darkness seemed to follow them as they emerged from the forest, flickering shadows that sought to hide their true nature. The mist blurred around their forms, shifting in colour, even as it was dispersed.

When Gawain had first encountered the knights, he had thought little of them. It was only after he heard the stories of those who had fought against them and survived that he realised the truth. Mordred's chosen were not men at all. They were demons. Immortal souls wrapped up in the approximations of men, squeezed and contorted until they fit the burnished plate of knights.

The armour they wore was bent and buckled, swollen out of shape by the figures within. Fleshy limbs extended out from where they shouldn't, insidious tendrils that seemed to grasp and move of their own accord. Growths blistered beneath breastplates, pressing against the steel like boils waiting to pop. And at their head rode the usurper himself.

Mordred had changed, or perhaps he had simply cast off the illusion he had borne before. He was larger now, taller than even the Jutlander giants Gawain and Theodoric had fought earlier that day. His armour, still scored with holes from the battle of Camlann, clung to his bulky frame in tattered pieces. A frayed red cloak hung from his shoulders, little more than rags now.

As Gawain stared, his vision flickered, and he felt a dull ache pulse behind his eyes. There seemed to be two realities, two visions of Mordred simultaneously trying to impose themselves upon the world. In one, Mordred's tattered cape was transformed into writhing tentacles. Hundreds of feelers thrashed about him, tasting the air with cavities that covered their veiny appendages. Mordred's helmed head twisted into a blackened maw, lined by razor-sharp teeth that extended out of the thing's head like unsheathed daggers. The air around him flashed grey and blue, like the bruised skin of a cadaver.

Gawain's pulse was racing as he watched the being—that thing that had once been his brother. The aura that surrounded Mordred shifted, rippled as the fell knight hurtled across the field. It was like a tear in reality, a window into another world. Something moved within, grey and membranous. Serpentine bodies squirmed, shaking off a mucous-like substance, and a thousand eyes turned to look through the widening tear.

Sir Gawain vomited into his helm.

A panicked yell tore him from his trance, and he snapped open his visor to heave the puke out onto the grass. He shook his head, his eyes watering from the sharp stench and sucked in a deep breath of air, glancing about the glen.

The lines were reforming all across the field, pikemen and greatswords quickly moving back into their squares to meet the coming charge. They hadn't seen what he had—not yet. Sir Bedivere and his entourage were trying to pivot around to face the traitor, but they were moving too slowly. Mordred was heading straight for them.

"God." He shivered, feeling his courage strain. He wanted to run, to flee the field, never to set sight on Mordred again. He gripped his sword tightly and stared at Theodoric. The Saxon was pale, his mouth covered in spittle and bile. He'd seen it, too—the shape that lurked within Mordred's soul. After a moment, the Teuton blinked and met Gawain's stare.

"We must," said Gawain, nudging Gringolet forward. He could see Sir Garin and more of his knights streaming across the field towards Sir Bedivere, rushing to lend their support.

"If we do not win here, there'll be no one left to win, ever again." He didn't know where the words came from, but he knew they were true. And so did the Saxon.

"Aye," Theodoric grunted. He hefted his axe across his knees and brought his charger up to a canter, gaining speed beside Sir Gawain as they headed towards the darkness.

THE GRAIL KNIGHT

When King Arthur died, Gawain had thought he'd come to understand the nature of despair. His heart had broken that day, never to be fully formed again. A piece of it was left in Camlann, where he'd found the king's mangled body half-submerged within the mud and dirt. The spark that had coloured Arthur's eyes was gone, put out by one of his own knights. A man he had once called brother. Gawain had shed tears then and cursed until his throat was raw. But then he had picked himself up and carried his friend's body from the field. Anger and vengeance had overcome his despair.

But when Bedivere was plucked from his horse, dragged from his saddle by a monstrous tentacle and torn in two, then Sir Gawain had known despair. True despair. What hope was left had dissipated, sucked out of him like an oyster from its shell. The other knights had felt it, too, and a low cry rose above the press of battle. Men exchanged hopeless stares, vacant looks as fear finally overwhelmed what courage remained.

There had been no honour in Bedivere's death. He had screamed as he was pulled apart, his shrieks cut short by his own demise while his entrails fell across the ground. Blood had fountained from his torso, drenching those around him in a red mist.

"No," Gawain breathed as he watched what was left of his fellow knight flung across the field. Excalibur glinted in the air for a moment before it fell from Bedivere's grasp, disappearing into the churned-up mud.

The thing that had been Mordred had swollen to gargantuan proportions, towering above even his own fell-knights. The black horse he'd ridden upon had all but disappeared beneath him, fusing into his rotting flesh like some accursed centaur. His aura had grown with him, a throbbing purple haze that stood out like a bruise against reality. Insectoid-like feelers had emerged from the tear, stabbing and ripping at anyone who came too close. Slimy bodies, serpentine in shape, pulled at the opening, slowly enlarging it. There was a glimmer of mucoidal green, and a myriad eyes stared out from the gaping wound of reality.

Gawain felt something press against his mind, a hateful presence. It whispered to him, sibilant words that made his skin crawl and his head ache. *Begone!* he urged, dragging his stare from that void of madness, from that place of ending.

Something had changed with Bedivere's death. The moment Excalibur hit the ground, Arall Myrddin pulsed in the sky above. Its red glow flared, overwhelming the pale light of the sun, and plunging the world into a bloody haze.

"We must go!" Theodoric shouted as the world morphed into a hellish scape. Inhuman shapes moved within the thickening fog, hunting the survivors of Bedivere's army. Bestial grunts paired with maddening laughter, cries and screams all conjoined to form a dread choir.

"It's over." Gawain shook his head. "There is nowhere left to go."

"Don't be a fool, man!" The Saxon leaned over to pull at Gringolet's reins. "We must ride."

The knight nodded slowly, turning to stare at the dissolving press. Perhaps they could run for a while, resist, survive. They could save as many lives as were willing and cross the channel for France or Saxony. Even as the thought materialised, he dismissed it. No place would be spared this evil.

Mordred's engorged frame waded across the dell, knocking aside a gibbering greatsword with a flick of its distended hand. A claw-like pincer shot out from the flickering chasm, cleaving a horse clean in two and sending its rider sprawling into the mist. The thing was moving with purpose now, the gaping maw that was its head flicking left and right as it searched the field for something.

Excalibur.

He dug his heels into Gringolet's flanks, pushing Theodoric's hands away from the reins as he lurched forward. The Sword of Kings. He could not let Arthur's blade fall into the hands of the Enemy. He would die to defend that legacy.

He heard the Saxon calling out his name as he thundered forward, his charger eating up the earth as they raced towards Mordred. Ghastly shapes appeared out of the mist, humanoid figures with reptilian faces. Gills flared at the sides of their necks, and Gawain saw more of them emerging from the riverbanks. Gringolet barged past them, knocking their chittering forms to the wayside as they rode on.

"Help me, God," Gawain whispered as he searched the field for the sword. Mordred had not yet noticed his approach and was swaying through the smog. Pieces of flesh were falling from his body, melting away as his aura quickened and convulsed. A slick, oily substance replaced the skin where it fell away, and Gawain felt his stomach heave as a rotten stench penetrated his helm. If he hadn't already disgorged the contents of his stomach, he would have again.

The knight breathed out a prayer as his eyes settled upon the sword, and he felt a moment's joy before he realised Mordred had seen it, too. The great lumbering creature chortled in glee, increasing its stride, even as its midriff throbbed and fell away, revealing more of the oily black skin.

Gawain braced in his saddle, urging Gringolet on to greater speeds. If he could get to Excalibur first…

A shadow darted towards him, sweeping out from his periphery, and he just managed to raise his shield to fend off a thunderous blow aimed for his head. Gringolet reeled beneath him, staggering as a monstrous, black charger tilted into its flank.

One of Mordred's fell-knights hammered down at Gawain, trying to break through his guard with a sickle-shaped sword. Foetid, hot breath billowed out from behind the creature's helm, jagged teeth just visible through the grate. The fell-knight's armour was twisted and curved, forced into shapes that made Gawain's eyes water. Blasphemous symbols covered the creature's plate, distorted mockeries of his own heraldry.

Gawain rocked back on his saddle, narrowly avoiding the edge of the fell-knight's blade, and then swung out with a deadly riposte. The dread-knight couldn't keep up with his speed, and one of his attacks pierced the creature's breastplate. Gawain lunged forward, sheathing his sword almost up to its hilt in the creature's chest. Black ichor spurted from the wound, burning through flesh and steel, even as he tried to pull away.

The creature cackled and sprung from its saddle with surprising agility. Gawain let out a grunt as the fell-knight barrelled into him, feeling Gringolet lose balance and tumble to the ground beneath him.

A sharp pain burst through his side again and again as the fell-knight stabbed him with a jagged, black blade. Gawain tried to push the creature aside, his gauntlets tearing against the sharpened edges of the knight's armour, but it wouldn't budge. With a panicked heave, he managed to shift out from beneath the devil and pin him to the ground. His sword was still embedded in the thing's chest, but he didn't have enough space to draw it or swing it. Instead, he smashed his gauntleted fist against the beast's head.

He rained blows down against the fell-knight's twisted helm until he felt it crack beneath his fist, until it twisted and bent, and a gooey black substance ran out the sides. He hit it until he felt his gauntlets break against the thing's teeth and his knuckles start to bleed. When there was nothing left but a flattened mess of gore and hissing ichor, he relented, finally rolling off the creature's body.

Gringolet wandered over towards him, lowering its head to inspect its master. Gawain's stomach had been punctured half a dozen times, and dark blood ran down the grooves of his armour. There'd be no fixing that, he realised, somehow managing to get to his knees. His eyes rolled inside his head, and he nearly fell back to the ground, gripping onto Gringolet's reins to steady himself.

Excalibur.

He had failed.

Gawain blinked into the gloom, shielding his eyes as a golden glow shone out through the fog. The thing-that-had-been-Mordred stood fully transformed, a glabrous mass of oozing tentacles, writhing serpentine bodies upon which were attached a thousand eyes. They curled and sniffed the air, twisting and turning as they wavered between this reality and another. Mouths appeared upon the vast tendrils, near as many teeth and fibrous tongues as there were eyes.

But something was wrong. Gawain sensed the warrior before he saw him, feeling a surge of hope course through his veins, even as his lifeblood left them. The hell-spawned creature was transfixed, its floating eyes all focused upon the figure that stood before it.

A golden light wreathed the knight like holy fire, burning through the shrouds of mist that surrounded him, drowning out even the glow of Arall Myrddin. His armour was radiant, forged from shining steel that made Gawain's own plate look like the ragged remnants of the iron age. A white mantle hung from his shoulders, as pure as snow, scrawled in golden filigree and symbols. An ornate chalice hung by his side, and Gawain sensed a hidden power emanating from it, infusing the man who bore it. The golden knight wore a closed-face helm, with curving antler horns that twisted up into the air above his head. And in his hand, shining even more brightly than his armour, was Excalibur.

Gawain let out a gasp. It was like staring at Arthur reborn.

A voice echoed across the field, barking out words in a strange tongue. The mist seemed to shudder, receding ever so slightly as the words buffeted against them. Gawain searched the dell for the source of the words, holding onto his side as he squinted into the mist. He thought he saw a crooked figure move past, the hunched back of an old man with a greying beard, but when he blinked, he was gone.

Another pulse of brilliant light drew his eyes back to the knight, and he watched in awe as the man moved into a jog, headed towards Mordred. The creature wriggled forward, its tendrils whipping out to meet this new threat. Darkness grew around the beast, gathering across its oily skin as it screeched out a challenge.

The golden knight dodged and weaved between its thrashing limbs with preternatural speed, lopping them off with elegant flicks of his sword. He was a blur, moving faster than Gawain's tired eyes could see. The creature cried out as its appendages were cut from it, groaning out in violent shrieks as its pieces were left to writhe upon the grass.

There was something about the way the knight moved, the grace and elegance with which he bobbed and weaved between the beast's clumsy attempts to catch him with its tentacles. Gawain recognised it. He had seen it in battle, and the training yards, too many times not to. Lancelot had come home.

His old friend rolled beneath the outstretched tentacles of the beast with uncanny agility, carving through a host of blinking eyes and gibbous limbs as he got up from his knees. The thing-that-had-been-Mordred lashed out again, opening its gaping maw to try and consume the knight.

Gawain grunted as he watched the golden figure spin out of the way, returning to a blur of light as he pivoted and pirouetted his way around the creature. An inky black substance covered the ground around them, hissing as it burned into the grass but never managing to land upon Lancelot. The man was too fast, too brilliant, too beautiful.

Gawain smiled, knowing that in that moment, there was nothing on this earth or another that could touch Lancelot. He had been chosen, as had Arthur before him, to wield the Sword of Kings, to set right the wrongs in this world. And if the chalice hanging from his side was what he thought it was, he would prove every bit as worthy as King Arthur had—if not more.

Sir Gawain never saw the final blow that killed the beast, his own life having run its course before Lancelot could end Mordred's. But if he had, he would have smiled all the more for knowing that vengeance had been done, and that, for the first time in a very long time, there was hope again.

The Breeding Mound
I

Night was drawing in, bringing with it an icy breeze that nipped at exposed flesh. It rustled through the pines, leaving shaking branches in its wake—a gentle reminder of the winter still to come.

It had rained that morning, and the smell of earth, and moss, and pine needles still clung to the air. And beneath them, the faint smell of forest rot.

Jens threatened a smile as he inhaled the natural odour of the woods, his eyes dancing across the boughs of ancient, still-wet firs and pines. Their roots rested deep in the earth, like the people that lived here. And their green tips rose high, clasping at the amber sky like outstretched hands, never quite able to reach the heavens. There was something to be said for that and the people that lived here, too, Jens thought.

But there, a piece that didn't fit.

"Wolf?" said Didrich, limping up beside him.

"No," said Jens, crouching down on his haunches to inspect the entrails. "Not in these parts. Not anymore."

A thin line of gristle ran lengthways beside the path, ending in a small clump of matted fur and exposed bone. From the look of the remains, the carcass had been gnawed on for some time before being discarded. A tattered ear, half-chewed, identified it as a hare.

"Then, what?"

"Fox?" said Jens, leaning against his flintlock as he drew himself back to his feet. "Marten? Badger? Some scavenger that finds its home in these woods. Whatever it was, it's got a full belly now."

"It's hunted the woods bare," said Didrich, letting his weight rest against his own flintlock and rolling a cigarette. "There hasn't been any game since we crossed into Vissenbjerg. Just this... dead thing."

Jens turned to consider his brother, wondering if he should share his doubts and then deciding that he should. "I don't think we're in Vissenbjerg. We should have made it home by now."

Didrich placed the rollie in his mouth and then patted at his pockets for a match. His blue fatigues had faded into a dull grey, and his poorly mended trousers were starting to fray above the right knee, where shrapnel had turned his once jaunty gait into a staggered shuffle.

"Here," said Jens, handing him his own box.

"So we're lost?" said Didrich, dragging on the cigarette and then flicking the match out. "Pa will have something to say about two Funen boys who couldn't find their way back after the war. He'll say, unless we're dead, we've no excuses, so we better be dead or find some good excuses."

Jens winced at that. There would be no laughter to greet them when they returned home. Perhaps at first, at the sight of Jens and Didrich. But then his mother's eyes would search for Erik, and his father would go quiet like he always did.

Didrich saw his look and sighed, exhaling a plume of silvery-white smoke and following its path into the canopy with his eyes. "They will have heard by now. Received his pension and his letters. Or else one of the Steinmann brothers will have let the news slip. They left before we did."

That didn't make it any better. The dread he felt at the thought of facing his parents had formed a knot in the pit of his stomach, tightening with each step they took closer to home. They would stare at him without blame, but the questions would come regardless. How could he have let this happen? How could Erik be dead? There was nothing he could have done. Erik's face flashed before him, disappearing as he clambered over the wall of the trench. Smiling, always smiling. A thunderstorm of cannon and muskets, the earth shaking with each pounding beat of the drum. And then Erik's mangled body in the mud, punctured by Prussian lead, his crooked grin hidden by blood. No more smiling.

"We still have some light," said Jens, shouldering his flintlock as he tried to push the memory away. He stepped onto the path, not waiting for Didrich to catch up. After a brief pause, his brother limped after him.

They followed the sloping path across a small river and past a shallow ravine. The last of the day's golden glow had just begun to fade when Jens brought them to a halt near the edge of the forest, where the trees had thinned.

"I don't recognise this place either," said Jens, squinting at the outlines of a village that occupied the centre of the small glen ahead of them. The river ran through it, spine-straight, like a sliver of light between grey silhouettes. The forest grew around the town like a great boundary wall, its densely packed confines keeping the world inside from prying eyes, while its towering peaks sent menacing shadows across the field and toward the buildings. A plume of cloud-white smoke curled up from the chimney of the nearest house, and Jens felt his stomach rumble.

"No," said Didrich, already walking out from the forest, his thoughts a step ahead of Jens's. "But I am hungry, and they will have beds for a pair of tired old soldiers. Come on. They can show us the way back home in the morning."

II

Jens returned the friendly waves of the few folk working on the outskirts of the village, toiling in the fields and gathering fruit from the orchard that grew along the river. Didrich scowled back at them, stomping a cigarette out on the path before a nudge from his brother yielded a... more friendly-looking scowl.

"Do you want them to send us on our way like a pair of beggars?" Jens said, keeping his voice low as they passed a bygmester and his cart on the road.

"Look at them," spat Didrich. "As fat and happy as pigs in a pen. Where were all these young folk when we were getting shat out of the Als?"

Jens frowned deep into his coat, his eyes darting at the figures in the field around them. His brother was right. Everyone they'd seen had been around their age or near enough. This close to Sønderborg, why hadn't they enlisted to defend Denmark's borders?

"Just... keep it to yourself. They'll have their reasons, as do we."

Didrich stabbed him in the chest with a tobacco-stained finger, his voice low to match Jens's. "This was everybody's war, Jens."

"I know," he replied, trying to keep his tone even. "But pick your arguments. Now is not the time. Unless you want to spend the night in the open again?"

Didrich snorted, showing his yellow-stained teeth like a snarling pine marten. But Jens's words made sense, and after a moment, he lowered his hackles with a begrudging nod.

The village dwellings were uniform in shape and size, single-story structures with white-washed walls and Victorian-styled roofs. Only the chimneys appeared to be fashioned from brick and stone, poking out from the rooves like rabbit bones. The village chapel towered over the surrounding dwellings, standing over them like a vulture guarding its brood.

A small crowd was gathering by the town well, and Jens met their warm smiles with one of his own, nudging his brother to do the same.

There were a few grey heads and wizened faces amongst the gathered group, though the number of unwrinkled faces far outnumbered the wrinkled. As did, Jens noted curiously, the number of men to women.

"Hello," said Jens to no one in particular. "We're from the war." He ignored his brother's barely stifled cackle and looked hopefully at the crowd until a short, squat man emerged from their fold and extended a hand.

"Bjerund Hansen," he said, his yellow eyes blinking as a smile appeared on his round face.

"Jens Oversen," said Jens, taking the proffered hand in his own. Bjerund's grip was moist, and he suppressed the urge to wipe his hand when it was released. "And this is my brother, Didrich. We are on our way home to Vissenbjerg."

"Vissenbjerg?" Bjerund looked confused for a moment, and then his wet eyes lit up again, and he nodded enthusiastically. "Oh, aye, haven't been along the coast in a time! But tell me, what news from the front?"

Jens crooked his head, like a crane staring down its beak at Bjerund's toad-like face. "It's... over. We lost. Hadn't you heard? They've taken Schleswig. Holstein and Lauenburg too. Cut Denmark in half."

Bjerund seemed to nod to himself, considering Jens's words. And then he shrugged. "News travels slow to Fødebjerg. We sometimes joke that the world has forgotten us here, and we it."

Fødebjerg, Jens thought, trying to place the village on the map. Fødebjerg, Fødebjerg. Yes, he recognised the name, somewhere north of Glamsbjerg, but still within the Assens municipality. They were about a half day's walk from home.

"But don't think we are blind to your sacrifice. We will not forget that so easily," Bjerund was saying, waving one of his chubby, wet hands at Didrich's leg. "We have bed and board for you both. I can offer you veterans a night beneath one of our roofs, a full belly, and a mind dulled by lager if you will have it?"

"How about it?" Jens turned to his brother, but the smile slipped from his face when he saw

Didrich's expression. His lips had curled into a snarl that was all too familiar, and his eyes were fixed on a face in the crowd.

"Aksel Bodin," Didrich hissed, his voice coming out like a saltwater spray, spittle coating his lower lip.

Jens followed his gaze, staring into the crowd. For a moment, he didn't recognise him. His hair was longer, his face gaunt, the tufts of beard not quite managing to conceal his weak jaw. But there he was. Aksel Bodin. Deserter. Traitor. Coward.

III

"Aksel!" Didrich bellowed, his head fixed on the wiry man standing behind Bjerund. His shoulders rippled, his jacket rolling like the wind through pines as he dropped his flintlock and knapsack to the ground. He barked out a low growl, and before Jens could stop him, Didrich was lunging forward, his arms extended before him, hands like claws.

Bjerund's eyes widened as the enraged veteran barrelled past, a long step followed by a short one in an attempt to reach Aksel.

"He's not worth it," Jen grunted, grabbing onto the hem of Didrich's coat. "Come on, Didrich. Let it go."

"It's your fault!" Didrich yelled, pointing a finger at Aksel even as Jens dragged him back. "If you hadn't deserted... if you hadn't abandoned us... Erik would still be here."

Their younger brother had taken Aksel's place in the line. He'd been the youngest in the group, hardly more than a boy, and the officers had let him hover in the back for the most of the war. But when the call up had come, and Aksel was nowhere to be found, Erik had taken his spot. And it had cost him his life.

Didrich tried to shrug off Jens's grip, but this wasn't the first time he'd lost his temper, and Jens knew to hang on until the storm had passed.

For his part, Aksel just stood there, meeting the barrage of curses and accusations with a blank stare, his hooded eyes red-rimmed and empty.

"Aksel?" said Bjerund, finally stepping between Didrich and the deserter, his palms held open. "But this is our dear Thomas. He's never seen the army, let alone a war. You must have him mistaken for somebody else, yes?"

"See?" said Jens, feeling his brother's shoulders relax beneath his hands, still wired and ready to spring but no longer tense with the prospect of violence.

He did look different, Jens thought, now that he was no more than a breath away from this 'Thomas'. His jaw was narrow, like Aksel's, but his skin had a faint yellow sheen to it, and his eyes were set deep inside his gaunt face, making him appear closer to the skeleton of their old friend than the man himself. But there was something else. Aksel had always had an air of confidence about him, an arrogance that made Jens want to rattle his teeth. Thomas was a weed in comparison.

"Let him deny it," Didrich spat, shrugging off Jens's grip. "I want to hear him say it."

"I'm afraid that's not possible," said Bjerund with an apologetic shake of his head. "Our Thomas is a mute."

IV

Didrich's temper had calmed by the time they reached their lodgings, ebbing back like the pooling waters of the Odense fjord after the first winter storms. Bjerund pointed them to a steel bath and a washhouse and promised to collect them for dinner before leaving them to clean up.

He had waved away Didrich's attempt at an apology with a smile. "No, boy. Save your apologies for those who have never felt their blood boil or their hearts sing!"

The room Bjerund had shown them to was small, with a flat roof and two beds. An old rug covered the dusty floor, and a solitary window stared out over the town.

Fødebjerg, Bjerund had called it. A distant memory stirred in the depths of Jens's mind. There had been disappearances, hunters who had gone missing in the forest, never to be seen or heard from again. But Jens knew of another story, too, one that had sat less well with him than the idea of missing hunters when he'd first heard it.

"It is him," said Didrich, interrupting his thoughts.

"What?"

"Aksel. I will never forget his face."

Jens turned from the window, facing his brother, who lay sprawled on his bed. His dirty boots were still on his feet, staining the covers with muck.

"Why would Bjerund lie to us?" said Jens.

Didrich shrugged. "Maybe Aksel is his kin or the kin of someone who lives here. You heard what he said about passions. Perhaps they are what drive his lie. I won't pretend to know his reasons, only that 'Dear Thomas' is the Bastard Aksel."

"And if you're wrong? You will have the death of an innocent man on your hands and a rope around both our necks."

His brother sneered. "You think of me as a beast, brother? Some criminal who would slit the throats of those who offer us shelter and break bread with us?"

Jens rolled his eyes. "I suppose earlier you had no intention of harming him, is that it? When I had to pull you away before you could sink your claws into his neck?"

"I never said I wouldn't hurt him," Didrich chortled, an ugly grin on his face. "I'll beat him black and blue until he screams my name to stop. And then the fools that live here will know he is no mute!"

Jens was about to dress his brother down with a fiery rebuke, his patience finally at its limit when his head snapped toward the door. He raised his hand to silence Didrich's laughter, peering into the gloom.

"What is it?" said Didrich, sitting up on his bed, his laughter forgotten.

"Someone's outside," Jens whispered, slowly drawing his hunting knife. He motioned at Didrich to keep still and took a cautious step toward the door.

He had heard a soft scraping sound, like tile slabs being pulled across the ground, and a gentle click, like long nails tapping against stone. But when he looked out of the door, there was nothing. No sound of retreating footsteps, no figure disappearing into the shadows. Just the empty gloom and the soft glow of the town lights.

"Your hearing hasn't been the same since Als," said Didrich, still staring out through the door. He sounded uneasy, despite his words.

"Aye," said Jens, slowly relaxing his grip on the knife's handle. "It must have been a rat."

But there were no rats in Fødebjerg, he thought, closing the door. Only Bjerund and Aksel and their smiling kin.

As promised, Bjerund collected them for dinner on the last toll of the night bell. Jens had bathed in the cold water of the wash house and had scrubbed his skin until it was nearly raw, shedding weeks of mud and grime beneath the hard brush and soap. There wasn't much he could do about the state of his uniform, though. And he'd felt a moment's shame when he'd pulled his shirt over his head and smelt the sour stink of musk and sweat that must have clung to him like a swarm of gnats.

Didrich had swept his hair back with some wax he'd found in the washhouse and had even managed to trim his beard. He ignored the look Jens gave him when he stepped out of their room and started limping toward the town the moment the smiling Bjerund appeared on the path.

"Eat. Drink. Sleep. And then we're going home," said Didrich over his shoulder, his voice low so Bjerund wouldn't hear. "These people smile too much."

V

Bjerund's smile never left his face as he led them through the town, chatting amicably as they walked.

"That there is where the remains of the first lindorm were found," he said, pointing to a row of hedges that ran along the fence to a neat garden. "A great serpent that crawled up from the well and ate all the children, some adults, too... if you believe the old wives' tales, anyway."

"And there, my grandfather told me where he caught his first nisse. I could never tell if he was fibbing or speaking the Lord's truth. He used to say, 'Bjerund, treat the little folk kindly, or they will treat you poorly, and that'll go the worse for you.'"

"Your grandfather was a Christian?" Jens asked, giving Didrich a look.

"Oh, yes," Bjerund replied without pause, his thick-lipped grin growing wider. "But that doesn't mean he didn't still hold to the old tales. There are truths in them, too, even for a Christian. Before we Christians ran the pagans out and forbade such things, there was a peace between us, if only for a little while. A gentle balance between we who gave unto the Lord that which is His, and to the Gods that which is theirs. There is no contradiction in that."

Jens exchanged another bemused look with his brother, who simply shrugged and shook his head. Following Didrich's lead, Jens decided to keep quiet, too, not wanting to offend their host. For contradiction was all he had heard.

Jens had expected to dine at Bjerund's home, to quietly sup while the town head asked them questions about the war and their plans now it was over.

But instead, Bjerund led them to an old longhouse, complete with a thatch roof and old walls made from wattle and daub. Runes covered the wooden frame of the entrance, and Jens recognised them as Old Norse. Fresh marks had been carved into the wood more recently—a Christian cross, a Danish flag, and a few Jens had not seen before.

He paused on the steps outside and stared at the nearest marking. The curling, artistic flourish of the symbol reminded him of pages from the Muslim holy book he'd seen at the National Museum when he was a boy. And yet, there was something more pressing about its shape—more ominous.

"Come on, said Didrich impatiently from the step behind him. "I didn't wash up to stare at lines in wood all night."

Jens snapped something back but then took the last step up and pushed open the longhouse doors.

Warm air rushed out to greet them, and a wall of noise—laughter and clapping, and the first notes of a violin on the other side of the hall. Jens immediately found himself salivating at the aroma that accompanied the sounds: fresh bread and stew, garlic and spring onion, fried butter bread, and pickled fish. It smelt like home.

A young girl appeared in front of Jens, her blonde hair neatly folded into a marigold braid. She stood no taller than his knee, and he was reminded of the flower angel from one of Hans Christian Andersen's tales his mother had read to him and his brothers growing up. Jens smiled down at her until she waved a hand at him, and Didrich's dry cackle broke the spell.

"She wants you to close the door. We're letting out all the warm air, you dolt."

Bjerund slammed shut the door, and the girl gave Jens a bright gap-toothed grin and skipped away toward the rows of benches that filled the hall.

"Let's find you two a seat, then," said Bjerund. "And fill those empty bellies of yours!"

He led them toward the nearest bench, sitting them down between a pair of dark-haired farm girls around their own age and one of the few elderly couples Jens had seen since they'd arrived. The girls took one look at him and Didrich and started whispering and giggling to one another. Jens felt his face flush red when he caught the eye of the nearest of the two. She was fair-skinned, with dark hazel eyes and a crown of flowers set upon her thick curls.

"I won't tell Inge if you don't," said Didrich with a grin. He dug his hands into the nearest tray, breaking off a hunk of bread and offering it to Jens.

"There's nothing to tell," said Jens, taking the bread with one hand and ladling up a bowl of soup with the other. Fresh carrot, onion and turnip, but no red meat. He stared down the table, seeing it absent from the spread. The feast consisted entirely of food that could be pulled from the ground or taken from the river, but nothing hunted nor slaughtered.

"Not yet, anyway," said Didrich, tearing into his own piece of bread. And then, between mouthfuls, "You think she's waited all this time for you? Or has Hannes managed to lure her into his bed in your absence? He always had an eye for her, and maybe she for him?"

"She has promised herself to me," said Jens between gritted teeth. His brother's taunts had always gotten under his skin, but when it came to Inge, he was particularly vulnerable. And Didrich knew it, too.

"It's been a long time," Didrich continued, that nasty grin of his appearing as he finished off his bread. "Who knows? Maybe you've got some bastards to raise when we get home, eh? Two of Hannes's wretches to call your own."

"Shut it," Jens growled, a hard edge in his voice. But Didrich was enjoying himself now.

"Do you think she'll have named one after you?" He sniggered. "Round-headed, with Hannes's bent nose and your name."

Didrich let out a sharp grunt as Jens's fingers pressed into his leg, digging into the skin just above his knee, where the shrapnel had turned his muscles into mince.

"I told you to shut it," Jens whispered, his eyes fixed on the couple across the table, a thin smile on his lips. The cold edge in his voice had turned to steel.

"Yes," Didrich croaked. His eyes were starting to water, and a bead of sweat made its way down his forehead.

"There will be no bastards when I get home and no talk of them until we do. Agreed, brother?" He turned to look at Didrich, who was nodding fervently, the pain writ across his sharp features.

"Here we are, then!" Bjerund bellowed above the chattering voices and Didrich's groans, slamming two flagons of lager on the table before them.

Jens gave Didrich's knee another squeeze, eliciting a muffled curse from him, and let go.

"Fødebjerg honey lager," Bjerund declared proudly, not noticing Didrich's red eyes or Jens's sheepish grin. "And what meal would be complete without a tot of akvavit?"

A pair of glasses appeared beside the flagons, filled with a sun-kissed liquid that seemed to glow in the light of the room.

Jens raised a brow at Didrich, who had gulped his akvavit down without pause, and was now sipping on his lager contentedly. "What? No toast?"

Didrich snorted, his eyes still laced with pain. "There is nothing left to drink to. Only reasons to drink."

VI

The honey lager was smooth and delicious after the flat beer and mulled wine they'd become used to on the front, and before long, Jens felt a warm buzz, and a smile broke out on his face. They were nearly home.

"Come on!" Didrich grabbed him by the arm, pulling him to his feet, their earlier disagreement all but forgotten. He shoved another tot of akvavit into his hand. "Schleswig may have fallen, but we are still Danes, eh?"

He slammed Jens on the back and raised his glass to the table, toward the laughing farm girls and the old couple—as deep into their cups as Jens and Didrich were.

"To God's chosen people!"

"To Denmark!" Jens roared, knocking back his own shot. The liqueur was like fire in his belly, and he felt his head spin as the spicy drink took hold.

Didrich threw an arm over his shoulder, half leaning, half supporting him, and winked down at the farm girls. "How do you two feel about dancing with a couple of war heroes?"

Jens had hardly blinked when he found himself in the middle of the longhouse hall, his body rocking to the beat of the drum, his arms pumping to the spasmodic rhythm of the violin. The benches had emptied, and the town's folk crowded the back of the hall beneath a small stage the musicians occupied. They laughed, clapped, and sang as they jostled with one another for space.

Didrich was laughing, too, his limp all but forgotten as he sang along with the two elderly folk from their table. He'd spilt honey lager down his front, and his beard sparkled with moisture. But he was happier than Jens had seen him in years, and his laughter made him grin all the wider.

Then the girl was in front of him, her crown of flowers tilting with her head as she curtsied. She held out a hand, and Jens took it before he could even pause to think. The honey lager and akvavit were coursing through his veins, pumping his heart in time with his feet. This was not the time for thinking.

The crowd whooped as he spun the fair-skinned forest princess in a pirouette too bold for a sober Jens. She spun across the floor, graceful as a nymph, her own smile lighting up their corner of the hall. And then she was in his arms, laughing into his chest, her hands gripping him tight.

Jens thought he heard his brother say something over the music, but he ignored him, closing his eyes as his hands went to the girl's waist. He felt her respond, nudging up against him until they were one writhing, sweating form, dancing on the path the music set for them.

He could smell the flowers in her hair and inhaled her fragrance deeply—she smelt of wet pine and needles, like the forest after rain. He pictured her naked then, beneath him, all but her flower crown discarded on the floor at her feet. Then her mouth forming an O as they became one.

His hands cupped her tightly, pulling her closer still. His fingers played along her hips, moving up her lithe body of their own accord. He felt her skin, warm and smooth beneath his touch. Promising him more. She was breathing into the nook of his neck, and he shivered as his manhood began to stir in his trousers. But he felt no shame. This was not the time for shame.

He inhaled her scent again, marvelling at her fragrance, at how it drew him into the forest around them. But there was something else beneath the aroma of pine and rain, and he struggled to recognise it. His brow wrinkled, and then he flinched, finally placing the familiar stench. It stunk like the trenches, like his brother's corpse when they'd dragged it back across the mud. It threatened to overwhelm him, a heady mix of musk and death. He tried to recoil, to pull away from the girl.

His hands felt wet against her skin, which was no longer smooth but matted—covered in damp fur like that of a dog.

He snapped his eyes open, lurching back a step, pushing her away with more force than he intended. The girl gasped, falling to the floor with a soft cry. She stared up at him with a look of hurt in her eyes and started pulling herself up to her feet.

"Wait," Jens called as she turned her back on him, pushing her way through the crowd.

"What's wrong?" Didrich chortled from beside him, the other sister's arms wrapped around his waist, a flagon of lager in each of his hands.

Jens shook his head and let out a deep breath. It felt like he'd been holding it forever. "Nothing. I'm going out for a piss."

VII

He'd drunk too much. He knew that even before he stepped into the cool night air outside the longhouse, and his head started to ache. His vision had blurred. He thought... before he'd pushed the girl away, he'd seen something, a shadow. Curving horns raised from the crown of flowers. Black nails and fiery eyes. It had been in the space before a blink, a moment within a moment.

He shook his head, ridding himself of the vision until all he saw was the hurt in her eyes when he'd shoved her to the ground. He'd drunk too much, that was all.

He took the steps down from the longhouse carefully, not trusting his own balance anymore. He spared the runes a glance but looked away when they started to move, blurring into one, making his head pound more than it already was.

After another deep breath, he wandered away from the warm glow of the longhouse and started unbuckling his belt.

"Jens, you idiot," he muttered, dropping his trousers to piss into the night. "Dancing like a fool with some farmer's daughter, you're—"

A woman's scream cut through the night, making bristles out of the hair on the back of his neck.

Wolf, he thought, already buckling his belt. The wolf had gotten into Fødebjerg and had already found its first victim. He remembered the carcass in the woods. Only gristle and bone had remained.

Another scream rent the air, a bloodcurdling cry of pain that faded into an almost breathless moan, like the last bit of wind through a ravine.

Jens glanced back at the longhouse, but the music and laughter continued. They hadn't heard the cry. He considered going inside and raising help, but they were all as drunk as he was, and by the time he'd rallied them outside, it might already be too late.

When the scream came again, Jens was already running toward it. His head started to clear with each stride he took, his mind clearing as adrenaline pumped through his veins. His shambling run turned into long, purposeful strides. He drew his hunting knife.

He came to a stop by the town well, his head tilted as he listened for another cry or the slopping sound of a predator gorging itself on its victim. He would need to chase it away if that were the case. To save something for the family to bury.

But the streets were empty, and there was no sign of the beast and its hapless victim. There are no wolves left in Funen, Jens thought, his brow knitted. But who had screamed? And why?

He stared down the nearest road at the neat houses that lined either side of it. They were quiet and dark, their inhabitants feasting in the longhouse with the rest of the town. His gaze came to a rest in the garden they had passed before dinner, where Bjerund had said the first lindorm had been found. A giant snake that feasted on the spines of those it caught in its venomous fangs. Jens shivered. He briefly considered peeking over the rim of the well, where the serpent was said to have come from, and then felt foolish for the thought.

He was about to turn back around and take a slow walk back to the longhouse when a faint light appeared on the road ahead. It hovered in the middle of the street, floating for a moment while Jens squinted at the silhouette in the shadows behind it. A young woman, he thought, in a flowing white dress. Even in the dark, Jens felt their eyes meet, and then she was gone, darting across the street into one of the houses on the other side.

"Wait!" Jens called for the second time that night. If there was something hunting these streets, he'd be damned if he let another victim fall to its teeth… or fangs.

He hurried along the road, inhaling the night as he scrambled through the dark. Finally, he came to a stop in front of the building he'd seen the girl disappear into. It wasn't a house like he'd first thought, but rather the entrance to the town's solitary church.

Its twin doors hung slightly ajar, and a soft glow spilt out onto the doorstep. Jens thought he saw a shadow move within and took a cautious step forward. It wasn't his place to intrude at this hour, but there was a wolf about… and he'd heard something.

"Damn it, Jens," he swore, suddenly aware that he was in no fit state to visit a house of the lord. He cupped his hand over his mouth, checking his breath. It stunk like lager and spirits and faintly of the sweat he'd never get out of his clothes. It would have to do, he thought, lurching up the church steps. His head was starting to spin again, and he had a horrifying thought that he might be welcomed into the church, only to spew his dinner all over the floor.

But before he could knock or call out, he heard a gasp from behind the door and the faint moans of a woman in great pain. He was too late.

He threw his shoulder against the door, swinging it wide as he stumbled into the church foyer. But instead of a woman struck down by a wolf, white dress rendered red by tooth and claw, he found himself staring at rows of cots. They lined both sides of the walls and every spare inch of the church itself. Almost two dozen of them, he guessed, forming aisles like pew benches, with just enough space to walk between.

Another moan filled the church, and Jens's eyes grew wide as he noticed the occupants. Each of the beds held a woman, naked but for a thin strip of cloth that covered their breasts. Their swollen bellies jutted out of them like fleshy mountains, engorged by the life they carried.

Jens covered his nose to the stink that greeted his entrance, like sour milk and shit. The smell clawed at his nose, and he nearly gagged. He clenched his jaw, just managing to maintain his composure, even as the honey lager and akvakvit sloshed about his insides.

After a moment, he glanced down at the nearest cot, flinching at the shape that moved within the belly of the woman who occupied it. Her child was kicking, pressing against the flesh chamber that had nurtured it for so long.

Sweat covered the woman's brow, and her face was pale, but a thin smile played about her lips when she saw Jens staring. She didn't seem to care that she was naked, and he a man.

He averted his gaze, embarrassed by her lack of shame. As his head turned away, his eyes caught on something at the foot of her bed, and he paused to look, knowing he should have left as soon as he'd stepped inside the church. But curiosity had him now.

A knotted string of what look liked leather had been tied to the bedpost. It was covered with beads and tiny teeth. As Jens's eyes adjusted to the gloom, he realised the cord was made of coarse dark hair. Human hair. Not leather at all. And that a pair of thin, nearly translucent bones hung from the end of it.

He glanced up at a sharp squawk from the other side of the hall. A red-faced woman was bearing down on him from between the aisles. A cry came from behind her, and Jens saw another midwife hunched over one of the church's occupants, her arms bloodied up to her elbows. There was something in her hands, a red smear, limp and lifeless. Another cry came from the bed, but not of pain this time, but despair as the mother looked down on her twisted child, dead before its first breath.

Jens tried to say something to the midwife storming toward him, but she wrung her hand at him like a priest in service, each sharp movement accompanied by a string of words he couldn't hear or understand.

Then one of her wrinkled hands wrapped around his arm, her grip as strong as a mason's. She pushed him back toward the door, still squawking. He blinked and found himself outside again, in the cold dark night air.

VIII

Wake up, brother.

"No."

They're waiting for us.

"Who is?"

Them. Get up.

"My head... it hurts."

Pay it no heed. You have your horns now. It is a blessing—a gift.

"From whom?"

Them. Get up!

Jens felt a kick to the leg, and his eyes snapped open with a jolt. He nearly blacked out again from the pain, a sharp blade cutting at the meat behind his eyes, his forehead. His vision swam.

"Here," came a voice. His brother's grinning face appeared above him. Didrich held out a glass, and Jens accepted it with a grateful nod, taking a deep sip before spitting it out and glaring at him.

"To take the edge off," said Didrich with a chuckle. "You were gone last night. Came back here well after dark, babbling about horns and wolves and pregnant churches. I couldn't get a word in. Then you just fell on your bed and started snoring. You wander into Fødebjerg's nursery? Drunk off your arse, that must have been a shock for the matrons, eh?"

Jens groaned, pulling himself up in his bed, and placing the akvavit on the table beside him.

Fragments of the night slowly started coming back to him: the longhouse, the dance, the girl and her flower crown, and then it blurred— horns and bleeding women. A wolf, and the stink of rot. He let out another groan and clutched his head between his hands.

"It feels like Thor is beating my head in with his hammer. Get me some water, please, brother."

"Thor?" Didrich gave him a bemused look. "A night in the longhouse, and we are suddenly invoking the Old Norse?"

"Water," Jens croaked, falling back against the pillows.

Didrich rolled his eyes but retrieved a tin mug from his knapsack by the door and filled it with icy cold water from the bathhouse. His limp seemed less steep, Jens thought as he watched him go about the task, his strides less cautious.

Jens took a deep sip from the mug, his brow unknitting as the water dampened the fire in his head.

"Who is waiting for us?" he asked, his eyes flicking to Didrich.

"What?"

"You said someone was waiting for us when I woke. Who?"

Didrich shook his head, raising his thick brows. "You were snoring so loud I couldn't hear myself think. The kick was from me… but anything else? You must have been dreaming."

Jens frowned into the mug. He was sure he'd heard Didrich talking to him. A blurry reflection stared back up at him through the water. He looked like shit: pale with dark rings under his red eyes, his hair a messy nest. But no horns.

"Let's go have a look around," said Didrich, nodding to the door. From the sunlight filtering through, Jens guessed it to be around mid-morning.

"Maybe find ourselves some breakfast too, eh? Or one of those farm girls." Didrich clasped his hands together and grinned. The wariness of the day before seemed to have left him, and his smile was genuine.

"Alright, brother," said Jens, the throb in his head starting to dull as he slowly swung his legs over the side of his bed. "But then it's time to go. Vissenbjerg is waiting. Our parents will need to know they still have two sons left."

Didrich's smile faded, and he let out a sigh but nodded.

"Where is everyone?" said Jen as they walked through the quiet streets. They hadn't seen a soul since they'd left their lodgings, the only sound coming from their boots against the road and the occasional snigger from Didrich at his brother's misery.

The day was warm, and Jens had unbuttoned the collar of his shirt and carried his coat.

"What day is it?" Didrich paused to adjust his bootlaces, taking a knee while his brother waited. "Maybe they're in church? Or all stuck in bed, their heads knocked in by Thor's Hammer."

"It's Wednesday," said Jens, only half-listening as he stared across the town. The forest appeared closer than he remembered, its roots and boughs sprawling across the fields, nearly atop the orchard by the river.

A warm wind stirred through the branches, for a moment exposing the recesses within. Dark woodland paths disappeared behind the thick gorse and crooked trees, winding their way to parts unknown. Shadows shifted with the wind, creating skeletal shapes and silhouettes that danced upon the woodland canvas.

"We'll go knock on Bjerund's door and see if anyone's home," said Didrich, getting back to his feet.

"Good idea," said Jens, distracted. His eyes were fixed upon a shadow in the woods. He'd thought he'd seen a splash of colour, a flicker of golden-yellow passing between the trees. But when he'd looked again, it was gone.

It was nearing mid-afternoon by the time they found the townsfolk of Fødebjerg. They had gathered on the edge of the forest, in the shadow of an old mill. Men sat on haystacks, smoking their pipes and gossiping, while the women tended to the children, chasing them through the field and splashing around in the river.

A crowd congregated near the trees, and Jens and Didrich came to a stop just behind them.

"What is that?" Jens said, peering over their shoulders at a wooden structure set up on the edge of the forest. He spotted Aksel a few feet away and tensed, waiting for Didrich to spring.

But his brother seemed unbothered by the doppelgänger's presence, his gaze passing over him without so much as a clenched jaw or balled fist.

"It's some kind of tower," said Didrich, his eyes fixed on the structure. Jens looked away from Aksel, taking in the assemblage of wood and scaffolding that stood over them. It was as tall as the lofty trees behind it and near as wide as the longhouse they'd feasted in the night before. A pair of what looked like arms hung by its sides, above the scaffolding and lumber that would be used to complete it.

"The Pyre of Saint Ansgar," said Bjerund, ambling over to them. He pushed his way past Aksel and came to a stop beside Jens.

"The pagan?" said Didrich, finally turning his gaze from the pyre.

"He was, he was," said Bjerund, nodding his head. "But after his conversion, he spread the word of Christ from village to village, until he met his end in this very forest."

"But he was a pagan first?"

"Oh, aye," said Bjerund. "We celebrate the life of the man, the good and the bad, each step a step on the way to his enlightenment. Even those that took him into the embrace of the old ways."

Jens and Didrich exchanged a look. "But you don't believe in the old ways, do you?" He remembered Bjerund's comments about God and the pagan stories working in tandem, existing in parallel, both true and non-contradictory. A blasphemy concealed by a smile.

"We do not believe," said Bjerund, opening his palms wide. "We fear. We fear many things, as should you: we fear the spirit of the earth, who raises storms, and whom we must fight to secure our livelihood each day. We fear the moon, we fear the sun, we fear want and hunger... disease... war. We fear malevolent spirits who would do us harm. We fear the souls of the dead, and of the animals we have killed... but we do not believe."

Didrich was nodding to Bjerund's words, but Jens snorted. "How can you fear something you don't believe in?"

"Because it is right to do so," said Bjerund, his broad grin unmoved by the question, though Jens thought he saw a flicker in the man's eyes. Annoyance? "The knowledge and experience of generations has been handed down to us by our fathers, in their wisdom. Though we may not know how they came to be, we keep these rules and traditions so as to live protected from evil."

"How did he die?" asked Jens, steering the conversation away from the matter of duality of faith. He'd never heard of this 'Saint Ansgar', nor any other saints from Denmark, for that matter. He didn't care what gods Bjerund held so long as they left him alone.

Bjerund shrugged. "Beasts, perhaps… or his enemies finally caught up with him—beasts of another kind. We remember his life here on Saint Ansgar's Day, not his death. You will stay with us for the celebration?"

"We really must get home," said Jens. There was something unnerving about the shape of Saint Ansgar's head, he thought. It was crooked and oblong. The wooden posts surrounding it seemed to him like the horns of a stag. It stirred an unsettling feeling in the pit of his stomach, and he shook his head.

"One more night won't hurt them," said Didrich, putting a hand on Jens's shoulder. "And I'd like to have another go at those farm girls you scared off, how about it?"

"You said you wanted to leave today." Jens glanced at his brother and then, under his breath, "You said these people smiled too much."

Didrich chortled. "Perhaps they've got good reason to smile. Look at this place! The sun is shining, there is food and drink… and tonight there will be more of it?" He gave Bjerund a look, who nodded in affirmation. "I'm in no rush, brother."

Jens followed Didrich's outstretched hand as it swept across the field, past the river, and the plumes of smoke from the men sitting beneath the mill. It was… peaceful, he had to admit. The only scars the men bore here were from working in the fields, and the women were free of the downcast expressions that usually accompanied seeing the loss of their loved ones to war.

"One more night," Jens conceded. "But we're leaving bright and early, so let's not overdo it, eh?"

"It's settled, then," said Bjerund, slapping his palms together and grinning, his limpid eyes near protruding from his head. "Your first Saint Ansgar festival! You'll never want to leave!"

X

The Saint Ansgar's Day Feast was held outside, on a patch of field beneath the old mill. Lamps and torches held the night at bay, while a great bonfire kept winter's creeping touch from the celebrations.

The longhouse's benches and tables had been arranged in a semi-circle facing out from the millhouse and toward the forest and the strange effigy that loomed beside it.

Jens waved away the akvavit, smiling thinly at his brother's curiously cocked head. "Not after last night. I have learned my lesson. I will stick to honey lager and thank myself in the morning."

"Suit yourself," said Didrich. He snapped back both shots in quick succession and burped loudly before wiping his mouth. "I intend giving Saint Ansgar the celebration he deserves, and if that means a roaring headache in the morning, I'll consider it penance for my sacred duty."

Jens rolled his eyes as Didrich quaffed down a giant sip from his tankard, the golden liquid spilling down his chin and beard. It had taken the better part of the day for him to put the hangover behind him, and he was in no mood for a repeat of the night before.

His eyes wandered across the tables, past the smiling Bjerun holding court to a captive audience—more tales of lindorms and nisse, no doubt. He paused for a moment on Aksel. The man had grown somehow paler and more gaunt overnight. He wasn't eating. In fact, he was barely moving, his eyes fixed on the towering effigy the feast was in tribute to.

Firewood had been stacked around the base of the structure, and hung from it like the hem of the saint's robes. Some of the scaffolding had been removed, but they wouldn't be done building it until the first winter moon, and then they'd light it. It'd be a blaze large enough to put the bonfire they had now to shame, and Jens wondered how they'd never seen the fire from Vissenbjerg before.

"Come, brother," said Didrich, his words pulling Jens away from the effigy. "A toast."

Jens sighed, but seeing his brother's sombre expression, he raised his tankard. "You said there was nothing left to drink to?"

"Only reasons to drink, aye," finished Didrich. He thumped his tankard against Jens's, spilling lager across the already wet table, and pursed his lips into a sad smile. "To Erik."

"To Erik," Jens agreed. He took a deep draught from his honey lager and slammed the empty tankard down onto the table beside Didrich's.

―――※―――

They drank until the early hours that night; Didrich hard and heavy, Jens slow and steady.

But when the moon was at its highest, and the town's folk took to the field in song and dance, Jens felt a warm buzz come over him.

It was only when he couldn't find her that he realised he was looking for her at all. The hazel-eyed farm girl of the night before. He saw her sister twirling in the grass beside Didrich, but of her there was no sight.

He felt a little of the shame of the night before come back to him as he stood alone amongst the crowd of revellers but tried to ignore it as he watched them churning the field with their feet. They'd all donned flower crowns and necklaces of barley. He'd even lowered his head to accept one of his own, and it now rested above his ears. He should've been laughing and singing with his brother, but it wasn't the same. And after another moment, he decided to call it a night and slunk silently away from the feast.

XI

The air was quiet and still as he made his way back to their lodgings, and he huddled into his coat against the sharp breeze that had followed him from the field. His head held low, his shoulders hunched, he wouldn't have noticed the forest if he hadn't looked up to the soft clicking sound coming from ahead.

Jens paused on the path, his head cocked to the side to stare at the trees. They had got closer this time, he was sure. Their branches now hung over the roof of their lodgings, like crooked fingers scraping against the wooden boards with each gust of wind.

Satisfied he'd identified the source of the sound, Jens carried on his way. But this time, with an eye turned toward the shrouded mass of the forest. The moon was bright enough to illuminate the edges of the woods, and Jens stared deep into the knotted confines and shadows that lingered there.

The sound of snapping branches sent his heart racing, and he froze in his steps. There was something there, something staring back at him from the woods. He couldn't see it, but he could feel it: a brooding presence drawing nearer.

Another crack echoed from the trees, and then a long, hollow tearing, like one of the ancient pines had just been uprooted and was being dragged across the forest floor.

There was a movement beneath the trees, in the corner of Jens's vision. He tried to follow it, but it stayed just ahead of his gaze, disappearing into the dark shadows beyond the moon's touch. The trees around the shadows began to sway, their branches rustling like some presence was pushing them aside as it moved through the forest.

Jens flinched as a bestial bark echoed from the forest. A challenge. Or warning. A promise from whatever lurked within the heart of the woods.

His heart pounding in his throat, Jens ran the last few steps to the lodgings and slammed the door shut behind him.

***

Jens peered out the single window of their lodgings, his flintlock gripped tightly in his hands. The weapon was reassuring, a cold certainty after the questions posed by the unknown that night. There was a presence in the woods, one that instilled in Jens a fear so ancestral, so primal in nature, that he'd had to fight off the urge to simply fall to his knees before the forest and surrender himself to it.

For a brief pause, he'd nearly succumbed to the instinct, joining his ancestors, the fire-worshippers and moon dancers, in a steady line of fear that had only ended when man took axe and saw to the dark places on the horizon. They had pushed back the unknown with fire until only man remained.

His musket was the legacy of this fact, and he had shrugged off the feeling long enough to pick up the weapon. His mind had focused after that, narrowing in on the smooth, repetitive process of loading the firearm. All other thoughts had faded into the backgrounded while he'd completed the task he'd done a thousand times before. Then he'd settled down to wait.

The moon had long since reached its zenith by the time Jens shifted from his knees in front of the door. His muscles had started to ache, and the gnawing sensation in the pit of his stomach had lessened with each passing moment.

Branches still tugged at the roof, but he'd gotten used to the sound, and the hair on the back of his neck no longer prickled when he heard it.

Maybe he'd been mistaken? Maybe his instincts were nothing more than a hand-me-down for a threat that no longer existed? What had Bjerund said? Some things we keep simply because those before us kept them too. Maybe his fear was like that.

Exhausted and still a little drunk, Jens slumped down on his bed. He'd keep an eye on the door, he thought, even as his eyes began to droop.

XI

Wake up, brother.

"Why?"

They're here.

"Who is? Come into the light. I can't see you."

A laugh, like bone scraping bone. You wouldn't like seeing me, brother.

Jens shifted on his bed but leaves rustled beneath him, and his legs were wrapped up in roots and branches instead of his blanket.

Come, brother. Join us.

"Who is us? Didrich? What's going on?"

A shape moved in the shadows around Jens, a figure shifting on its haunches. Jens gagged as a wave of rot filled his nostrils, a stench of old bones—meatless and dry—and dead flowers. He pulled himself up, eager to escape the smell and whatever lurked in the shadows.

"Didrich!"

Jens's eyes snapped open, and he rolled in his bed, still retching from the dream. The stink lingered for a second, like the grey, rotten meat of an old wound, but it was gone by the time he drew himself up on the mattress. He wiped his mouth with the back of a hand.

It was only then that he noticed that the door was open. He glanced at the cot beside his, expecting to see Didrich sprawled out on the blankets, dirty boots and all. But the bed was empty, the blankets undisturbed. Didrich hadn't returned yet.

He was about to turn back to the door when his eyes settled on a thin string of hair hanging at the foot of Didrich's bed. Gooseflesh covered his skin when he saw the same charm hanging at the bottom of his own cot. Dark curls, frayed at the end, platted into a tight knot. Small teeth—no larger than a child's—had been knitted into the string, beside small bones... a child's, too?

Jens crawled forward in his bed to take a closer look when a shadow stepped in front of the moonlight spilling in from the door.

There was that smell again. Rotten, like old bones and barren soil. Rotten meat gone grey. A soft clicking sound, rusted nails dropping on wood, like the trees scratching on the roof. Only, it was coming from the silhouette standing at the doorway.

"Aksel?" said Jens, recognising his wiry frame. What was he doing here? Thomas. Before he could correct his mistake, the man spun around and started walking back out into the night.

"Thomas!" he called, leaping from his bunk, his fears all but forgotten. He remembered his brother's words, his doubts about this 'Thomas'. Where was Didrich? Had Aksel done away with him and now come to do away with the last Oversen brother?

Jens burst out of the lodgings in time to see Thomas disappear behind the washhouse, glancing over his shoulder to meet Jens's eyes with his own. They were bloodshot in the moonlight and... scared, he realised. But he wasn't running, and Jens caught up to him with ease.

"Where's Didrich?" Jens demanded, grabbing Thomas by the arm. There was nothing but skin and bone to hold onto, and it felt like he was holding onto a broom handle, like it might snap beneath too much pressure.

He relaxed his grip and pulled Thomas around to look him squarely in the eyes.

"What were you doing outside my room? Speak, man. Speak!"

Thomas remained quiet, his thin lips curling until a crooked smile covered his face. Yellow teeth appeared like chipped tombstones from his mouth. Jens shoved him back with a sigh.

"You're mad," he said, shaking his head. "All of you are mad. Did you leave that token by my bed? Where did you get those teeth from? Disgusting."

Thomas stiffened at the mention of the string, and Jens raised a brow. "Not you, then?"

Thomas shook his head once and then lifted a hand to point across the town.

"The church?" Jens asked, staring across the uniform dwellings. The steepled roof of the church and its twin arched wings made it look all the more like a carrion bird, hunched and brooding in the night.

Thomas nodded. Another single, curt motion.

"It is you, isn't it?" Jens took a step toward the man, half expecting him to flinch or to leg it like a frightened rabbit. Thomas remained still, meeting Jens's questioning stare with his bloodshot eyes. A vein pulsed on his forehead, so thick and raised, Jens thought it might burst.

Again, that tombstone smile. This close, Jens could see the discolouration in Thomas's gums and the bloody pits where two of his teeth had been forcibly removed. His lips were slightly swollen around the area, cut by whatever tool had been used in the extraction.

"What happened to your tongue?" said Jens, even as he realised the answer.

Thomas opened his mouth wider, revealing the full extent of the damage. The skin around his molars was black and scarred. Jens winced at the graveyard breath that flooded out from the open maw but stared long enough to see the scarred tissue and meaty stump where a tongue once sat. It looked like it had been pulled out at the root rather than cut, and a tattered tail of meat still flicked around in the back of Thomas's mouth.

The mute wagged what remained of his tongue, flicking it against the roof of his mouth. The sound it made was immediately familiar—

the soft echoing clicks that Jens had heard outside his door.

He felt a momentary relief. He'd been right, after all. There was nothing here, just a mad, half-starved mute poking around outside their lodgings at night. The relief was short-lived as another thought pulled its way to the fore: why had they taken his tongue?

"Aksel," Jens said, no longer a question. "Who did this to you? Was it the people that live here? The church?"

Before Aksel could confirm it, Jens felt him tense beneath his hands. He started wriggling, pulling away, his eyes fixed on something behind Jens. On the church.

Jens let go, raising his hands to show that he didn't mean him any harm. But Aksel bolted the moment he let go, and this time he did not look back.

Jens considered chasing after him again, plunging into the darkness after the frightened rabbit like a wolfhound, and then thought better of it. He was still feeling the effects of the akvavit and lager. Aksel would have disappeared down the first hole he found, anyway. Where would he even begin looking?

He let out a tired sigh and turned to stare back at the church. Aksel had been spooked, but by what?

As his eyes adjusted to the gloom, he started making out figures moving in the darkness.

People. Dozens of them, until it seemed the whole town was streaming toward the church.

Jens stared past the slow-moving crowd, down the road toward the old mill. They were coming from the Feast of Saint Ansgar.

An evening service? Jens wondered. It was well after midnight, and the church, from what he remembered, was in no state for midnight mass.

Jens's speculation was cut short by the shrill cry, an aching scream as long as a breath. His hand went instinctively to his hunting knife before he remembered that there were no wolves here, no predators left to challenge man's dominion.

His brow knotted as he watched the town's folk increase their pace, moving quickly toward the church. As they got closer, Jens could just make out their faces in the night. Didrich had been right, Jens thought, walking toward the church. These people smiled too much.

XII

The cries grew louder as Jens approached. He realised, with some discomfort, that not all of them were moans of pain. Some of them were closer to the throes of a woman in great pleasure rather than suffering. Though, he was acutely aware, the distinction was not always obvious.

The others hadn't noticed him join their procession, or else they didn't care. Jens recognised some of their number: the violinist from the longhouse, the young girl who'd greeted him at the door, he even saw the sister of the woman he'd danced with—but not her. He stared over the heads of the crowd, hoping to glimpse her flower crown and curls.

Bjerund's toad-like face appeared ahead of him and then disappeared through the church doors before Jens could call to him.

He shuddered as another scream washed over him. He shook again when he realised he couldn't tell if it had been a scream of pain or pleasure, or of both.

The church doors were open wide, like the mouth of a cave, drawing him in as those behind pressed forward. A soft light filled the room, and Jens blinked as the midnight gloom was replaced by a warm glow.

The same stink that had heralded his last visit hit him as he stepped into the church. He was expecting it this time and tried breathing in from his mouth instead, but it only made it worse.

The cots were lined up in neat rows, like before. Only this time, the aisles between were filled with people, plodding forward like livestock in butcher lanes toward the back of the church.

Jens paused to look at the woman writhing on the cot beside him. Her pupils had disappeared into the back of her head, and blood-laced white orbs stared up at him.

A hand nudged him gently from behind, and he stared up, seeing for the first time what they were moving toward.

The two midwives were hardly recognisable in their yellow robes. Their white eyes stared out from their black painted faces. Twin, curling antlers had been fastened to their heads, tightened with bits of hair and bone.

They stood to either side of another of the cots, above a writhing figure clad in a simple nightdress. Her belly protruded out beneath her breasts, a swollen orb that seemed well past due.

As Jens watched, the shorter of the two matrons—the one who had chased him out of the church the last time—drew a thin dagger from her robes. It sparkled in the warm light, its ridges etched with elaborate shapes and runes.

He knew then that he was about to witness something he shouldn't, that his mere presence in this church—no, this hall, now empty of any of God's graces—was evidence of his complicity. He wanted to turn around and run, to push through the line of town's folk and to leave this charnel house behind. But he couldn't. His eyes remained fixed on the blade and the woman who wielded it.

A low murmur filled his ears, and he managed to draw his gaze away long enough to see that those in the line ahead of him had begun to sway on their feet. They moved from side to side like rafts on the tide. Their lips moved almost imperceptibly. Soft words escaped them, hardly louder than a breath.

Bjerund appeared beside the priestess, his wet hands clasped together as he spoke. Whatever he said was too soft for Jens to hear. A prayer? A litany for the Devil?

The matron turned her horned head to Bjerund, the knife held high, her white eyes blazing. A silence descended upon the hall. A tense anticipation as all eyes fixed on Bjerund. The town's head smiled deeply, and nodded.

A shrill ululation swept through the hall, starting with the priestess as she cried out in joy, before she plunged the knife deep into the still writhing woman's belly.

The blade sunk up to its hilt, spraying blood across the white nightshift and yellow robe. Before the gasp had even escaped Jens's lips, the matron began to cut into the womb, tugging the blade in and out of the torn meat like a wood saw.

Gorge started to rise in the back of Jens's throat, and he covered his mouth with a hand. Murder, he thought—not yet able to voice the words. A mother and her child butchered in some pagan spectacle, all in the name of a Christian Saint. The evil of it all hit him like a physical force, and he felt his eyes ache.

The matron let out another ululating shriek, and the dagger fell from her fingers.

Somehow, the pregnant woman was still alive, her legs kicking out on the bloodstained mattress. The matron pulled back the torn and bloodied shift, exposing the wound in her belly, and her swollen labia. She gestured to the other midwife, motioning at her to hold the woman down while she lowered her horned head until she was staring right into the torn meat she'd made from the belly. After a moment, she cocked her head to the side, the hair and bones that hung from her horns tracing the movement.

She tilted her head again, but this time she did not pause, plunging her hands into the bloodied mound of flesh, until both of her wrists were concealed by it.

The murmuring voices began to fill the hall again. Whispers that tugged at Jens's ears softly, like the wind. They were growing louder, until he could finally make out the words, though they meant nothing to him. A flowery, guttural language that reminded him of the script he'd seen on the longhouse door.

Beads rattled from somewhere within the hall, adding to the sickly rhythm of the chant. The matron's hips began to sway in time to the beat, her own howls echoing off the walls.

Her shrieks reached a sickening pitch, and Jens felt his vision swim and the bile in the back of his throat rise.

He caught sight of the woman splayed out on the bed, their eyes locking for the briefest of moments, before the yellow robes hid her from him again. He knew her. He knew those curls and dark brown eyes. The flower crown was gone, but it was the same girl he'd held in his arms that first night.

How. It wasn't possible. She'd been as lean as a dancer when he'd seen her, when he'd felt her. Had she another sister? A third farmer's daughter Jens had confused for the same?

The midwife shrieked again, this time in triumph. The horned woman started pulling her hands out from the pit of the girl's stomach.

There was a sickening plop as the matron disentangled herself from the womb, drawing her hands back out into the hall. But they did not come out empty. A bloodied bundle quickly disappeared into her robes, while the other midwife snapped the birthing cord with an experienced twist of her wrists.

The midwives huddled together, staring into the shape now concealed by their bloody yellow robes, leaving the girl to quietly expire on the bed. Jens could see her properly now, and he knew without a doubt that it was the farmer's daughter he had danced with. The forest princess. But she would never dance again. Her ribcage had been bent open, and poked out from her skin like fence posts on a bloodied field. Her eyes were closed, and the ragged breaths from her heaving chest were growing fainter.

Jens felt his gaze drawn down toward her broken body, and for a moment he was staring into her womb, into the gaping chasm that had birthed a child into the world. But even as he stared, he knew it was no child that lay concealed within those tattered yellow robes. And that what he was gazing into was no womb. It was like staring into a cave of glass, at a thousand blinking eyes that all turned to meet his gaze. Vomit burst past his lips as something shivered within that infinite space, another foetal shape with a horned head, coiling tendrils wrapped around its midriff.

Jens managed to break his gaze away long enough to see the matron raise the thing swaddled in her robes, lifting it above her head for all to appraise. Her triumphant cries were echoed back to her by the watching townsfolk, their faces shining with glee as they built themselves up into a feverish frenzy. They were chanting now, and singing, and fighting, and making love—a sharp roar of pain and pleasure and faith.

Jens felt the last colour drain from his face as a child's cry joined the cacophony. A paternal instinct stirred somewhere deep within him, one he could hardly suppress—he wasn't even sure he wanted to. His legs nearly buckled when the newborn lifted its head to stare across the church floor, holding him in its black eyes. Its infinite gaze. Bony nubs had already started to protrude on its forehead, where the horns would grow.

XIII

"What is it, Jens?" Didrich was sitting on the doorstep of their lodgings, smoking a cigarette, when he returned.

"Get your things," said Jens, breathing heavily. Sweat covered his shirt and brow, like a fever had taken him during the night, only to break with the light of dawn. "We're leaving, back to Vissenbjerg. Hurry up."

Didrich cocked his head, moving his legs to let Jens through the door. "Right this minute?" he called over his shoulder to the sound of Jens stomping through their lodgings, looking for his flintlock. "But brother, will you not wait to hear my news?"

"This very minute," Jens hissed, cradling his musket in one arm while he shouldered his knapsack. He didn't bother with his blanket or mug and made for the door before pausing. "What news?"

Didrich stomped out his cigarette and rose to his feet, a sheepish grin on his face. "I am to be made an honest man. Would you believe it? Me! Last night, with Emma—the farm girl. I felt something, Jens. Not like before, this is different. We are to be married."

Jens seemed not to hear him, turning instead to stare back at their beds. "The tokens—hanging from the bedposts, where are they?"

"The what?" Didrich shook his head, a look of annoyance edging the grin away. "Did you not hear what I said?"

"The bits of hair and teeth," said Jens. "They were here when I got back from the feast. I thought Aksel had left them for us, but I was wrong."

"Aksel?" Didrich's smile disappeared entirely, and he eyed his brother with concern. "I thought we had decided I was wrong? That this Thomas is someone else...."

"I saw what they did to him," Jens said, suddenly turning to him. He pointed to the corner of his mouth with a finger. "They cut out his tongue and left his mouth to swell so that he cannot talk. So that he cannot speak of what he has seen in this place."

"You're not making any sense," said Didrich, walking toward his brother, his hands open at his sides in a calming gesture. It reminded Jens of Bjerund, and he took a step back.

"Your limp?" he said, his eyes darting from Didrich's hands to his knee. The patchwork repairs he'd done to his trousers were still there, but the limp was barely more than a subtle affectation in his stride.

"It's the damnedest thing," said Didrich, stretching out his leg in front of him, the smile returning. "There's something healing about Fødebjerg. Can you feel it? It feels like... like life! When I woke up this morning, I could hardly feel the ache in my knee. I think I'm nearly whole again."

"It is the work of the Devil," said Jens before he could stop himself. "Or some spirit of the forest. They consort with it. Breed with it. I saw for myself last night." His voice was raised despite himself, and spittle flew from his mouth like a torrent of rain. He knew how it sounded—like madness had taken hold, that the cannons of Als had done to his mind what they had done to his brother's body. "You heard what Bjerund said about the old ways. They still hold to them, and it to them."

"Breed with it?" Didrich snorted, disbelief writ upon his face. "Listen to yourself, man. You've been babbling since we got here; horns and churches and crooked things in the trees. There's—"

"I saw it," said Jens, throwing caution aside as he moved a step closer to Didrich. His brother could think him mad all he wanted, as long as he left this place with him and never looked back. "You remember the girl I danced with that first night? Your Emma's sister?"

"Oh, aye." Didrich frowned. "She's taken ill, tucked up safely in bed until the fever breaks, God willing."

"She's dead," said Jens bluntly. "Her belly carved out by the matrons last night. I was there, in the church when they did it."

Didrich snorted again, though this time, he looked less certain.

"She let them do it willingly," Jens continued, the memory of the night coming back to him. Her crown of flowers and the smell of wet pine. "They butchered her to get at the thing within, and then they tore that from her belly and let her bleed out in her cot."

"What... thing?"

"A god. A demon. Both. I don't know." Jens tightened the grip on his flintlock and stared past his brother out the doorway into the town. The morning lay subdued behind a grey palette, thick wintry clouds keeping the sun's light from Fødebjerg. Nobody stirred beyond their lodgings, but they would be up soon, their muscles aching from the revelry of the night before. Jens blinked and looked back at his brother. "Will you come with me?"

"Aye," said Didrich with a slow nod. "But I must take Emma with us. If what you say is true, then she is in danger here."

"She was there, too," said Jens, remembering her face amongst the crowd walking toward the church. "She is one of them, Didrich. You must leave her behind. There will be other women."

"I have promised myself to her. If I go, then she goes, too," said Didrich.

"But—"

"If I go, she goes," Didrich growled.

There was a stubborn grit in his voice, and Jens knew he wouldn't be changing his mind. He thought about leaving them both behind for a moment and making the trek home alone. The rotten thought had been a candle in his mind for no more than a second when he put it out. He'd already left one brother behind; he wouldn't be leaving a second.

"As you say." Jens sighed and then nodded to Didrich's things, still strewn about the floor. "Get your things, and then we'll get your wife to be before anyone knows what we're about."

"It's better if I fetch her alone," said Didrich, already packing up his kit. "I'll have to sweep her out from under her father's nose, and if he sees one of us, he'll bring the town down on our heads."

"Meet me in the orchards, then," said Jens, peeking back out the door. He thought he saw a movement at the end of the road, but he couldn't make anything out in the gloom. When no frenzied townsfolk appeared, he nodded to his brother and stepped out onto the porch. "If you're not there by mid-morning, I'm leaving without you."

Jens waited until it was nearly noon before shifting off of his haunches beneath the cover of the orchards, and staring across the field into the town. His brother hadn't come. Either he'd thought him mad and disappeared beneath the farm girl's covers for the rest of the morning, or he thought him sane and had been caught in the act of trying to retrieve her.

There was nothing Jens could do in either scenario. Damnit, he thought. He should never have let Didrich go alone.

He let out a soft sigh, allowing his gaze to sweep across the hunched rooves of the town houses and then over the crooked spine of the church. Its doors had remained open throughout the night, like a black pit, like the eyes of the spawn it had seen birthed within its walls.

He felt his eyes drawn to another shape beyond the path of the river. The effigy of Saint Ansgar loomed above the treeline as a triumphant finger pointed toward the heavens. But that was not quite right, Jens thought as he started walking toward the forest. From a distance, he could better make out the shape of the tribute. What he had first taken to be scaffolding had been fashioned into a pair of curling horns; the flowing habit of a saint had been transformed into a ragged robe, and additional appendages had been fastened to the figure's side. A bovine snout now pressed out from behind the hood of the robes.

The effigy stood in defiance of God, not in celebration of Him.

As Jens took his first steps into the forest, already promising to return for his brother, a shape detached itself from the trees and followed.

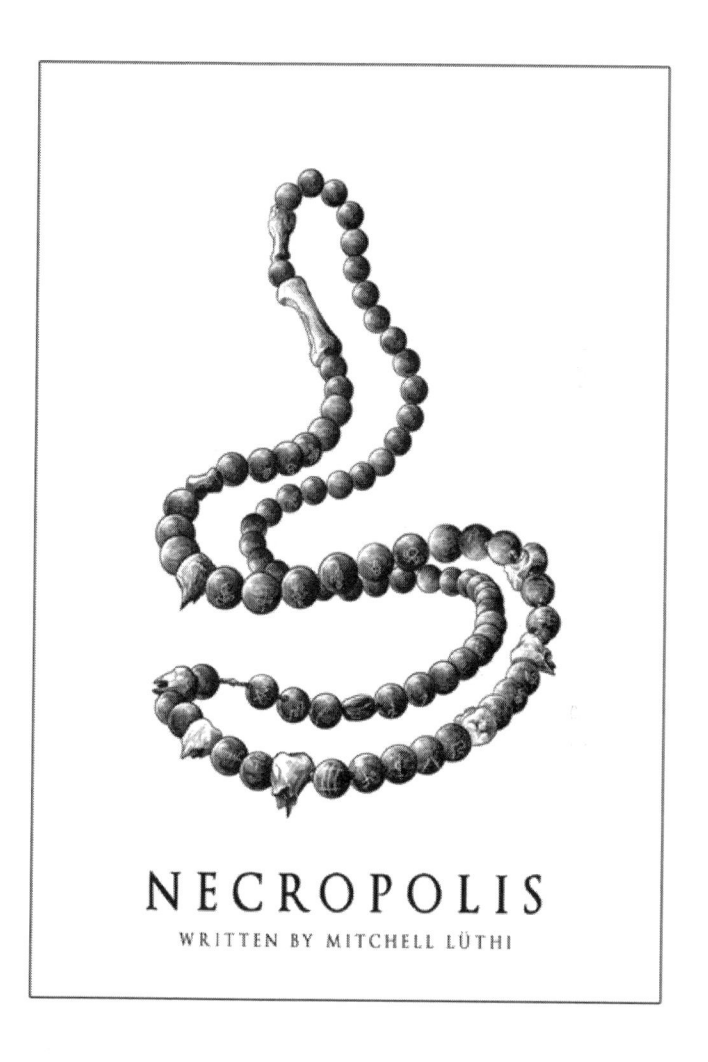

NECROPOLIS
WRITTEN BY MITCHELL LÜTHI

Necropolis

THE GRAND LITURGY OF THE KEEPER

The Necropolis, that great mass of portentous and tortuous architecture, hovers in perfect balance within the gravitational pull of the moon. Its form equilateral—in principle, if not in deed—spun in a steady, languorous motion upon its axis. For each ponderous rotation made, the moon completes another revolution of its own, and so the years pass by. But time is slower on the Necropolis. Initiated by minute oscillations, the very structure seems to jitter in a manner peculiar in itself. Such vibrations, of varying strength and measure, were most disruptive closer to the centre of the monolithic polyhedron, where time itself seems to have taken pause.

From beneath the failing light of Dartuan, the Blessed Sun of the Ten Thousand Pilgrims, the tomb-ship concludes another cycle. Twisted towers and rugged spires appear from out of the shadows, piercing the blotchy inkiness of space like broken fingers extended against the heavens. Row upon row of jutting buttresses press against the tiered walls, encroaching upon the massive steps that form the levels of the Necropolis and its broken teeth of black obsidian. Finally, as the shadows withdraw and the faint light of the sun begins to reflect off myriad clerestory windows, the Necropolis is revealed in its entirety. The basilica in the void—a pyramidal mausoleum.

A thousand souls once resided within these walls, their lives dedicated to a twofold purpose: life and death. The one fleeting, the other eternal. But now, like so many others, their bodies are interred within the catacombs below; and of those former denizens, only one remains.

💀 💀 💀

Septimus Acculei cupped his long, sinewy fingers together and brought the icy water to his face. He gasped as tiny, lucent droplets ran down his face and neck, leaving a trail of goose pimples in their wake. His body quickly adjusted to the cold, and he found that wakefulness was less elusive, now that this first task was complete. He flicked his hands sharply—once, then twice—and reached for the small washcloth beside the basin; the motion was precise, calculated to exactitude, redolent of the meticulous nature of Septimus himself. His face now clean, he turned to the rest of his body.

Adjacent to the basin, on the opposite side to the washcloth, sat two grey bowls. In the one, a blend of finely ground ochre and white powder. In the other, a crimson paste. Septimus pinched an index finger and thumb together and dragged them through the powder, leaving a furrowed channel behind. He rubbed his digits together, spreading the fine dust across his leathery hands, and carefully applied the mixture to each of his cheeks. Next, Septimus swirled a pinky through the water and dabbed it in the second bowl. Satisfied that the dilution was acceptable, he lifted his finger to his brow and drew it down from the centre of his forehead, past his pursed lips, to the cleft of his chin. He licked his lips, careful not to smear the paste beyond the ridge of his mouth, and tasted the bitter paint on his tongue. Finally, Septimus drew his robes from the ground. He dusted down the yawning sleeves, tightened the belt around his waist, and adjusted his hood. He was now ready to perform his duties.

Septimus had been a curator on the Necropolis for an imprecise period of time. In some parts, where infinitesimal vibrations had shifted the very fabric of reality, and time had slowed down to a faltering pace, Septimus had only just accepted his post. In others, the cold hand of centuries had waved itself none too gently, and the curator had been dead for a long, long time. Such contradictions are commonplace in the vast burial ground of which he was custodian, though he was careful not to dwell on them too often. To do so would be unwise, and Septimus was anything but that.

The curator blinked myopically at the door to his cell, then peeled back one of his sleeves and flashed the microchip embedded in his wrist. With a mechanical whir and the hiss of pneumatics, the door slid open. Septimus pulled at the hem of his robe, clutching handfuls of the material between his gnarled fingers, and stepped out into the passageway beyond. Stark, strong light blared down from the fluorescents above, and the soft humming of rotary machines filled the air around him. In the bowels of the Necropolis, where there was no need for spectacle or ceremony, the walls were dreary and unadorned. Grey, fibrecrete tiles blended with ever-rusting metals and sparse, windowless walls. The space was narrow, with only enough room for one person to walk comfortably—not that he needed more. His former colleagues were long dead, their corpses sealed within the chilly niches of the main crypt. He'd put most of them there himself.

The passage terminated in a tarnished door, and Septimus scanned his microchip once more, and waited. Humid air rushed through the corridor, and the slow creak of metal whined in a jarring, syncopated rhythm from above. Finally, with a grating thump that echoed along the walls, the tedious song came to a halt, and the sealed door opened. Septimus entered the lift and thumbed a sequence of digits into the interface beside the door. A luminous green light shone in acceptance, and the steel cage took off, racing toward its destination above.

The curator slid his fingers through the barred frame of the lift as it screeched and rattled, holding tight when the shaking steel floor threatened to throw him from his feet. The amber light flickered once, and then went off entirely, leaving the curator in a darkness so thick he could almost feel it pressed against his skin. The lift itself began to falter, slowing in speed as the mechanism within shut down. It was running on fumes at this stage—the whole ship was. The curator felt around with a hand, his fingers extended out toward the dark, until he felt the cold face of the console. He muttered a few words and pressed his palm squarely against the glass face. His murmured incantation was met by a high-pitched wheeze from the roof of the cage as the bulb sputtered back on. This was followed by the reassuring drone of the lift's mechanism, and everything returned to order. Septimus let out a relieved sigh. He'd have to see to that.

The lift took him to one of many landing stages. This one filtered out to a passage not unlike the one before his cell, and he strode toward the door with purpose once he'd disembarked. It opened without the need of his chip, and he pushed past it into an oblong chamber. The room contained dozens of wall-mounted shelves, each holding hundreds of dusty, leather-bound tomes. There were many rooms like this scattered throughout the Necropolis, and the curator spent much of his time digitising their contents. It was the toil of lifetimes, but Septimus was nearly done. He breezed through the room, barely glancing at his most recent work-pile, and exited through a door on the other side. He had other duties to fulfil that day.

Before Septimus, a large, cavernous hall materialised. Annular in nature, rows of concentric rings rose up around a gaudy black spire in the centre of the room. In each of the concrete layers surrounding the steeple, hundreds or more niches had been formed. Carved out with the use of hydrocentric drilling, the holes gave the chamber the appearance of one colossal honeycomb. Tiered steps mounted the area before the central tower, and four pillars stood steady and strong beside it, like those of a temple—but this was no place of worship. Every opening that pinpricked the outer rings was garlanded with a decorative crest and inscription, as well as a simple polylithic mound that rested before them. And within each of the alcoves, a single body lay entombed—for this was a place of the dead. The largest of all the chambers in the Necropolis, the ossuary was lit by the cold light of a dozen floating lamps. They hovered like the bees of a hive, zipping from one vault to another at dizzying speed, buffeting each other in their eagerness to illuminate the darkest corners of the chamber. Hundreds of keepers had once looked after the souls resting here, monitoring each of the interred like an obsessive mother would a child—but now it was only him.

He strode into the gallery, making for a recess in the furthest corner of the ossuary. Flights of stairs rose beside him, following the curving walls of the chamber ever upward. More resting places awaited him above, spiralling up into the darkness, where even the ambitious little lamps struggled to reach. The alcove in question was some distance away, so he lifted the hem of his robes and increased his stride. The soft click-clack of his sandals upon the tiled floor was the only sound in the echoing chamber, and he quickly fell into a steady rhythm. When he arrived at the niche, a sheen of perspiration had formed on his brow, and the red paste he'd so fastidiously applied that morning was threatening to smudge. He dabbed gently at the sweat, careful not to disturb his earlier efforts, and wiped both his hands upon his robes when he was done. He could not move to the next task if the labours of his previous became undone. Such a thing would be... heretical.

Septimus knelt, lowering his knees one at a time in a staggered sequence of movements, and came to a rest in front of the mound. From his robes he drew a tangled string of beads that he wrapped around a knuckled hand. They felt dry and uneven against his skin—chipped and worn by time, but comforting nevertheless. Carved from the bone of one of his precursors, and coupled with the black stone of the ossuary, the prayer beads were as sacred as the place itself. He steepled his fingers and rested his palms on his chest. The beads hung low, hovering in front of his midriff, swinging gently with each breath like a slow moving pendulum. Next, he lowered his head and closed his eyes. He held this position, his lips moving soundlessly, until his knees began to ache beneath him. As if prompted by some unheard command, Septimus rose to his feet and stepped past the mound, and into the alcove itself.

The niche was shallow—hardly a couple of feet cut out from the grey rock—and Septimus found himself pressed tightly from all sides, against the shelf in the centre of the recess. The teeth from the drill that had formed the narrow inlet had left great furrows in the walls, akin to erosive watermarks left by the ocean's tides. The curator stared around him, basking in the dim light of the closest lantern as he read the walls. More than a dozen shapes had been carved into the face of the stone, a complex weave of iconography and glyphs. The inscriptions commemorated the life of the figure laid bundled up on the ledge. By all accounts, it had been an impressive life.

Septimus pressed a hand against the mantel, pushing a finger into a hidden compartment beneath. Feeling the flat sheeting of the screen, he swiped his thumb over the surface, and stood back from the shelf as a ripple of neurthatic energy emanated from within the room. It brushed gently against the curator's skin and robes, wrapping itself around him. He shivered for a moment, feeling the cold energy coil its way beneath his flesh and wriggle inside of him. And then it was gone. Whatever last reservoir of life remained in that room had now departed, flickering out like the light of a candle. Septimus tilted his head, staring down at the empty corpse lying flat on the table. It was only the strongest of souls that lingered after death. One in a million, perhaps. Whoever this was must have been very impressive indeed. The curator sighed deeply to himself and began the administrations.

Septimus knew that when his time came, he would not find himself interred within the Necropolis. He would not be afforded the great honour of the eternal rest. No, his was a life of service, of hardship. His body would be incinerated like those who held the post before him, and his soul offered up to The Silent King so that it may aid in the continuation of the great work. Even in death, he would have a purpose.

The curator placed a hand upon the cold, hard skin of the deceased. His touch was gentle, and he took care not to bruise the flesh where he pressed against it. First, he pressed his thumb and forefinger against the corpse's chin. Then, he pressed his hands against the man's cheeks, squeezing softly in a circular, massage-like motion. He continued this process, moving down toward the man's throat and neck. Finally, he rested his palm against the man's chest and began the final incantation. When he was done, he stood motionless and stared down at the body. The corpse was now an empty vessel, completely bereft of even the memory of the life force that had once powered it. Septimus nodded to himself, satisfied that his duty to the dead had been completed, and pressed the screen beneath the mantle. The mechanism whined for a moment, and then purred contentedly as it began lowering the corpse into the floor. The curator stepped toward the opening, but glanced back before leaving. He watched as the body was slowly lowered, as the steel slide began to close across the tomb below. Here the dead would rest, in the peace and quiet, in the absolute darkness of eternity. Septimus envied him that.

A DIVINE INTERLOPER FROM THE VOID

When next the keeper emerged from his cell, he was notified of another presence aboard the Necropolis. It was a single heat signature, confined to a landing bay far above the labyrinthine corridors he inhabited. Setting aside his duties for a moment, he took a lift to the highest floor, and emerged at the tip of one of the tomb-ship's great spires.

The way here was empty, and it was seldom that he found himself traversing the narrow bridges beneath the silver dome. The landing platform was rarely used—it had been rarely used when the vessel was a densely populated place, too. But now it seemed decades would pass between each visitor—not that Septimus minded. He had always preferred the solitude of his own company to that of others.

The dome itself was a translucent screen. Beyond it, the white light of distant suns twinkled defiantly against the black vastness of space. The tomb-ship was in the middle of one of its leisurely rotations, and the dome spire faced away from the crater-riddled moon below. Instead, its steepled towers stared unblinkingly into the empty black, at long dead stars and the blotchy stain of the Hubris Constellation. He'd come here often as a novitiate, and pondered his own fate, and of those entombed beneath the heavens. Such visits had become less frequent over the years, until they had stopped altogether. *Why was that?* he wondered briefly as he came, at least, to a heavy door. He shook free the thought, and swiped his chip. After a brief pause, the door opened, and Septimus stepped inside.

The heat signature had been registered here, the ships automated systems picking up the interloper the moment he or she had set foot aboard. Septimus stared about the landing post, looking for the tell-tale signs of a vessel that had just completed atmospheric diffusion. About a dozen ships were still docked in the bays, though their occupants would no longer require their services. The curator hesitated beside one of the raptor-like Radius vessels, but the marks were old, the paint chipped and rugged from use in years gone by. He ran a hand over the worn-down steel and conchrite of the ship's corrugated exhaust, and wondered at the places this transporter must have seen.

A sound to his left—the soft click of boots on marble—made him turn.

So young, he thought as he appraised the new arrival. A girl, no more than five or six, stood before him. She had wispy brown hair that hung across her eyes, and full, round cheeks. She wore the grey robes of a novitiate, which hung from her too-small limbs. The girl wrinkled her nose up at him, and Septimus found himself quite unsure of what to do.

Eventually, after an awkward silence, Septimus gathered himself and approached the child, extending a hand toward her. "Come, child," he said. "This is no place for one such as yourself." He clasped her little hand with his own, and began to walk back toward the lift. "What is your name?" he enquired as they strode across the arching bridges, through the narrow chambers of the boarding platforms.

"Shima." She seemed unafraid of her surrounds, confident in a way only a child could be. "Who are you?"

"Me?" he smiled despite himself. "I am the keeper of this place, but you may call me by my name: Septimus."

"Sep-eh-mis." She stumbled over the words, her glinting blue eyes narrowing as she confronted the consonantal sound. "Septimus."

"That's right," he said, nodding encouragingly. He could not remember the last time he had conversed with anyone, let alone a child. He glanced at her, a grey brow raised. Shima was dragging her feet through her long robes—he'd have to hem them in for her—and was now chewing quite happily on one of her nails.

The caretaker ushered her across the last bridge, and spared a final look up at the dome. He felt very small beneath the countless stars, and smaller still in the face of the impossible void. The hazy band of light in the distance provided some comfort, though. The Hubris

Constellation, the realm of The Silent King. Someday soon he would join him there, and continue unhindered by the shackles his mortal form provided. A wave field flickered somewhere overhead, spreading blue light across the bulbous screen that encased the upper spire, and obstructed his view. Septimus sighed to himself and nodded Shima forward, toward the lift. She wasn't what he'd expected, but she'd have to do.

💀💀💀

Over the next few hours, Septimus familiarised the girl with her various roles and duties upon the Necropolis. She was a quick learner, and took to her tasks with ease. He found himself impressed with her enthusiasm, and with the knowledge she'd already accrued on the topics he instructed on. Apprentices he'd had in the past had proven... unsuited to the task.

"Thread slowly, and be careful not to poke yourself." The curator gently pressed the strand through the canvas, and watched to see her mirror the task. "Wounds made with an aethertic blade are not prone to healing."

"But these are needles."

He nodded, a thin smile on his lips. "The principle remains the same. It is the *substance* of the tool that counts, not the name. That this is an aethertic needle, and not a blade, is of no consequence; the result will be the same."

The girl furrowed her brow, and digested the information as she continued with her task. She was good with the needle, and threaded it through the Hessian sacking without issue.

"Can you tell me what these are for?" Septimus opened a palm to the row of bags lined up on their work table. Varying in size and length, they covered most of the table, and would take hours more to complete.

"They are for moving the dead," said the girl indifferently, "from their home to here."

"And why are they important?" The curator looped off the last strand, and clipped the end of the thread off deftly with a small cutting blade. His bag complete, he placed the tools on the table and watched Shima finish hers.

"Once made holy—"

"*Sanctified*, yes."

"Well, when that's done, the bags are like a little piece of this place that can be carried anywhere." She stopped threading for a moment, and met Septimus' eyes. Those bright blue orbs of hers shone unnaturally in the light of the underhive. "It is what *He* wills."

"Correct." Septimus clasped his hands together, the hint of a smile becoming more apparent. He had found that he was quite enjoying the conversations with the girl. Corpses, he'd found, were good listeners, but little else.

"Do you know the *Words of the Keeper*?"

Shima nodded, though she seemed more hesitant than before.

"I would like to hear them, if you wouldn't mind?"

The girl put down the needle and thread, and placed her hands in her lap. She squeezed her eyes shut for a moment and then began reciting the words of his vocation.

From life's pale light
Stark but true
To Death's delight
A life that's due
In throes of the end
Where the sun cannot go
His garden we must tend
His seed we must sow

The words delivered, Shima picked up her tools and began to thread again.

"That was well said." Septimus opened his eyes, having closed them during the recital. The intense brightness of the workroom made him flinch, and he blinked back the light. "You learnt the *Words* during your trials, I take it?" he said once recovered.

"Yes, Keeper." The girl was squinting hard at the thin thread, scrupulous concentration on her young features.

Septimus stared down at his own thin, aethertic needle and considered his words carefully before next he spoke. "How many of you were there?" He watched her from the corner of his eye, looking for a reaction, but she was stoic in her work, her head slumped over the material.

"Seven," she said. "Eight, if you include me."

"I do." Septimus pursed his lips. "Indeed, I would be remiss not to... given how things have turned out."

Shima beamed at him, her cheeks creasing as her smile revealed a perfect row of white teeth. Then she returned to her work, her face fixed in a tight-knit mask of focus.

He couldn't imagine one as young as her competing in the trials, vying against others twice her age for the honour she had been awarded. There must be a hidden strength within this girl, he concluded. "And of the others, what became—"

The lights went out, plunging the workroom into darkness absolute. Septimus carefully stood up from his seat, his hands patting the table as he moved toward the entranceway. "Place the needle on the table and be still," he said, turning to where he thought Shima would be. The girl was deathly quiet, but he thought he heard the soft shift of her utensil being laid down. "This won't take a moment." He hoped that were true, but the sporadic shutdowns were becoming more common, lasting longer. He walked away from the table, relinquishing his grip on the seat nearest, and stumbled to the doorway. His hands held out in front of him, he finally came into contact with the cold steel tiling of the wall.

"What can I do?" Shima's voice came softly from beside him. He hadn't even heard her cross the floor.

"I thought I told you to be still." He wasn't annoyed, but she would have to learn to follow instructions.

"I'm scared," she said. "I don't like it down here."

It was almost a relief to hear her act her own age, however fleetingly, and Septimus felt around until he had her shoulder beneath his hand. "Don't be afraid," he said, patting her in what he hoped was a reassuring manner. "I'll have this fixed momentarily. She said nothing in reply, but he felt her shoulders relax beneath his grip. "Now, if I could just find..." He felt around the wall, searching for the access console. "It should be—Ah! Found it!"

Septimus let out a deep breath, flexed his fingers, and concentrated. The room was already getting colder, the rest of the systems having shut down with the lights. If he left it like this, they'd eventually freeze to death—if the oxygen supply wasn't depleted before then. A crypt without a Keeper. A tomb without its guardian. He shuddered at the thought, and then pressed his palm against the screen.

It took a moment before he could feel it—a slight tingling sensation along the tips of his fingers. The feeling quickly moved across to his palm, and then to his wrists. The words he recited were not of the common tongue, nor the archaic spiel commonly associated with his station. No, the words were far older than that. He created a link with the beating heart of the Necropolis, and beseeched it. He showered it with adulation, and made promises that would bind him even further to the ship. But most importantly of all, he brought with him a gift. And the gift he brought was the only gift the Necropolis valued: life.

The incantation took longer this time, and he could feel his life energy leaving his body at an alarming rate. It wouldn't be long before a more precious energy— that of his soul—was syphoned off, too. A bead of sweat ran down his brow, rolling down his forehead and past his lips. He was almost at the bottom of his reserves.

He was about to concede defeat, and take a step back to recoup his losses, when he felt a soft hand press against his own. He looked down, but Shima was swathed in as much darkness as the rest of the room.

"Try again," she whispered, clasping his hand. Her grip was surprisingly strong, and Septimus decided not to question the girl. He closed his eyes, forcing his will upon the heart of the Necropolis once more.

A jolt of electrifying energy raced through him, bursting out from the small hand he held with such force that he gasped. His heart rate elevated, and his eyes dilated. There was so much power he could barely contain it. He remembered his duty, before it could overwhelm him, and he began the incantation again. It didn't take long for the system to reboot, not once their combined energy had been used to kick start it. The lights sputtered back on, as did the temperature control. In the distance, he thought he could hear the soft purr of the Necropolis. Deep down, beyond the twisted passageways and narrow archways, below the winding bridges that criss-crossed above, the heart of the place was pleased.

THE SILENT KING

Septimus Acculei flexed his tired fingers and clenched his hands as icy water ran over them. He rubbed his palms against his cheeks, letting the water splash against his face and neck, and flinched as a chill ran through him. Next, he patted down his skin with a small towel, paying special attention to his throat and neck. Then, Septimus applied the grease paints. He was less scrupulous with his application than normal, knowing the mask he would soon don, and the paint was smeared on unevenly in places. From the grey bowls adjacent to the basin, he retrieved a darker blend of fine ochre and grease. He applied the black paint beneath his eyes, stroking a finger gently against his skin as he layered it on. The grease paint stung where he'd been careless, and his eyes started to water. He rubbed at them gently with the back of his hand and then shook his head, staring down into the water of the basin. The image that met him was hardly recognisable. Grey tufts of hair jutted out above his ears, while the rest of his head was a barren place— empty of hair, and covered with liver spots. Folds of skin, lathered in powder, hung from his neck and cheeks. The whites of his eyes glowed visibly against the contrasting paints he had applied, making him look even wilder than normal. How many times had he done this?

How many times had he completed this never-ending task?

Septimus bent over to retrieve the robes by his feet, feeling the tension in his back and legs as he did so. With a deep sigh, he smoothed down the sleeves and tightened the thin belt across his waist. The belt was growing tighter each time; it wouldn't be long before he'd have to pierce another hole in it.

The mask he picked up from the table beside him was old and heavy. Wrought from burnished steel and gold, the thing was expertly carved. Set in an expression of neutrality, the face that Septimus drew over his own was that of a young man in the prime of his life. Complete with accompanying curls, and light dimples beneath the cheeks, the artistry of the mask was beyond reproach. Intricate shapes had been woven into the golden face, and lavish forms wrapped themselves around each other in a ceaseless dance that covered every inch of the mask. The dance was one of life and death, of duality. A celebration of coexistence. For without one, you cannot have the other. The last embellishment added, Septimus was now ready to perform his duty.

Darkness crept through the corridors, trailing behind the flittering lanterns that tracked their route. Dense rows of shelves lined the walls, but were mainly empty. Covered in dust, their contents had been added to the already vast number of tomes waiting to be digitised for posterity. Septimus saw a few less sparsely furnished sills as they wandered deeper into the library, but ignored them. He would get to those in due course.

"Come, child," he said, locking arms with Shima. "The way is close; we are nearly there." The girl nodded beside him, content to let him guide her through the passages. She was becoming more familiar with the layout of the Necropolis, but one can never quite *know* such a place, not completely.

As they closed on their destination, the lanterns raced ahead of them, ducking narrowly beneath the great archway at the end of the walkway. Then they hovered, casting their luminescence against the walls of a small room some distance away. They seemed more animated than usual, visibly buzzing with excitement.

They were deeper in the Necropolis than he had been for an age, than she had ever been. The air was different here—heavier, more prone to deep silence. The whir of mechanisms, and the deep hum of the tomb ships engines—something he took for granted—had faded, and then disappeared entirely. Within these cavernous tunnels, thinly disguised as corridors, time flitted by inconsequentially. With each step, it seemed to slow further, dragging him with it.

When they reached the room, Septimus could feel hot sweat running down his forehead, mixing with the ochre and greasepaint that covered his face. The concoction of bodily fluids and oils stung his skin and made his eyes water more than before, further aggravating the problem. The Mask of the Keeper was making him more uncomfortable with each passing moment, but he couldn't remove it—not until this final task was complete. He squinted through the eyeholes, blinking back the burning sensation until he became numb to it. "What do you know of this place?" Septimus unwound his arm from Shima's and stepped into the centre of the room.

The girl hesitated for a moment, and then followed him, twisting her neck to stare about as she did so. Tangles of wires hung from the corners above, clinging to the walls like knotted webs. A red light blinked along the cables, moving from one side of the room to the other, and then repeating the circuit. Beneath the cords, thick panels of black steel had been bent into shape and forced together. They formed separate rows, tiers of steps that spanned up to the shadowed ceiling of the cell. Upon each of these steps, black-mirrored screens rested, waiting to be activated and put to use. Shima gazed about her, her soft breathing the only sound in the room. "I haven't seen it before." She frowned, her brow knitted in concentration. "It was not in my lessons. Where are we?"

Septimus was silent as he moved toward the steps, red light blinking as it completed yet another trip. The lamps had calmed, and now hovered silently above their heads, barely moving as they tracked their master's movements. "We are in the heart of the Necropolis," said Septimus finally. He swiped a hand against the nearest screen, and began to chant beneath his breath. These were the old words again, the kind that hang in the air long after they've been voiced, the kind that spoke to the spirit of the place, to its very *soul*. He felt his heart rate increase as he uttered them, and the screen go warm beneath his hand.

As he watched, a handle emerged from the moulded black steel beside him, seeming to come out from nothing; such was the perfection of the cut lines in the step itself. Septimus pulled at the handle gently, coaxing it out with more words, and then with more force, until it responded. A simple drawer materialised from behind the handle, and hung out over the step like an uneven tooth, ready to be pulled.

The box contained therein was less simple. Dozens of silver tubes ran across the surface of the thing, so dense and tightly wrapped it seemed impossible to differentiate between them. Two rows of sockets ran down the one side, culminating in a nest of wired springs and inputs. A simple, opaque window sat between them, and stared back up at the Keeper.

"It's time, then?" Shima's voice was soft, and the heavy air of the place threatened to smother her words entirely.

"It is time," Septimus agreed. He was sombre as he input his code into an ancient screen beside the panel, resulting in a hiss emanating from the drawer itself. The lid of the box began to rise, hesitantly at first, until it flopped open entirely, revealing the space within. Septimus said nothing as he bent down over the open box, and retrieved a little bundle of rags from within. He was quiet as he walked across the room, stopping only to wave the hovering lamps away, and stepped outside. There was a clink as whatever was contained within those rags bounced against one another on the floor, and then there was silence.

Septimus returned, his expression hidden behind the impassive mask he wore, but his eyes flickered for a moment, moving from Shima to the drawer, before settling on her face. "Did you recite *The Words* when you awoke?" he asked. His hands were clasped before him, his shoulders hunched.

"Yes, Keeper."

"Did you pack away your tools?"

"Yes, Keeper."

Septimus nodded, his lips pursed behind the mask. It was the greasepaints that irritated his eyes, that made them water. He let out a yielding sigh, and turned to the open shell. Thinner wires ran along the inside, flowering across the small seat positioned inside like numberless veins. A dim light pulsed through them, a glowing pink that throbbed intermittently.

Septimus brushed a hand across the small seat, wiping his paint-stained fingers against the smooth material. It was rough beneath his hand, and he could feel a hint of moisture—residue from its previous occupant. He rubbed his fingers together, feeling the fine grains of bone and cloth between them. "Then you know your duty," he said, looking to the girl.

"He wills it." Shima's voice was even, devoid of any hint of hesitation or nervousness. She stepped toward the shell, her grey robes clutched between her hands to stop them getting in the way. He hadn't got round to hemming them in. *No matter*, he thought as she approached. *The time for that has passed.*

She extended a hand, and Septimus accepted it, helping her up over the top of the drawer. She clambered over the sill and onto the seat within, arching her back and wiggling down until she was comfortable. The Keeper squeezed her shoulder gently, and then pressed his hand against the screen beside the chamber. The lid clicked, and then jolted at his activation, whining softly as it began to close.

Septimus could still see the girl's face, and watched through the panel as the lid tightened over her. She was whispering *The Words* to herself, her eyes squeezed shut as the sarcophagus was sealed.

The light that ran through the dense wiring within the shell began to throb brighter and more persistently. The pink glow turned a shade of red, and then green, as the lid was finally shut. Septimus was forced to look away as the beam grew in intensity, until it was like staring at the sun. The entire room turned a sickly, blaring green, and even the flashing red light was blotted out from view.

Septimus placed a hand upon the shell, flinching at the heat that coursed upon its surface. The tubes that surrounded the cylinder were beginning to glow themselves, pumped full with neurthatic energy that quickly spread to the wires on the floor and walls. From here it would make its way across the rest of the Necropolis, coursing through the veins of the ship, reinvigorating the heart of the place. It was enough energy to sustain the tomb-ship for an age—perhaps forever.

As the blazing light began to fade, Septimus opened his eyes and stared down at the sarcophagus. He still couldn't look through the panel, such was the force of the energy that emanated from within. Instead, he comforted himself with the thought that the little girl was content—that Shima was pleased to take her rightful place within the tomb-ship. It was *such* a duty for one so young. Regardless, to be interred within the vessel for all eternity, like so many others before her, was a great honour. Perhaps the greatest.

Septimus smiled to himself, and then stepped away from the glowing sarcophagus. He had many duties to fulfil that day, and the next. He clicked his back and rolled his shoulders. His old bones were starting to feel better already.

💀💀💀

The Blessed Tomb

The Blessed Sun of the 10,000 Pilgrims, the last ghoul star in the Hubris Constellation, was dying. Even now, its light had started to fade, and torrents of flame rippled across its surface, pulsing waves of radiation that heralded its end.

But it would not die alone.

Monolithic tomb ships hung in orbit around the many moons of Dartuan, their twisted spires stretching out into the inky black void of space. Obsidian towers lined their bloated bellies, marring their smooth surfaces like knucklebones, twisted and scarred by centuries of service.

The great brooding basilicas spun slowly, tracking the rotations of the moons beneath them as wan light reflected from a million viewing ports and clerestory windows. Some of the ships were as old as the civilisation that once thrived beneath the light of Dartuan. Others were older still.

The last surviving Pilgrims filled their enclaves, waiting patiently in cells and chambers for what was to come. The star that had given them life would now give them death. Such was their privilege; such was their duty.

But not all who had toiled beneath the light of Dartuan were deemed worthy of such a fate. The realm of The Silent King must survive, must prosper so that He might continue his great work and build a bridge between Life and sacred Death.

☠ ☠ ☠

"So, that's it then?" Artella thumbed a glyph, rotating the view of the screen in front of her. "It seems... a little underwhelming."

"What were you expecting?" Plemus wiped his own screen clear and stared up through the viewing port. The two pilots sat in the nose of a Vanguard-class scout ship, a thin needle of a vessel built for stealth rather than comfort. They were one of several such ships that had just entered the system ahead of the fleet, each equipped for long-range observation and able to bounce between moons in the blink of an eye.

Artella shrugged, the movement constrained by the dozens of wires embedded in her skin, connecting her to the pilot's thrones. "Something less bleak, I guess. This doesn't look like the home of a God, much less a home for us."

Her companion snorted, turning his grey eyes to her. "The first Arcs haven't even arrived yet, Tel. Give it time."

"I'll be an old woman by the time they do. And you, Plem. Well, you'll probably be dead long before they're done turning this place into Paradise."

"And not a moment too soon," said her companion with a thin smile. "Eternal rest after a lifetime of service... Yes, I think I might quite like that. Or is it eternal service after a lifetime of rest? I can never remember."

"You can warm my spot in the catacombs." Artella thumbed another glyph, tapping her spider-like fingers over the green and yellow sigils that appeared on the screen. "I've got too much left to do, eternal service or no."

Reels of data scrolled beneath her finger: topographical charts, air purity levels, temperature readings, atmospheric pressure, grids identified for potential settlements. She swiped them all away until she found what she was looking for.

A pixelated image glowed up at her, illuminating her ghostly pale features, her regal nose, with its yellow sheen. Rock formations stretched toward the horizon, basking in the rays of Guah, the system's primordial sun.

"The Cradle of Creation," she whispered reverently. Her free hand went unconsciously to the prayer bones around her neck, clasping them gently as she examined the landscape.

A ravine slithered out from beneath the rock formations, winding its way toward the shadowed horizon on the other side of the screen. Atmospheric distortion had played havoc with their long-range lenses, and a smudge crowned the nearest of the canyon walls, a dark spot that couldn't be removed. If Artella zoomed in enough on the shape, it looked almost human—like some skeletal figure risen from the mausoleum, its empty eyes staring out across the infinity of space.

"Perhaps," said Plemus, his brow raised. "We don't know that for sure. It could be just another valley on another planet... one of countless millions."

"Hush, Plem." Artella expanded the image, stretching its already distorted form until it filled her screen. "It's here, alright. I can feel it. There's something different about this place, about this system. It feels old, like it's seen things, like it holds secrets it wants to share with us."

Plemus shook his head and turned back to his own screen, inputting coordinates while he spoke. "Even if it is, there's no way to be certain. It's been millennia, Art. Places change... secrets are forgotten."

"We'll know," said Artella softly. And then louder, "There will be patterns, signs left over. You saw what we found on Atlas IX. Repetition at a molecular level. Artificially reoccurring patterns nature cannot explain, that our Keepers could not comprehend. Because they were beyond nature, beyond comprehension. God-touched."

Plemus nodded, only half-convinced. He'd seen the scarred stone and markings that covered the asteroid, been privy to the confused communications of the adjuncts aboard the tomb ship. It'd been like looking into the pre-history of the universe, at its building blocks. Atlas IX had been old. Older than anything they'd seen before. And it had come from the planet in front of them.

"One way to find out," said Plemus, easing their ship forward. "Let's see if anyone's home."

💀 💀 💀

The vanguard ship cut through Eden's atmosphere like a knife through bone, leaving a trail of nethartic energy in its wake. The ship's travel was as silent as a tomb, its every action deadened by the perfect slipstream it carved through the air. Once it broke the atmosphere, it hovered above the clouds, slowly rotating as its polyhydronic form adjusted to in-atmosphere travel, and then it shot off again, racing over the yellow sand and mountains below.

"There it is," said Artella as the ship began to decelerate, nearing the coordinates Plemus had set for it.

The silver-grey cloud cover broke, revealing a vast complex of ashen caves and a mountain range that disappeared into the horizon. Dusty yellow sand covered the floor, like it did everywhere else, though it seemed darker here, tainted by a coppery tinge.

Cavernous chambers riddled the canyon, flanked by steep slopes that cast long shadows, concealing that which only the Blessed technology of the Silent King could reveal.

"How deep do they go?" Artella leaned forward in her throne, staring down into the dark hollows that covered Eden's surface. The ground beneath the mountains looked to her like porous skin, stretched tautly and cracked from exposure. Empty riverbeds spread out around the hollows like veins before splintering off toward the mountains.

"Pretty deep," said Plemus, not looking up. A string of glyphs flashed green and red in front of him, repeating the pattern over and over. "There's too much distortion. I can't see anything past 1,500 feet. We'll have to wait for the arcs to arrive to boost our signal."

Artella nodded. The void fleet would emerge from inter-system travel any moment and begin preparations for the arrival of the Arcs. Then, settlement would begin, and life on Eden would slowly be moulded to suit the requirements of the denizens of the tomb fleet.

"Must be iron pockets nearby or something else that's turning the soil red." Plemus banked the ship, slowly easing it down toward the canyon. "Any volcanic activity in the logs?"

Artella glanced back at her screen, swiping away the image and absorbing reels of data in the blink of an eye.

"Nothing active," she said. "But I'd like to get a sample, maybe take a closer look at those caves. Before the fleet arrives and douses everything in enough decontaminates to drown us in."

"And washes away your precious patterns."

"Take us down," said Artella, ignoring the jab. "Let's go stretch our legs a little."

💀💀💀

Eden's air was hot and dry, and Artella's first breath felt like fire in her lungs. She drew her hood over her head, blocking out Guah's scorching light. The primordial sun was still powerful here, far from the energy-draining tools that had been deployed in the Hubris constellation, and had eventually led to Dartuan's demise.

Plemus followed her down the boarding bridge, adjusting his own hood as he stepped out on Eden's red sands.

"Still underwhelmed?" he asked, looking pointedly at the towering canyon walls and their shadowy enclaves. "Or does this now meet your expectations?"

"I am satisfied," said Artella, striding down the ramp. She pulled her robes up by their hems to stop them dragging through the sand and headed toward the nearest chasm. After a moment, Plemus followed.

"What made this?" Artella asked, staring over the lip of the hole, into the empty void below. The sand was soft beneath her boots, and she steadied herself against Plemus's shoulder. "It's edges are smooth, like they were cut with purpose, by some methodical hand."

Her companion snorted. "If you search for the Divine in all things, you will find it…." He drew a data slate from his robes and was silent while he read through a series of glyphs. "But no," he said finally. "These were once methane pits. They must have burnt hollow sometime in the past aeon. Nothing purposeful about them."

Artella frowned, staring deep into the rift. The inner walls were ridged, like someone had scooped them out with a spade, leaving thin grooves behind. The markings spiralled downward before disappearing into the shadows. She was about to ask how fire could create such perfectly symmetrical walls when she felt Plemus stiffen beneath her arm.

"What is it?" she asked, turning away from the chasm.

"That's strange." Plemus pursed his lips, still staring at his data slate. He took a few steps back from the hole and looked up at the canyon walls surrounding them, a bemused look on his craggy face.

"What?" Artella asked more forcefully this time.

"The walls around us are hollow too. But I think there's something inside of them?"

Artella followed Plemus's gaze toward the steep inclines. The stone was dark, covered by centuries of mud and dust. But there appeared to be gaps between them, narrow passages to follow deeper into the gorge.

"Something?"

"Don't get your hopes up." Plemus lowered his data slate. "It could be anything... Iron pockets distorting my readings... More sand."

Artella smiled. "But it could be something. Let's go see what."

💀💀💀

Naturally forming pillars crowded their approach to the nearest corridor. They stood as tall as their ship in some places, obscuring the shadowy passage from view. The air was cooler within the shade of the canyon walls, and Artella felt the sweat on her back and brow chill against a soft wind flowing from within the corridor itself. The ground, too, was harder, though it maintained its ochre tinge.

"I've seen such readings before," said Plemus conversationally. "In an ossified Necropolis once thought lost, only for it to reemerge centuries later from within the Urzuan Strain. Of course, its Keepers had long since perished, and the mausoleum was barely on its last reserves, but—"

"But?"

"Gas deposits had formed within its sealed chambers, highly pressurised concentrations that looked like shapes to our readers. Once we broke them open, however... nothing."

Artella mulled this over, walking in silence with only the sound of her boots scraping against the dirt to fill her ears.

"And you think... Plem?" She paused in her steps, staring around at the place her companion had been not a moment ago.

"Plem?" she said softly, feeling the cool wind tug at her robs. A soft whistle followed the breeze, and she turned to stare into the corridor. He couldn't have gotten ahead of her, could he? He'd been right... there?

"Plemus!" Her voice echoed off the ravine walls, bouncing back at her as she twirled on her feet, her robe swirling in the dirt. Her call sounded strange as the canyon played it back to her—hollow, like it wasn't really hers. There was no sign of him, just the soft whistle of the wind.

Artella was about to call for him again when she hesitated, her eyes coming to a rest on the canyon walls. She hadn't noticed it before, but the same markings she'd seen in the methane pit covered it, row upon row of thin grooves that looked to her like the growth rings of a tree.

"Ple—"

"I'm here, I'm here," Plemus said, stepping out from behind a crooked pillar, his eyes still fixed on his screen. "The caves are playing havoc with my readings... I thought I might get a clearer one further from the passage."

"And?"

Plemus simply shook his head.

"Well, don't disappear like that. I thought you'd fallen down one of those holes."

He looked up from his slate with a wry smile. "There'll be no catacomb for me if that happens. No rest, either. Who knows if those pits even have a bottom?"

"Let's not find out." Artella turned toward the corridor, adjusting her hood as another gust of cool wind swept through the ravine. Shadows stretched out toward her, growing long as Eden continued its ponderous circuit around the primordial sun. It would be dusk soon, and the temperature would drop rapidly. They would need to hurry if they wanted anything more than a cursory look at the cave system.

Plemus raised a brow at the grooves on the wall when they reached the passage but only shrugged when Artella met his eye.

"They could be tide marks," he offered when she didn't look away. "Perhaps there was a river running through here before Guah got too hot and drained it all away. Or maybe..." Artella didn't wait for him to finish, turning on her heel to stalk deeper into the passageway.

The corridor grew narrower as they walked, and Artella began to fear they were headed toward a dead end. Plemus's data slate had stopped working entirely, despite his best efforts, and beeped miserably from within his robes. Artella was about to declare their expedition a failure and return to the ship when the path began to widen, and a few moments later, they found themselves in a hollowed-out clearing. The canyon walls fell back a little but still towered over them ominously, allowing only a faint grey light into the gloomy recess.

Artella came to a stop at the entrance to the hollow and let out a faint gasp before a smile formed on her lips. The path disappeared into the clearing, reappearing on the other side where the canyon walls imposed themselves once more. But it was not that which had caught her attention.

Resting in the centre of the hollow, hewn from the same dark rock as the canyon walls, was another pillar. This one, however, could claim no natural origin. Its body was perfectly smooth, as though sanded down until even the most minute of impurities had been whittled away. Each of its four corners culminated in edges so thin and sharp that it was a marvel they hadn't crumbled away. The same furrowed growth lines they'd seen in the methane pits and canyon walls covered the pillar but far more densely, leaving almost none of its surface free of them.

"I told you," said Artella, getting over the momentary shock to hurry forward. "I knew there would be a sign, a pattern, something… but this? Not even our most zealous Keepers would have expected this. A marvel of creation!"

It was only when she stood beneath it that she realised how gargantuan the pillar really was. It rose well above the columns they'd seen in the canyon, and she had to crane her neck to see the top. The growth lines spiralled their way all along its surface, tightening nearer to the peak until she couldn't make out anything but the dark rings. But there were other markings too, incisions that had been cut, not formed, between the lines. Artella stared at those quizzically while she called back to Plemus.

"Could this be the first form? The first creation of our Creator? That would make it the oldest thing in existence. Should we take a sample? Or would that be… frowned upon? We'll have to notify the fleet once they arrive. We can't have them stumbling around here before archotheologists get boots on the ground.

"Easy, Art," said Plemus, entering the clearing more cautiously than she had. "I'm sure there's an explanation for this. There always is."

"Come, look at this," said Artella, waving him forward. "These are… words? Between the growth lines. They are, aren't they? Some form of ancient script. Perhaps the first words?"

"I recognise some of these," said Plemus, coming up beside her. He touched the smooth stone column with a hand, his brow knotting as he stared at the markings. "This here, this is the Anadeun word for life. And these... I have seen these glyphs in some of our most ancient mausoleums."

"What do they mean?"

"I'm not sure," Plemus confessed. "My ancient Anadeun is not what it used to be. It has something to do with 'a closing', I think. But more final than that."

"An ending?" Artella suggested, not taking her eyes off the glyphs. There was something unsettling about them, though she wasn't sure what. They repeated all around the pillar, each repetition an exact replication of the one before it. They looked less like copies to her eyes and more like... She wasn't sure how to explain it, but she got the impression that they were all the original, and not merely copies of it. They were too... perfect.

"An end... That could be it, yes." Plemus tilted his head in a nod and then stared past the pillar, his brow furrowing further. "Art, look."

"Hmm?" She hesitated before following his gaze, half-distracted by the motifs in front of her. Then she blinked. "Oh."

"Oh," Plemus echoed, already striding across the clearing. They hadn't noticed it at first, partially obscured as it was, within the shadow of the canyon, but an incision had been cut into one of the walls on the opposite end of the passage. It bore the same markings as the column, though its edges were round and smooth rather than sharp and narrow. And what looked like a handle had been carved into its face.

"This must be the entrance," declared Plemus, barely containing a note of excitement that had found its way into his voice. "You were right. There is something here. We might have uncovered the last resting place of a civilisation that died before we even crawled out of our caves. Such a discovery would be unparalleled... Art?"

Plemus turned to look at her. His eyes shone with excitement, with ambition. He was right. Such a discovery would change everything.

"I don't think we're supposed to be here." The words formed on Artella's lips unbidden, but she found herself agreeing with them as she said them. "This place... it's not for us."

"Nonsense," said Plemus, turning back to the door. "You're the one who wanted to come here. Maybe you were right, Art. Maybe you've always been right. This could be where it all began... Now, come help me open this. I want to see inside."

Artella crossed the clearing with a few lengthy strides and watched Plemus as he threw his weight at the door. It remained as immovable as the canyon wall it had been carved into.

"Fine," said Artella, meeting Plemus's glare. She added her own weight to his efforts and, after a tense moment, felt the stone begin to move against her shoulder.

"Almost there," gasped Plemus, a vein pulsing on his forehead.

Artella groaned as the door ground against the stone floor beneath it. Then, finally, with one last bit of effort, it swung open.

"There," said Plemus, brushing off his hands. "That might be the first time it's been opened since Creation."

Artella ignored his smile and peered into the shadowy space beyond the door. Darkness met her eyes, and she blinked against the gloom until she was able to make out the outlines of a small chamber and the faint impression of the shapes within. She flinched when Plemus ignited an Ossuary Lamp and cast it into the room. The light flittered for a moment, its power source adjusting to the subtle differences in Eden's gravitational pull, and then it stabilised, hovering with a gentle hum in the centre of the chamber.

"Fit for a king," said Plemus, staring into the now glowing hollow. The amber light revealed a room no wider than the cockpit of their vanguard ship, though it stretched back deeper into the canyon's walls until even the Ossuary Lamp couldn't penetrate the inky black shadows. A pair of steps rose from the entrance, coated in dust and a pale white powder Artella didn't recognise. Funeral dust? The steps led into the narrow chamber, its stone roof held up by a pillar, not unlike the one outside but smaller.

The same growth lines and script covered every inch of available space in the chamber, the scrawl carved into the walls so densely that Artella could barely distinguish one glyph from another. The chalk-like substance from the floor had been smeared into the recesses, making them glow in the light of the lamp.

"Or a God," she whispered. She didn't know why she'd said the words so softly, only that the room before her demanded reverence... Worship.

"And there, his crypt," said Plemus, matching her tone. He nodded, uncurling a finger to point at the shape beyond the steps. A mausoleum. Its smooth surface seemed to absorb the light of the Ossuary Lamp, swallowing it whole without spitting anything back out.

Artella took a hesitant step up the stairs, feeling the dust and grit crunch beneath her boots. The air was stale, untouched for a thousand thousand years. She breathed it in like it was sacred, part of a ritual, a rite, and then strode toward the tomb.

Even in the light of the Ossuary Lamp, the mausoleum was the blackest thing she'd ever seen. Its surface seemed to occupy a negative space, barely allowing any refraction from the amber glow that hung above their heads. Artella knelt down beside it, squinting to try and decipher the inscriptions that covered it. The act made her eyes hurt, and she blinked away after a handful of seconds, but not before recognising one of the symbols as the same she'd seen outside on the pillar. Life.

Plemus sidled up beside her, staring down at the tomb, his own brow furrowed. Slowly, hesitantly, he extended a hand to touch its surface. When his palm touched the stone, he drew it back with a start and then chuckled, turning to her.

"It's cold," he said. And then, placing his hand back down on the stone, "Frozen, like ice, but without the... ice."

Artella slipped off her gloves, tucking them beneath her armpits, and then placed her own hands gently onto the inky black stone. Plemus was right. The surface was freezing, and she felt her body temperature dropping just from that initial contact.

"What is it?" she asked, sliding her hands back into her gloves. "Some type of obsidian?"

"None I've ever seen before," said Plemus. He shivered and then crouched down right up beside the mausoleum, staring into its oily sheen. "This must be...." He wrapped his hands within the drooping sleeves of his robes and pressed them against the stone, then leaned forward as he started to push.

"Plemus," Artella said, shaking her head. "We don't know what's in there. It could be anything. A pathogen, dormant for millennia, who knows. It could be—"

"A God," Plemus grunted, straining as the lid of the tomb started to scrape open. "But we... won't... know... unless... you... help... me."

But this time, Plemus didn't need her help, and the topmost part of the crypt seemed to slide open of its own accord, Plemus's weight simply guiding its path. Artella thought she heard a soft click as the lid was drawn over and a whistle, like breath being exhaled through a gap in someone's teeth. The light flickered as the sound grew louder, but when Artella blinked, it was gone. And Plemus was smiling back at her, the tomb open beneath his shivering fingers.

"It really is freezing," he said, rubbing his hands together as he turned to stare into the vault. The Ossuary Lamp buzzed closer above their heads, as if the mechanical intellect guiding its rotation was trying to catch its own glimpse at the contents of the mausoleum. Artella stepped forward to get a better look.

"Oh," said Plemus.

"Oh," Artella repeated. She let out a sigh and shook her head as she realised it was relief she was feeling. "I hope you didn't catch your death for that."

"A poor reward," Plemus admitted, still staring into the empty vault. A disappointed smile turned the edges of his lips, and he shrugged. "But it would have haunted me if we..."

Plemus blinked, the words fading on his lips.

"What?" said Artella, staring into his unfocused eyes. He was looking past her, back down toward the steps. She turned to follow his gaze, searching the entrance for a sign of whatever had caught his attention. Light shone in through the doorway, the dust and powder they'd disturbed hovering in the rays like the ash of a funeral pyre. But nothing else. Again, that rasping breath, a soft whistle. The wind... or...

Plemus snorted, shaking his head when she glanced back at him and smiled. "Sorry, I thought I saw something. My eyes are getting tired... not to mention old!"

He seemed uncertain, the false confidence in his voice betraying his unease.

"What did you see?" Artella pressed, barely hiding the unease in her own voice.

"Just a shadow," said Plemus with another shrug. "As if this place doesn't have enough of those. Still, I think it's time we started heading back, don't you?"

Artella nodded and was about to help him push back the lid of the tomb when Plemus's data slate started beeping loudly from within his robes.

"I thought I switched that thing off," he said, clawing it out from a fold in his sleeve. Red glyphs covered its screen, and Plemus swiped at them as he tried to switch off the wailing alarm. Artella looked up and frowned as the Ossuary Lamp started spinning faster, its tiny engine whirring in time to the beeps. It drifted across the room, as if pulled by some invisible force, dragged down by a magnetic field they couldn't perceive.

Without knowing why, Artella felt her eyes drawn back to the tomb. She could make out the symbols now, even though her head felt like it would split from the ache of staring at them. The same marks had been carved over and over again, perfectly etched with a precision she knew she could never match.

A Closing. Life. An End. A Closing. Life. An End. A Closing Life. An End.

"Something's wrong," she said, pulling her eyes away from the tomb and moving toward the door. "We aren't supposed to be here. Leave it, Plem. Come on."

Before she could make it to the steps, the Ossuary Lamp let out a high-pitched squeal, flickered once, and then plunged them into darkness.

"Plem?" Artella took a deep breath, her heart pounding in her chest. Her voice sounded thin to her ears, weighed down by the rock and dust of the crypt. "Plemus?

"I'm right here, behind you." She heard scratching on the floor, boots on stone, then a reassuring hand on her shoulder. "Head for the door."

Artella turned toward the entrance, letting out a soft sigh when she saw light still flooding in through the doorway. She shuffled forward, her hand held out before her until she felt the grooves of the nearest wall against her fingers. The stone was cold to her touch, even through the glove, and she could feel the ashen powder crumbling out from the markings.

"Almost there," said Plemus, his voice soft in her ear.

Artella froze. A low whine filled the chamber, followed by a soft clicking, like a nail scratching against gravel. She snapped her head in the direction of the sound, staring into the pitch-black void of the chamber. Her eyes strained against the darkness, but it was like looking at a wall, and she could see nothing, not even the outline of the pillar.

"It's just the lamp," said Plemus. "Let's go before Guah decides to leave us too."

"Right," said Artella, turning back to the door. She followed the curve of the wall, taking careful steps until she reached the top of the steps. Just as she was about to descend, the surface beneath her fingers changed abruptly, the cold stone replaced by something soft... something sticky.

"What?" she said, pausing her steps. She slowly removed a glove from her fingers, not moving forward even when Plemus's hurried breathing blew against the back of her neck. I should just leave it, she thought, even as her hand moved back toward the wall. *Do I even want to know?*

She winced as her fingers pressed against the stone, meeting the wetness that now covered it. There was another crackle from where the broken lamp lay, and then it flicked back on, its brilliant amber light illuminating the chamber.

Artella flinched against the light, still blinking as she stared down at her hand. Black ichor coated her fingers like oil, the watery substance oozing between her nails. She wiped her hand against her robes, and looked up at the wall beside her. It was slopping wet.

"Where did that come from?" Plemus asked, his voice barely steady. Artella didn't have to turn around to know that his face had gone pale, his lips thin. She knew the same look now covered her own features.

"I'm not sure," said Artella, watching the black discharge trickle down the stone. It filled the growth lines and the glyphs, too, covering everything in its path as it rolled toward the ground. She tracked its progress across the ground, stepping aside as the ichor seeped past her until it reached the pillar in the centre of the chamber. The oily fluid was no longer as smooth as it had been when she first felt it, and thin tendril-like pieces bubbled up along its exterior, dragged along in an inexorable journey over the cavern's floor. The ooze puddled at the base of the stone post, and then, impossibly, it began to flow up the column.

"Look," said Plemus, tugging at her sleeve and pointing back toward the mausoleum.

The barely suppressed unease Artella had been feeling since arriving on Eden finally bubbled to the surface, and her hands started to shake as she turned to look back at the tomb. The oily black substance was flowing from the crypt, spilling out across the chamber in waves. But something else was happening too. A shape was forming, pressing itself against the now fluid matter that made up the mausoleum. A figure was imposing itself from within the tomb, pushing against the crypt—trying to get out.

"Run!" cried Artella as wispy black tendrils shot out from the tomb. They were followed by a shape, a mass of swirling darkness congealing into a twisted skeletal figure the consistency of oil. In the glimpse she caught before turning, she was given the impression of a shape, vaguely humanoid, but its proportions were all wrong, its limbs too long, its sloping brow too deep and curved.

Then Artella was running, her legs pumping beneath her as she tried to put as much space between her and it as possible.

A Closing. Life. An End.

The words appeared unbidden in her mind, and she finally realised what they meant. Not God, but destroyer. They were a warning. One that they had not heeded, not fully understood. And now it was too late.

Artella shot out of the chamber, shielding her eyes against the sun as she raced across the sands. She glanced back in time to see Plemus stumble out of the cave, his own eyes shining bright with confusion and fear.

"For the ship," he gasped, dragging his robes up to give himself the freedom to run. The doorway behind him looked like a gaping maw, thin appendages clawing their way out, like veins spreading against the canyon walls, pulsing with life as light shone upon them for the first time in how many years.

"Go!" Plemus pushed past her, dragging her by the arm as he raced through the sand.

Artella let him pull her, her own feet pounding against the dirt as they hurried away from the crypt. A low groan echoed out from the doorway. It was deep, like the wind being funnelled through mountains or the engines of an Arc warming up. Artella resisted the urge to look back, even when the rumble of stone walls collapsing, breaking, filled her ears.

They sped past the pillar in the clearing, blinking away the dust and grit that was billowing out from the chamber behind them. Artella ground her teeth, her nostrils flaring as she exhaled deep breaths. If they could make it to the ship... warn the fleet.

They slipped into the narrow passage, barely slowing as they navigated the winding ravine. The light of Guah was fading, leaving darkening shadows in its wake. Artella skipped over loose stones, careful not to lose her footing in the half-light. She could feel the temperature dropping, and her tight breaths misted in the air before her. She didn't want to turn around—she didn't want to see if that thing had followed them into the ravine.

Artella's heart nearly stopped when she heard a sharp cry behind her. Plemus. Had he tripped? Or... She risked a glance over her shoulder, slowing to turn, willing herself to face her fears. Her co-pilot was sprawled out on the ground a few feet behind her, his legs caught up in his robes. Blood covered his hands where he'd cut them against the sharp rocks, and he was scrambling to get back to his feet.

Artella's eyes widened as she lifted her gaze, her breath caught in her chest. An oozing mass of formless shapes, of tendrils and appendages, was sliding through the passage, pullings its way toward Plemus—toward her. Ichor dripped from its black surface, so dark it seemed to suck in the last of Guah's light. And in that amorphous mass, Artella thought she could just make out that inhuman shape. Watching her.

"Plemus!" she shrieked, backing away.

Her co-pilot stumbled to his feet, lurching into a sprint that defied his years. But it wasn't enough. His fall had cost him too much time.

Artella cried out, spraying spittle into the air as she watched a tendril materialise behind her friend and then coil itself around his waist. Plemus tried to pull free of its grip, but it was like trying to fend off a cloud of mist—his hands scraping at emptiness even as he was dragged from his feet. Ichor splashed across his face as more of the coiling tendrils latched themselves to his skin, tearing at his flesh as they drew him into their embrace.

Welts were forming all along Plemus's hands and face, and blood flowed freely from wherever the tendrils touched him. Steam rose from the oil on his robes, and Artella could see it starting to burn through the fabric and then his flesh. The shadow extended itself over his limbs, and a low hum filled the air, and then a sickening tearing sound that made Artella want to throw up. Plemus let out a strangled scream as his skin was flayed, pulled from the bone of his hands like gloves. The discarded flesh fell to the ground, a growing pool of blood spilling onto the sand around it.

The black mass of shadow seemed to consider Plemus for a moment, an unknowable mind scrutinising its prey—toying with it. More tendrils swirled around him, tearing at his robes until he was bare, naked to the world. Plemus let out another haggard scream as his legs were skinned and then his arms and chest. Then, like a child tugging at the legs of a fly, the swirling mass pulled Plemus apart. Muscle and cartilage fell to the floor in meaty chunks, blood misting the air as his organs ruptured. Limb by limb, until Plemus's head slumped forward, before it too was removed from his body.

This time Artella did vomit, and then she was running again, leaving the ravine behind.

When she emerged from the passage, the last light of Guah, that accursed sun, was nearly gone. The forest of pillars at the entrance to the ravine was just empty silhouettes to her now, dark shapes that stared down at her while she moved. Sweat covered her brow, but her adrenaline was waning, and she was starting to feel the cold. Her hands shook, and her lips felt chapped beneath her tongue. But still, she ran.

By the time she reached the vanguard ship, her lungs were burning from the cold mouthfuls she was inhaling. Her skin had turned a shade of frosted blue, and her legs felt like lead beneath her. She stumbled up the boarding ramp, blinking into the warm glow of the cockpit, into the safety of her ship.

She dropped her gloves into the seat beside hers, and jabbed the wires from her throne into the plugs in her arms. Then she slumped into her seat and punched a series of glyphs on her screen. The Vanguard burst into life all around her, its engine whirring as it was activated.

Artella let out a relieved sigh as the ship lifted from the ground, its softly vibrating interior a comfort after what she had just seen. Plemus. She blinked away the wetness at her eyes and clasped the prayer bones at her neck. There would be no catacomb for him. No peace... Not after that.

She glanced down at her screen, adjusting the view so that she had a better look at her surrounds. She could see the swirling mass of black energy moving across the ravine, only exiting the gorge now that she was out of its reach. It was growing, its oily black surface shuddering and convulsing, the silhouette inside now completely hidden from view.

Artella hissed through her teeth, swiping away the image to enter in a new set of coordinates—ones far from Eden and its false promise of renewal.

She didn't notice the oily tendrils curling beneath her nails, nor the bubbling ooze slowly peeling off her hands from where she'd touched the mausoleum. It was going to be a short flight.

Printed in Great Britain
by Amazon